The Schuyler

I've always been fascinated by the enormously rich and powerful Anglo-American families who dominated social, political and financial life in England and the USA between 1860 and 1945. So when I decided to invent one I took Commodore Vanderbilt, the piratical American who founded the Vanderbilt dynasty, as the model for Ghysbrecht Schuyler, the founder of my family who is 'The Captain' of the *The Captain's Lady*.

Gerard, the Captain's grandson, who later becomes Lord Longthorne, settles in England and rises to be a power behind the scenes of the British Government as he steadily increases his family's influence and wealth. The men all marry women who are also strong characters in their own right. Three more of the Schuyler Chronicles, *Touch the Fire*, *The Moon Shines Bright*, and *An Affair of Honour*, feature heroes and heroines who are at the centre of public affairs.

But what, I asked myself, would happen if a Schuyler did not want to live a life dedicated to political and financial success? *The Wayward Heart* tells the story of Gerard's youngest son, Nicholas, who, in the late nineteen-twenties, rejects the values of his family's world in order to find happiness, fulfilment and true love far from power and luxury. I hope that you enjoy reading it as much as I enjoyed writing it.

Paula Marshall

Paula Marshall, married with three children, has had a varied life. She began her career in a large library and ended it as a senior academic in charge of history in a polytechnic. She has travelled widely, has been a swimming coach, and has appeared on *University Challenge* and *Mastermind*. She has always wanted to write, and likes her novels to be full of adventure and humour.

The Schuyler Chronicles:

THE WAYWARD HEART

Paula Marshall

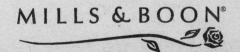

MILLS & BOON®

All the characters in this book have no existence outside the imagination of the author, and have no relation whatsoever to anyone bearing the same name or names. They are not even distantly inspired by any individual known or unknown to the author, and all the incidents are pure invention.

*First published in Great Britain 1998
Harlequin Mills & Boon Limited,
Eton House, 18-24 Paradise Road, Richmond, Surrey TW9 1SR*

© Paula Marshall 1998

ISBN 0 263 81233 2

*Set in Times Roman 10½ on 12 pt.
04-9810-81901 C1*

*Printed and bound in Great Britain
by Caledonian International Book Manufacturing Ltd, Glasgow*

The Schuyler Family

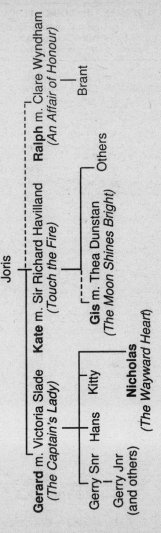

Ghysbrecht Gerhardt
(The Captain's Lady)

Joris

Gerard m. Victoria Slade
(The Captain's Lady)

Kate m. Sir Richard Havilland
(Touch the Fire)

Ralph m. Clare Wyndham
(An Affair of Honour)

Brant

Gerry Snr   Hans   Kitty   Nicholas
(The Wayward Heart)

Gerry Jnr
(and others)

Gis m. Thea Dunstan
(The Moon Shines Bright)

Others

Solid line=legitimate
Broken line=illegitimate

Prologue

1926

'Not since his poor performance at Oxford have I been so disappointed in Nicholas's behaviour, Victoria. For a time I thought that he had reformed—but this tells me otherwise.'

Gerard Schuyler, Lord Longthorne, flung the copy of the *Daily Mirror* which he had been reading, and which had arrived in the post that morning—forwarded by some unkind friend—across the breakfast table at Padworth, his country home, so that his wife might read it.

Torry, Lady Longthorne, picked the newspaper up, sighing a little. The depth of her husband's distress could be gauged by his calling her Victoria, something which he did only when greatly disturbed.

She winced at the screaming headline which was featured on its front page. 'Peer's son in trouble—again!' it shouted in bold black type.

Beneath it was a photograph of Nicholas Schuyler—always known to the younger members of his family as Claus—leaving the magistrates' court where he, along with several others, had been fined after a night in the cells for misbehaviour on boat-race night. Policemen's helmets had been knocked off and carried away in a drunken brawl. The magistrate had commented scathingly on his conduct.

Torry put the paper down and said placatingly, 'It's not really so dreadful this time, Gerard. Not like the other trouble over that actress's divorce.'

'And the trouble before that, and the one before that,' returned Gerard, with his rarely shown fierceness which reminded Torry of his fabled grandfather, 'the Captain', whom he physically, as well as mentally, resembled.

Who Nicholas Allen Schuyler resembled was open to doubt. He might look like his father and great-grandfather, but appeared to possess little of their hard-headed determination and self-control.

Torry, who loved her youngest son dearly, the more so, perhaps, because he was the youngest and the prodigal, tried appeasement again. Nicholas was due to visit Padworth on the following weekend for the annual family get-together, and she was fearful that the simmering dislike which father and son felt for each other these days would break out into open warfare.

'Be patient with him, Gerard, please. He was not always like this. Remember how wild Gis Havilland was, and look at him now. A model citizen, a loving father and a man of consequence. Use some of the diplomacy for which you are famous the next time you see him, and all may yet be well.'

'My dear Victoria,' returned Gerard wearily. 'I have been exercising both patience and diplomacy with Nicholas for years and, somehow, it never seems to answer. As for Gis Havilland, even at his wildest, he was a gifted and hard-working scholar and after that a Great War air ace. He is now hard at work establishing a successful business.

'What has Nicholas ever achieved other than a succession of thick heads and lurid headlines in the popular press?'

'He has been a champion racing driver at Brooklands,' ventured Torry.

'Is that all that you can find to offer on his behalf? If so, Victoria, you merely bolster my belief that, at twenty-six, Nicholas should be given some kind of ultimatum as to his future. Kindness hasn't worked with him. It is time we tried severity.'

It was also time, Torry thought ruefully, that she gave way. Her attempts to intervene on Nicholas's behalf were merely hardening his father's heart against him. It had to be admitted that Nicholas's behaviour would try the patience of a saint and although Gerard was no saint, he had been very forgiving towards Nicholas until this last piece of nonsense.

There were, she knew, two strong reasons for Gerard's exasperation with his youngest son. The first was that Gerard's father, Joris, had been idle and self-indulgent, and Gerard was fearful that Nicholas was following in his footsteps. The second arose from the fact that Nicholas's two older brothers were cheerful and hard-working men, devoted to their duty and their wives. Nicholas resembled them only in being cheerful.

Torry left the breakfast room and wandered distractedly into the big drawing-room where a table held the Schuyler family photographs. She picked up two taken the previous year when all the family, including Ralph and Clare, plus Gis Havilland, his wife Thea and his two children, had been present. They were group portraits, conversation pieces, and meant to be reasonably serious.

In the first, a memento of a happy afternoon, Nicholas was in the centre—clowning as usual. His brothers and sister, and most of the guests, were laughing at his antics. The children, who all loved Uncle Claus, were overjoyed. Only Gerard stood there, solemn and disapproving, a frown on his face.

The second photograph was the serious one. Nicholas, quietly rebuked by his father, had been persuaded to behave himself, and now stood at the edge of the group, straight-faced and a trifle sullen, whilst the rest of the family, including his father, smiled happily at the camera.

Torry sighed and put the photographs back. Nicholas would be with them soon, and somehow she must try to heal the growing breach between father and son before either of them did anything irrevocable.

Nicholas Schuyler drove his big Bentley down the avenue which led to the front of Padworth House. He wished that he had had the common sense to ring his mother and tell her he had been detained in town. Which would have been a lie and one which would have stuck in his throat.

There was nothing back in London now which he could honestly claim ought to detain him. Pamela Gascoyne, the girl whom he had escorted about town for the past year, and had hoped to make his wife, had told him two nights ago that she had at last accepted her cousin Nigel Townsend's offer of marriage.

'It was only a bit of fun with us, do admit,' she had told him cheerfully, 'and you're not ready for marriage yet, but I am.'

She was, he knew, speaking nothing less than the truth. But her rejection, coming on the evening of the day on which the head of the merchant bank for which he had worked since he had left Oxford with a pass degree had sent for him and informed him coldly that his services were no longer wanted, was something of a last straw. Particularly when he remembered the brutal fashion in which his master had dissected his lack of competence—and his unfortunate public reputation—before he had dismissed him.

'I want your desk cleared by tomorrow lunchtime at the latest,' he had finished, turning away from Nicholas when he spoke as though the sight of him was distressing to a man of sense.

Nicholas had thought that if he married Pamela she might have a steadying influence on him even though, if he were honest, he did not love her. She was, however, a jolly good chum—downright and sensible—which was almost certainly why she had decided on Nigel after all, rather than on flighty Nicholas Schuyler.

That he had lost his post at the bank would be sure to infuriate his father, and losing Pamela as well would be yet another black mark, for Gerard had quietly approved of her.

He sighed and braked sharply on the gravel sweep before the Doric portico which some long-dead eighteenth-century architect had designed. The whole place reeked of wealth and privilege, and in his present mood Nicholas was not sure that he approved of either.

There was no time to philosophise. Servants were appearing out of the woodwork. An under-chauffeur seated himself in the Bentley ready to drive it round to the stables once one of the footmen had removed Nicholas's luggage—not that he had brought much with him.

'Tea is being served on the lawn, sir,' the footman carrying his luggage told him. 'You are in the blue room, as usual.'

The blue room was at the back of the house. It overlooked the big lawn where he could see the entire family assembled. Even his older brother, Gerry, always known as Gerry Senior to distinguish him from his son of the same name, was there. He had come over for a short holiday from France where he had his home. He was talking animatedly to his cousin, Gis Havilland, while their children played together on the grass watched by their mothers.

Nicholas looked around for his uncle, Ralph Schuyler, his father's half-brother. Of all his Schuyler relatives he liked him the most. There was a cynical earthiness about Ralph which he found attractive, but he was not one of the group on the lawn.

Afterwards Nicholas was to ask himself how different his life might have been if Ralph's baby daughter had not been taken ill, causing Ralph to cancel his visit at the last minute. He had been intending to ask his uncle for advice about his future, but in his absence he was disinclined, as always, to confide in Gis.

It was not that he disliked his cousin, but he was unhappily aware that his father was always comparing him unfavourably with his Aunt Kate's eldest child, the clever and handsome paragon who was also a war hero.

'It's not my fault that I wasn't old enough to take part in the War,' he had told his father once, to meet an uncomprehending stare. Remembering the argument which had followed, Nicholas sighed and ran downstairs, past the portraits of the original owners of Padworth before Gerard had bought it, and finally past the twin studies of his father and mother by Sargent which graced the entrance hall.

Everything at Padworth was perfect. Even the group on the lawn, idly disposed in the late afternoon sunshine, was perfect: a twentieth-century conversation piece of the rich, the famous and the clever, thrusters all. He, the only unsuccessful member of the family, felt like an interloper as he walked towards it.

His mother's warm greeting cheered him up a little. 'Ah, there you are, Nicholas. How nice to see you. We didn't expect you before the evening. You managed to get away early?'

She was pouring tea as she spoke, and didn't require an answer which was, Nicholas thought wryly, just as well, for he could scarcely destroy the happy spirit of the party by informing her that the reason for his early arrival was that he had been dismissed from his post and had left the bank for good before lunch!

He took his cup of tea and sat himself in a basket chair beside Gis. He asked him if he knew where Ralph was, and was told the reason for his absence. He was aware of his father's hard eye on him, doubtless waiting to question him about the brouhaha on boat-race night.

Gis said idly, 'Merchant banking going well?'

'So-so,' Nicholas replied hardily. 'Planes still flying?' Gis designed and built aircraft as well as flying them.

'Sometimes,' said Gis with a friendly grin. 'My latest effort isn't exactly a world beater yet. So-so describes it well.'

'So-so describes everything well,' said Nicholas, his tone bitter, keeping his own eye on his father. The old man was dying to get at him, he was sure, but etiquette demanded that he wait until later.

One of Gerry's children hurled himself at Nicholas. 'Tell us a story, Uncle Claus. Another one about the dragon.'

Nicholas took small Brant on his knee. 'You mean the Great Worm of Enfield Chase.'

'Yes, yes, the one you told us about at Christmas. The one that nearly ate the princess! Make it eat the princess this time!'

'Bloodthirsty child,' said Nicholas, ruffling the little boy's hair affectionately. 'I can't do that. Princesses don't get eaten. They get married.'

By now all the Schuyler grandchildren had seated themselves around him, begging him to tell them another story about the dragon. The little girls were complaining that the boys in his stories had all the fun. 'Girls only get married or rescued,' they wailed.

'Better than being gobbled up by the dragon,' Nicholas told them, unaware that Gis, who had been lying back in his chair, quite relaxed, was now sitting up, an odd expression on his face, watching his cousin entertain the small Schuylers. 'But I'm only too happy to oblige you. Here goes. ''Once upon a time…'''

He was away. His audience, enthralled, laughed and cheered as he told them the saga of the cowardly son of the Great Worm who liked reading and writing more than he liked eating people, unlike his elder brothers and sisters who were proper dragons.

His mother, like Gis, was also watching him, but where Gis's expression was enigmatic, hers was loving as she listened to him explain how the oldest girl dragon had rescued her cowardly brother when a bold knight had tried to steal the dragon's treasure. Of how that had shamed the cowardly dragon so that he set off to perform a great deed of his own, but all that he managed to do was get himself rescued again—by the smallest dragon in the family this time. After that he didn't even fly home, but walked all the way, his forked tail tucked between his legs.

Little Joris, the youngest of his nephews, looked wistfully up at him and murmured, 'Did he never do a brave deed, then, Uncle Claus?'

'Yes, Joris, although you might not think it brave. He decided that he would not try to imitate his brothers and sisters again, but would retire to his cave to write the history of their exploits instead.'

'What's exploits?' asked Joris.

'Brave deeds,' said Nicholas.

'Writing a book's not a brave deed,' announced Gerry Junior loftily.

'It is if it's hard work, and because you're a dragon you find it difficult to hold a pen or use a typewriter,' Nicholas told him.

Before Gerry Junior had time to argue further, his father called out to all the party, 'Time for cricket on the back lawn—coming, Claus?'

Nicholas shook his head. 'Too tired.'

'Lazy as usual,' Gerry Senior reproached him, his father dourly nodding agreement behind him.

Gis excused himself as well, which left him and Nicholas as the sole remnants of the afternoon tea party.

'Had a hard week,' he had claimed earlier. Now he was lying back in his chair, his panama hat over his eyes.

'Did you?' queried Nicholas when they were at last alone. He was aware that his tone was a little antagonistic, but Gis, as usual, made nothing of that, merely drawling lazily,

'Did I what?'

'Have a hard week.'

'So-so. Did you?'

Was he being mocked? Did it matter? Nicholas decided not. He wished that he could see Gis's face. He settled instead for saying, 'Only if you call getting the sack being so-so.'

Even when this bombshell was dropped in his lap Gis neither took his hat off his eyes nor sat up.

'Did you, indeed? Relieved, were you?'

This polite and indifferent response delivered in Gis's flattest drawl was so far removed from any comment that his father might make that Nicholas began to laugh. The only trouble was that once begun, he couldn't easily stop.

His eyes running, his face red, he finally stammered out,

'I can only hope that my father's reaction will be as indifferent as yours. After all, I have just succeeded in proving once and for all that I am the family's one and only failure. Surrounded by success, I have distinguished myself by being dismissed from the sinecure which he found for me by twisting the arm of someone who owed him a favour.'

'Ah, yes,' murmured Gis, sitting up at last and removing his hat. 'The cowardly dragon. Why not try doing what *you* want for a change?'

'What *I* want?' Nicholas's voice was bitter. 'And what is that? I suppose, though, that coming from the man with all the talents, who finds everything easy, it's a reasonable question to ask.'

Gis was thoughtful. 'Of course, I forgot that you don't like me very much, but then, you don't like anyone very much, yourself least of all.'

He put out a hand to touch Nicholas's arm, an affectionate gesture which surprised them both—particularly when, at the moment of impact, Gis froze, his eyes widening.

Nicholas flung off the friendly hand. This, then, he thought furiously, was the absolute living end: that Gis should have one of his fateful turns when he saw danger and disaster facing the person who had provoked it, and that he should be the subject of it.

Even as he thought this Gis blinked and said, 'Don't look at me like that, Claus. Yes, I saw something, felt something, concerning you and your future, but it wasn't danger. Far from it.'

'What, then?' Nicholas's voice was nasty. 'What was it?'

'Happiness. Fulfilment. How I don't know—only this: you must follow your wayward heart, Nicholas Allen, wherever it takes you. That's all.'

These last sentences were so emptily cryptic, so pointless, that Nicholas flung away from Gis in disgust, exclaiming furiously, 'Well, that's a great help to take with me when I confront the Patriarch, the Lord of All—including Padworth—isn't it?'

And why call him Nicholas Allen in that odd way when he had always been Claus to him before? He was so angry that he scarcely took in what Gis was saying.

'Look, Claus—' so he was Claus again, was he? '—when I was young and foolish I was nearly weighed down by everything that was expected of me, and I think that you're in the opposite case. You're weighed down because nothing is expected of you. Somehow you have to find a way out of the maze you're trapped in—and only you can do it. That's all.'

'I would say that it's quite enough, wouldn't you? Training to be a parson, are you?'

Having shot this unpleasant dart at Gis, who hardly deserved it, Nicholas jumped up, and began to walk towards the House, away from his cousin and his unwanted advice, away from everything. There was only one thing left for him to do, and that was to prepare himself to tell his father of his latest twin disasters—three if you counted the boat-race brouhaha—and there was no way he could think of to make them palatable.

'Been dismissed from his post! They were so eager to get rid of him that they paid him a month's salary in lieu of notice. Regardless of anything that you might argue on his behalf, I told him that I was finished with him. He must make his own way in future. To Hell, one supposes, if he keeps up his feckless way of life. One might think that the example of the rest of the family would inspire him, but no.'

'Oh, Gerard,' Torry said sadly, 'you didn't tell him so.'

Gerard's anger and disappointment were briefly aimed at

her. 'Why, Torry, you're as bad as he is. He told me that
he was sick and tired of being assailed with the achieve-
ments of the Schuyler and Havilland clan and his one wish
was that he might find some nook or cranny where no one
had ever heard of them, for he never wanted to hear their
names again. I told him that if that was his wish then I
would be happy for him to have it fulfilled, for I was sick
and tired of the name of Nicholas Schuyler who had
brought nothing but disgrace on the family.'

'No, Gerard, you didn't—how could you? Oh, the poor
cowardly dragon.'

This last allusion flew by Gerard who had not heard his
son's impromptu fairy story.

'I could and I did. He needs a shock, something to make
him behave himself. When I look at him I see my worthless
father.'

'No, Gerard, that's not true. You see yourself, your
young self. Of all the children and grandchildren he resem-
bles you the most.'

'Oh, come, Torry. I was never like Nicholas, I was always responsible.'

'You were wild, Gerard, you know you were. But you
were never born to love as Nicholas was. You had to make
your own way, your father being what he was, and that
steadied you.'

'So we loved him too much! Is that it? Should I have
thrashed him?'

Torry shook her head sadly.

'No, we all loved him. You have forgotten what a dear
little boy he was. I think that he hasn't found his way in
life; you were lucky, you found yours early. He's been
trying to live up to the expectations of others without knowing what his own are.'

'Excuses, excuses,' Gerard flung at her. 'Well, that's

that. Time to dress for dinner. I hope to God he's been put as far away from me as possible!'

But when the Schuyler family were in the drawing-room waiting to go into dinner, Nicholas was late appearing. So late that the furious Gerard sent one of the footmen to his room to remind him at what time dinner was served.

After five minutes during which Gerard fumed in silence the man returned, looking harried.

'I visited Mr Nicholas's room, m'lord, but he was not there. Jackson, the footman who guards the entrance hall, informs me that Mr Nicholas ordered his car to be brought round half an hour ago. He had his luggage taken down to it and drove off at once, after tipping Jackson and telling him that he would not be back.'

The footman took in his master and mistress's stricken faces. 'Beg pardon, m'lord, Jackson took the liberty of asking Mr Nicholas if he was returning to London so that he might inform you, m'lord. Mr Nicholas said…' He coughed and fell silent.

'Yes?' said Gerard. He was looking his most formidable as Torry had only seen him once or twice in his life. 'Go on, man.'

'Here, m'lord? You wish me to tell you here?'

Gerard said in the voice which had quelled a recalcitrant House of Lords more than once, 'You might as well continue. Everyone present knows what Mr Nicholas is capable of.'

'He said, "Tell Lord Longthorne that seeing that he no longer has any interest in my destination I shall not give it. You may also tell him that I shall never visit him or Padworth again." And then he drove off.'

'Good,' said Gerard. 'You may go, but not before telling the butler to announce dinner. Torry, my dear, take my arm.

We are already late, and I do not wish to delay matters any longer.'

It was useless. Gerard was at his most implacable worst. Torry sighed and did as her husband bid her. Later, in private, she might try to move him, but for the moment, for the sake of peace and propriety, she held her tongue.

But, oh, where had her cowardly dragon gone, and how would he make his way in the world?

Nicholas drove steadily towards the southwest. First on main roads easy for the Bentley to negotiate, then on roads which were little more than tracks, one vehicle wide. He had driven back to London from Padworth, given his man a month's wages in lieu of notice, piled his most personal belongings into the Bentley, written to his landlord saying that he would have the flat cleared of his possessions before the three months' rent which he had already paid had run out, and then started off on his odyssey to God knows where.

Oddly as he drove through the morning, having slept for only a few hours, he felt a sense of exhilaration, of wild freedom. He had no plans, no idea of where he might finally stop to rest his head. He only wanted to be somewhere where no one knew or cared about the Schuylers.

He remembered the old story of the sailor who had left the sea and wanted to retire as far away from it as possible. He started walking, a pair of oars over his shoulder, and decided that the first place he reached where someone asked him what they were he would stop and put down his roots.

Driving into Devonshire in the late afternoon, he began to whistle. He had lunched at a little pub on bread and cheese, forgone strong ale and drunk shandy instead, and when he reached the places where the habitations of men were few and far between, he occasionally stopped to admire the view.

Around teatime he began to feel hungry. His road map told him that he was approaching a small market town called West Bretton and he decided to break his journey there and enjoy one of the cream teas for which this area was famous.

He had never visited north Devonshire before, so all that he saw was new and interesting. West Bretton turned out to be a town full of character with an imposing Town Hall in its centre. A stone butter cross stood in the middle of a market square which was surrounded by small shops. One of them advertised cream teas so he parked the Bentley in front of it and indulged himself.

Everything in the tearoom was spotless. The china was delicate, the tea in its silver pot was Earl Grey, the sandwiches were excellent, the homemade scones, cream and strawberry jam melted in his mouth.

The motherly woman who served him made a fuss of him; he was the only customer that afternoon. 'Not like it is on market days,' she told him. 'Passing through, are you?'

'I'm not sure. I might stay overnight—or even for a few days,' he said as he paid the bill.

His sense of exhilaration grew rather than lessened. He walked round the square, peering into the windows of the little shops which were full of things familiar—and things unfamiliar. A noticeboard over a large shop at the corner of the square proclaimed that it was the home of the *West Bretton Clarion* newspaper.

Pasted to the glass of its door was a placard advertising the job of general assistant to the editor, John Webster. 'Must be prepared to undertake any task' it said in crabbed, old-fashioned writing.

Amused, Nicholas stared at it. He obviously wants a tea-boy, a general factotum, as well as someone to report on the flower show and the school concert, he said to himself with a grin. Just the job for my cowardly dragon.

The grin disappeared. The one thing about his old life which he was going to miss was telling his nieces and nephews the stories which kept them quiet while their parents relaxed for a short time, secure in the knowledge that Uncle Claus would relieve them of their duties for the best part of an afternoon.

Well, he would have to live without their friendly voices and their unquestioning adoration, so different from the disapproval of their elders.

Bidding them a sad goodbye he walked on, following a road which led into the country. A couple of miles outside the town was an imposing house about two hundred years old, built in the local stone. Through the iron gates to its drive he could see in the distance a large lawn surrounded by flowerbeds, several gardeners with their wheelbarrows, and a tall old man leaning on a stick.

Beyond the house was open country with blue hills in the distance, and a stretch of water which he decided that he would visit on another day.

An idea was fermenting in his brain. Gis had said in effect, 'Why not do what you want?' He had not asked him for advice as he would have done Ralph, but he had been given it all the same.

Why not do what he wanted? He thought of the eager faces of the children as he had entertained them, of his tutor at Oxford, handing back an essay to him and saying, 'Have you ever thought of writing, Schuyler? I have the feeling that if you could only put your mind to it you might do well.'

He remembered his inward amusement at what his father

would say if he had told him that he wanted to be a journalist—he was destined for grander things than that.

Not that working for the *West Bretton Clarion* would make him a journalist!

But he must do something, and what better in the long summer days than to live and work in this sleepy town, to read the books he had always meant to read, far from the distractions and dissipations of his London life of which his father had so often disapproved.

Damn his father for wandering into his thoughts! He had come here to forget him, not to erect mental memorials to him. His feet had brought him back to the newspaper shop again with the tantalising advertisement on the door. General assistant wanted. Could he be that assistant?

Why not? He had had a good education. He could write a little—and knew how to make tea. He could learn the rest.

Nicholas Schuyler pushed open the door to find himself in a small anteroom painted white. Behind a counter stood a tall elderly man, white-haired with a thin clever face. Mr John Webster, undoubtedly.

He cleared his throat, and said, and he did not remember Gis Havilland as he spoke, although he should have done, 'Good afternoon, sir. My name is Nicholas Allen. I've come about the job.'

Chapter One

Three years later—1929

'You really should have come with us to Redroofs last night, Verena. I met the most divine young man, just when I thought that the whole district was devoid of everything but bumpkins and bores!'

'Handsome, was he?' asked Verena Marlowe drily, as her widowed stepmother flung herself down in an armchair and began to insert a cigarette into a long ivory-and-silver holder. Verena was busily engaged in playing Snakes and Ladders with her half-brother, Chrissie's small son, Jamie.

'Not really,' returned Chrissie, puffing vigorously in the direction of both Verena and Jamie, who began to cough distressingly. He was asthmatic, but Chrissie could never be persuaded that cigarette smoke was harmful for him.

'Big and dark and stern-looking, rather like your lamented papa, but amusing, very. You really ought to have come with us, you know.'

'Jamie had a bad asthmatic attack yesterday,' said Verena quietly. 'It wouldn't have been wise to have left him on his own.'

'Oh, pooh to that. Priddie could have looked after him. After all, that's what Sir Charles pays her for.'

Verena sighed. She was a slender young woman, quietly dark where Chrissie was boldly fair, retiring where Chrissie was forward. So she did not say that it was Chrissie's duty to look after her son rather than Verena's or Miss Pridham's, for she had long known that her stepmother never let anything stand in the way of her enjoyment.

'Miss Pridham's grown too old to spend night after night caring for a sick small boy,' she replied gently.

Chrissie shrugged. 'Then Sir Charles ought to put her out to grass and hire someone who isn't. He's too sentimental. I shall tell him so.'

Useless to inform her that Miss Pridham, their governess, was Sir Charles's last link with his three dead sons, Peter and John, who had both been killed in the Great War, and Hugh, her father and Chrissie's late husband.

'Oh, well!' Chrissie dismissed Sir Charles, Miss Pridham and Jamie from the conversation. 'To get back to this man, name of Nicholas Allen—does it ring a bell?'

Verena shook her head. She had left Marlowe Court, her grandfather's home, ten years ago with her father, an Army officer, when he had been posted to India. Her mother had recently died giving birth to the long-awaited son who had died with her.

'No, I don't remember a Nicholas Allen. I knew quite a number of the local boys. Grandfather kept open house in those days. He was still hunting and fishing—it was before he had the accident which disabled him.'

Chrissie, who had met and married Hugh Marlowe almost immediately after he had arrived in India, so that Verena had acquired a stepmother who was little older than she was, yawned her indifference about her father-in-law's hunting and his accident. She continued to pursue her latest obsession.

'Must be new here, perhaps. He's John Webster's assistant at the *Clarion*.'

John Webster was the owner of Redroofs and a cousin as well as an old friend of Sir Charles. His only son, young Jack, had been killed in the same offensive as Peter Marlowe.

Chrissie's determination to tell Verena of what she plainly thought was her latest conquest had brought Jamie's game of Snakes and Ladders to a temporary end. Playing had taken his mind off his breathing problems, but stopping had started them off again.

He began to cough and wheeze painfully.

His mother glared at him, exclaiming angrily, 'Oh, do pull yourself together, Jamie. No one would think that you were a soldier's son.'

Verena opened her mouth to say something as sobs provoked by Chrissie's heartlessness began to punctuate Jamie's tortured breathing. She closed it again. It was quite useless to remonstrate with Chrissie over anything. She had learned long ago that her stepmother's world consisted only of herself and her wants.

She contented herself with taking Jamie's right hand and beginning to stroke it. His fingers clutched convulsively at hers for a moment before he began to relax and his breathing steadied.

'There,' said his mother triumphantly, 'I knew that if he tried he could stop that awful noise.' She puffed smoke in Jamie's direction before rising in order to saunter out of the room.

'By the way, I've persuaded Sir Charles to invite Nick Allen and John Webster to dinner on Saturday evening. I suppose that I can trust you to inform the housekeeper and make all the arrangements. It's time that we started enter-taining again. We can't mourn Hugh forever.'

It cost Verena all her strength not to return acidly, but truthfully, that as his widow hadn't mourned for him at all, mourning him forever had never been on the cards.

His mother's absence restored Jamie sufficiently to allow him to continue playing Snakes and Ladders—which Verena lovingly allowed him to win.

'You're not so good a player as Mama is,' he informed his half-sister as he put the board and counters carefully away in their box. 'She always beats me, you know.'

'Yes, I do know.' It was one of Chrissie Marlowe's less lovable characteristics that she never allowed Jamie to win any child's game she played with him.

'Would you like to walk to the Parson's Pool when I've seen Mrs Jackson about Saturday's dinner? We could take Hercules with us—and try out your new kite.' Hercules was the dog which Sir Charles had given Jamie. His name was a joke, for far from being huge and fierce he was a small and usually obedient Yorkshire terrier.

Jamie, a sensible child when not being harried by his mother, shook his head. 'Not now, Vee. I'm still not breathing properly. Later this afternoon, perhaps.' A pro-posal to which his half-sister assented.

Late afternoon saw them on the path to the pool which took them past Jesse Pye's lonely cottage and down to the hollow in which the pool lay, shaded by trees.

'Why do they call it Parson's Pool, Vee?'

'Grandfather once told me that about a hundred years ago there was a parson at St Benedict's in West Bretton who liked to swim in the pool—hence its name. Grandfather said that the locals thought he was mad. He also said that he was a distant cousin of the Sir John

Marlowe who owned Marlowe Court then—and sometimes used to join him in the pool.'

They were now at the end of the steep track—for that was all it was—which led directly to the water. As they walked the last few yards Verena stopped dead.

'What is it, Vee? What have you seen?'

'Nothing,' lied Verena, taking Jamie by the arm and turning him in the direction in which they had come.

She lied because she had seen, under one of the trees which lined the pool—more properly a lake—a heap of men's clothing, carelessly discarded. Some man—or men—was undoubtedly swimming in the pool. The question was, how decently was he dressed?

She turned Jamie around, trying to think of some excuse to move him on. Unfortunately at that moment they both heard distant splashing, Hercules began to bark, or rather yap, and Jamie said excitedly, 'Someone's in the pool, Vee. Do let's go and see,' for the pool was not yet clearly visible from where they were.

About to say, 'No, we mustn't intrude,' Verena was prevented from doing so by Hercules, who, still yapping ferociously, charged happily towards the lake and its still-invisible occupant. Jamie, of course, ran after him, shouting, leaving Verena with no option but to follow them both.

She arrived to find that Hercules was now yapping at the swimmer who was doing an impressive Australian crawl in their direction. Any fears that she might have had about the swimmer's mode of dress was dispelled by his stroking arms revealing that he was wearing an orthodox one-piece black bathing suit.

When he had almost reached the bank he stood up, shaking his head to scatter water from his glossy black hair and greeting Jamie with, 'Hello, young shaver, that's a fierce beast you have there.'

'Isn't he just!' exclaimed the delighted Jamie. Like Verena he was impressed by the magnificence of the stranger's physique and his flattery of small Hercules.

'Beware of the dog, eh? Do you think it will be safe for me to come ashore?' His strange amber eyes dancing, he smiled at Verena who stood transfixed, staring at him.

This must be Chrissie's divine man, Nicholas Allen. He was certainly not orthodoxly handsome; his face was too strong and stern for that, his nose too big, his jaw too prominent. But his body in the revealing black suit was beyond anything in its strength and power. And, despite that strength and power and the sternness of his face, his manner to Jamie had been kind.

Jamie was blossoming under it. He was usually fearful of strangers, but when this one said to him, 'Would you be good enough, young fellow, to throw me that big towel, there, by my clobber, and then restrain your monster? I would like to come out of the water before I die of cold. The day may be warm, but the water isn't—if you don't object, ma'am,' and he turned his dazzling white smile on Verena again.

'No, no, of course not. And we really mustn't intrude. I told Jamie he was to leave you to enjoy yourself, but then Hercules went mad.'

The stranger deftly caught the towel which Jamie threw to him and, wrapping it round himself, began to wade ashore.

'Hercules, is it? What an apt name for such a ferocious beast. I suppose I ought to introduce myself, but I'm not sure of the etiquette when caught trespassing in someone else's lake. Anyway, here goes, I'm Nicholas, Nick, Allen at your service.'

Now on land again he towered over them both, not because he was abnormally tall—he was, Verena judged dazedly, just under six foot in height—but because of his strongly muscular build. She really ought to return his courtesy by introducing herself and Jamie to him—although he had almost certainly guessed who they were.

'I'm Verena Marlowe, Sir Charles's granddaughter, and this is my brother Jamie. I believe that you met my stepmother last night at dinner at Redroofs—and now you must allow us to go on our way. You will be wanting to towel yourself off and change into dry clothes. It's much too cold for you to stand about in wet ones. Come along, Jamie. At once. We can fly your kite more safely away from the water.'

She really could not wait for Nick Allen to answer her for she felt that she had to get away from his overwhelming presence as soon as possible. She could quite understand why Chrissie had called him divine.

Jamie took some moving. Anyone who admired both him and Hercules—apart from Verena, that was—was a rarity in his young life. For different reasons both his mother and his grandfather disapproved of them most of the time. Reluctantly, dragging his feet a little, he did as he was told, called Hercules to him and took Verena's hand again before they set off in the opposite direction.

Nicholas, towelling his head vigorously, watched them disappear through the trees. When he had first heard their voices in the distance he had supposed that the boy must be with his mother, the gorgeous blonde who had favoured him with come-hither looks from the moment John Webster had introduced her to him.

Instead he had been accompanied by a slender dark girl with great eyes who had stared at him as though he were the monster which he had named Hercules. The blonde had been nearer to his own age, pushing thirty, but this woman looked younger—and shyer. He had begun by wondering whether she might not be the child's nursemaid, but something about her had soon told him no, even before she had called Jamie brother.

Sir Charles had said that the boy was frail, and he was certainly small for his age, 'Which I blame on his being so long in India. No climate for a white child—and he's been allowed to play the invalid, his mother tells me, much encouraged by his sister. Supposed to be asthmatic. What he really needs is more men in his life, not a pack of indulgent women. Cold baths and a little firm discipline would do him the world of good.'

And it was the pale-faced scrap he had just met of whom his grandfather had been speaking so callously!

Nicholas felt a rush of anger such as he had not experienced since he had walked out of Padworth three years ago. He quelled it. This was no business of his, and after all the sister appeared to be looking after him—but for how long?

The pale-faced scrap was enjoying himself flying his kite. He ran up and down shouting until he was exhausted, then flinging himself on the ground to let Hercules dance joyfully around him. Verena had brought a small bag of boiled sweeties with her, and they sat and sucked some of them while enjoying the sun and the view.

'Time to go home,' she said at last.

Jamie pulled a face. 'Don't want to,' he said defiantly. 'I'm happy here. You don't scold me all the time, Mama does.'

'That's because she's worried about you.'

'No, she isn't. She told the housekeeper I was a nuisance—a thundering nuisance.'

Verena sighed—she seemed to be doing a lot of sighing since they had come to England. In India they had been surrounded by servants. Jamie had had an *ayah* as well as

Miss Pridham to look after him, and Chrissie had arranged her social life so that she had barely seen her son. He had been brought to her each night before dinner to be kissed on the cheek and be told to carry on being a good boy.

Now, in the relative confines of Marlowe Court, she was constantly with him. Worse, she had lost not only her husband but a circle of adoring admirers, attracted by her charm and vivacity. Neither the charm nor the vivacity had been much in evidence since she had come to England—until she had met Nicholas Allen.

It had been left to Verena to give Jamie the ungrudging love and companionship which ought more properly to have come from his mother.

So she refrained for the umpteenth time from saying anything unkind about Chrissie to her son, but firmly urged him homewards. He responded by dragging his feet in the dirt and grumbling under his breath.

Disaster struck when they had almost reached Jesse Pye's cottage. Hercules, headstrong again, ran off the path into the undergrowth, Jamie, still cross with Verena, let go of her hand and tore after him, plunging headlong through the scrub until he tripped and fell. Verena, following him more gingerly, found him lying on the ground, a repentant Hercules licking his face.

Even her equable temper snapped at the sight of his scratched hands and his bleeding knees as he wailed at her, 'I'm sorry, Vee, I'm so sorry. I didn't mean...'

'You never do,' she said tartly, but her hands were gentle as she carefully examined him for broken bones before she allowed him to sit up.

Neither her pocket handkerchief, nor his, was large enough for her to be able to stem the flow of blood from his right knee; the left seemed less damaged by his fall. He had begun to cry gently, but without Verena needing to say anything he sniffled wanly, 'Mama would tell me not to make a noise because I'm a soldier's son, and soldiers don't cry when they are wounded, so I won't.'

'Good boy,' she told him. 'Do you think that you could manage to walk to Jesse Pye's cottage? It's not far, and he might have something handy to help stop the bleeding and bandage your right knee. The left one is only slightly grazed.'

'If you help me, Vee, yes. I'm sorry, truly sorry.'

'Shush—now lean on me. Yes, like that. We're almost there.'

Jesse Pye's garden and the cottage behind it were neater and cleaner than Verena remembered them to have been. He had been an old man when she and Miss Pridham had taken him fruit and vegetables from Marlowe Court's gardens, and he must be a very old man now. Most likely he had a son or a daughter, or even a grandchild living with him.

She knocked on the door. Someone shouted, 'Coming.' Verena willed them to be quick. Jamie was shivering and was already in the throes of a severe attack of asthma. They did not have long to wait. The front door was thrown open.

But it was not Jesse Pye who stood there smiling at them. Instead it was Chrissie's young man, Nicholas Allen, now fully dressed, though his dark, curly hair was still sleekly damp from his swim.

'Miss Marlowe, what is it?' And then he saw the shivering, spluttering Jamie, blood running down his leg, a disconsolate Hercules cringing behind him.

'Oh, you've had an accident, old son. Do come in, please—that right knee looks as though it needs instant attention.'

'You're not Jesse Pye,' Verena said stupidly, overwhelmed by Nicholas Allen all over again.

'Indeed not. He entered an almshouse just before I came to West Bretton, and I rented the cottage from John Webster. Do come in, though, Jamie looks ready to collapse. Had a fall, did he?'

He didn't wait for an answer, simply scooped Jamie up in his strong arms and carried him into the little living-room at the back which overlooked the pool and the hills.

I really must pull myself together, thought Verena dazedly, as she followed him in. I've never been so silly in a young man's presence before and goodness knows, I've mixed with enough of them not to behave like a green girl at her first grand party!

Nicholas laid Jamie down on a settle which stood in front of an old hearth containing a blackened cast-iron kitchen range. A kettle was just beginning to boil on the fire. He motioned Verena to a large easy chair whose loose cover was made of heavy-duty cream linen ornamented with giant cabbage roses.

'Good thing the kettle's almost on the boil,' he told them, making for the small lean-to kitchen which stood at the side of the cottage. 'We can have a cup of tea after the operation's over. Give me half a mo and I'll be back with cotton wool, bandages, lint, iodine and scissors.'

Verena looked around her curiously. The small room was an odd mixture of the shabby and the grand. The dining table in the middle of the room was a battered deal one which she remembered from Jesse Pye's day, as was the brass oil lamp with its white opaque shade. But standing on a desk in the window was a new and expensive typewriter, and the curtains and the loose cover on her chair were not run up from cheap pieces of fabric but were Sanderson's best.

The small rug on the board floor was a fine piece, too, but the ornaments on the mantelpiece and on the top of the

bookshelves which covered one wall were inexpensive fair-
ings and small seaside trophies. The shelves themselves
were filled with an extraordinary variety of books ranging
from Latin texts to the latest thrillers by Sapper and E.
Phillips Oppenheim.

There were no photographs of friends and relatives such
as filled the living-rooms at Marlowe Court. Instead, on a
bulletin board by the window were pinned postcards and
small reproductions of famous paintings, most of them
showing dragons and other mythical animals. The largest
was Uccello's rendering of St George killing a ferocious
beast with giant wings.

Below that was a lively pen-and-ink drawing of a large
dragon snorting fire and cowering in front of a small boy.
Both pictures attracted Jamie's attention. Unlike Verena,
who was examining her surroundings discreetly, he was
twisting about and exclaiming at all the odd treasures which
filled a bachelor's living quarters. There was even a very
dead trout in a glass case above the hearth.

'And look, look, Vee, over there, a dragon. I say, what
a jolly place this is!'

'Glad you like it,' said Nicholas, coming in carrying a
tray with a bowl of warm water and the promised first-aid
kit on it. 'Bit of a mess really, but I like it, too.'

'I'd sooner have jolly messes than tidy places where I
can't play properly because I might break something,'
Jamie told him as Nicholas began to minister skilfully and
carefully to his knees. For a man with large hands, he was
very deft, Verena thought.

He must have sensed that she was watching him for he
said, without looking up from his task, 'Do *you* like jolly
messes, Miss Marlowe?'

'Depends,' she said gravely, 'on the mess. I wouldn't
say, for instance, that this room was a mess. It's clean to

begin with, and everything looks as though it has some order in your mind—which, since it's your room, is the only mind which matters.'

She was rather proud of this noncommittal answer. Nicholas, however, looked up long enough to give her his white smile and say, before turning back to Jamie whose knee, having been cleaned and dabbed with iodine—an ordeal which he bore bravely—he was now bandaging, 'You should be in the *corps diplomatique*, Miss Marlowe. That was an answer to keep everyone happy, without giving away your true feelings.'

For some reason this stung Verena a little. She thought that he was patronising her, and worse, that this was not the sort of conversation he would have engaged in with Chrissie. He wouldn't have been patronising *her*.

'Oh, do call me Verena. I agree with Jamie. I like your room, particularly the dragons.'

She had pleased him. After securing Jamie's bandage with a neat bow he rose to his feet preparatory to removing his first-aid kit, and bowed in her direction.

'Thank you…Verena. I rather winkled that compliment out of you, didn't I? Forgive me, and as a penance I shall not only make you a cup of tea, but will serve you Nice biscuits, chocolate biscuits and raspberry cream wafers. How's that for luxury?' His strange amber eyes shone merrily in her direction: their effect on her was immediate and shocking.

Oh, he was a heartbreaker, no doubt about it, and probably every woman he met got the benefit of his practised charm—and his eyes. Well, he wasn't going to charm her, even if Jamie was rapidly succumbing to him.

Verena would have liked to refuse the tea, but that would have been mannerless, and besides, he had once again been kind to Jamie, who was already bouncing up and down at the promise of unlimited biscuits.

'That would be splendid,' she said, still grave, trying to stop her heart from beating so rapidly that she thought that it was about to leap out of her breast. Plainly nothing of her inward confusion showed. Rather the opposite, for it was apparent from his manner that Mr Nicholas, or Nick, Allen thought her a cold fish.

Fortunately he had no access to her betraying inward feelings or he would be even more conceited than he appeared to be.

This thought—which was particularly unkind in view of his sympathetic treatment of Jamie—was forced upon Verena's consciousness as an act of self-defence, for she had no business mooning after a man whom she had so recently met for the first time—and that briefly. She could only resist his attraction for her by denying him any saving graces!

'Good, then you'll excuse me if I leave you to fetch the biscuits, the teacups and the pot. I have to be my own servant these days.'

Verena blinked, dragging herself back into the cottage again. What was he talking about? Oh, the promised tea! She really must get a grip on herself!

'Shan't be long,' he said. 'If you like dragons, Jamie, there's a big book about them on the bottom shelf of the bookcase. Perhaps your sister would like to show it to you. There are some stunning pictures in it.'

So there were. Verena carefully opened it to allow an entranced Jamie to admire the various beasts portrayed in all their colourful glory while Nicholas came and went, putting a linen cloth on the table and standing teacups, milk and sugar on it, together with the promised plate of biscuits. Finally he lifted the blackened kettle off the fire and made the tea in a big brown pot, just like the one in Jamie's nursery which Miss Pridham, now resting back at Marlowe Court, used to entertain him and Verena.

'Milk and sugar, everyone?' he asked cheerfully. He seemed remarkably domesticated for such a masculine man, thought Verena acidly. Only to reproach herself—of course, being John Webster's dogsbody almost certainly meant that he couldn't afford servants.

'Yes, please,' she told him. 'Lots of milk for Jamie. He's not allowed strong tea.'

Presently they were all arranged companionably before the fire. Nicholas had lowered his large frame into another armchair, a companion to Verena's. To Jamie's delight he toasted the company with his cup before he drank his tea.

'Have you been living in West Bretton long, Nicholas?' Verena asked him. 'Or is it Nick?' It wasn't etiquette, she knew, to ask personal questions of this kind, but Nicholas Allen not only attracted her, he intrigued her. What was he doing in a backwater like West Bretton?

'I prefer Nicholas, but I also answer to Nick—John Webster calls me that when we're working. He says that it saves time. I've been here three years.'

'You have relatives in the district?' Another forbidden personal question, but Verena couldn't help herself.

Nicholas shook his head. 'No, I was touring in the West Country when I was at a bit of a loose end, and happened to see, quite by chance, John's advertisement for an assistant. It seemed like a good idea to take advantage of it—and so it proved. I had another piece of luck when this cottage became vacant and John rented it to me.'

Verena noted that Nicholas called him John, not Mr Webster, which told her something of his relationship with her cousin.

'And you,' he asked in his turn. 'I gathered from Sir

Charles and your stepmother that you have been living in India for the past ten years and that Jamie was born there. How do you like being back in England?'

'Very much. I can only be unhappy, though, that it took Papa's death to bring us back. I miss him very much—and so does Jamie. But Sir Charles has been very kind and has offered us a home for as long as we wish to stay. Chrissie, my stepmother—she likes me to use her Christian name, she's not so much older than I am—wants to settle in London, but agrees with Sir Charles that she will wait until Jamie is a little stronger before she moves into the city.'

'I *am* strong, Verena,' Jamie announced indignantly. Under Nicholas's ministrations he had recovered from his attack of asthma, and there was some colour in his cheeks for the first time since he had returned to England. Living in India was hard on English children and the sea voyage home, far from strengthening him, had taken a lot out of him.

'Of course you are,' Nicholas told him, pouring them all another cup of tea. 'But you need to be stronger still. Country living will soon put more roses in your cheeks. So will plenty of biscuits,' and he offered Jamie the plate again.

Tea over, all the biscuits scoffed by Jamie, and Hercules fed in the kitchen, Verena stood up. 'We really must be going. I said that we wouldn't be long. Chrissie will be worrying over what might have happened to us.'

Jamie opened his mouth to say something on the lines of, 'No, she won't. She never worries about either of us,' but caught his half-sister's eye and grumbled instead, 'Do we have to go now? I'd like to see more of the dragon book.'

'And so you shall. You must visit me again when your knee's better. I know quite a lot of stories about dragons.'

'You do? Oh, do say we can come again, Vee! And I like your cottage, sir. Much nicer than Marlowe Court!'

This artless comment set both his elders laughing.

'But a little cramped, wouldn't you say?' offered Nicholas. 'But thanks for the compliment, young 'un.'

Verena could not stop herself from coming out with, 'It won't be long before we meet again. I understand from Chrissie that she intends to ask you for dinner tomorrow. She will be sure to want to thank you for looking after Jamie.'

Nicholas nodded. 'Yes, she came round this morning with the invitation. She was worried about the short notice, but fortunately, West Bretton's social life being somewhat less than hectic, I was able to accept at once. I look forward to seeing you again.'

So she would have the pleasure—if that was the right word—of sitting opposite to, or near him, at dinner. Which was probably as near to him as she would ever get. By what he had just said Chrissie was in the process of annexing him, adding him to the long list of her admirers.

She would also have the dubious pleasure of watching her stepmother make yet another conquest. Since Verena's father's sudden death and their return home, Chrissie had walked the straight and narrow path of virtue, but she had obviously decided that mourning was over and she could resume the headlong career which had caused her late husband—and her stepdaughter—so much misery.

Verena checked herself. No, she would not think of Major Roger Gough, she would not. That was over and done with and she must make a new life for herself in England.

If she had been free to go her own way she would have left Chrissie and Jamie to go theirs, but her father had begged her on his deathbed not to abandon Jamie to the untender mercies of his mother.

'Promise me you'll look after him, Vee. She won't, you know she won't. She doesn't care for the little fellow.'

So she had promised, but she was fearful of what that promise might yet cost her.

And Jamie, of course, was right about his mother's indifference to him. Chrissie stared crossly at his bandaged leg, and ignored his excited cries of, 'Oh, Mama, we had such a splendid afternoon...'

Instead she exclaimed scornfully, 'Do be quiet, Jamie. Really, Verena, can't I trust you to do anything right? Take him upstairs to the nursery and let Priddie have a look at that knee. I knew I should have insisted on her taking Jamie for his walk—look what happened when she didn't.'

Jamie, trying to mend matters, but only succeeding in making them worse, shouted defiantly, 'It wasn't Vee's fault, Mama, it was Hercules who—'

His mother cut him off again. 'If that's so, I shall have to think about getting rid of him. That dog is nothing but trouble. For the present go upstairs—at once.'

This piece of unthinking cruelty was enough to cause Jamie to suffer another, and more severe, asthma attack, since all his pleas on Hercules' behalf were ignored by Chrissie, who simply walked out of the room, still railing against Verena *and* Hercules.

Every time Verena considered leaving Jamie to his mother, Chrissie's heartless cruelty had Verena renewing her vow to her father all over again. Perhaps if Chrissie married someone like Nicholas Allen, he might persuade her to be a little kinder to her son. But the possibility of her marrying Nicholas Allen wasn't a happy one, either.

Chapter Two

'Piers!' Chrissie's excited exclamation floated up the stairs as Verena walked down to dinner that same night.

She had dressed herself with some care in a blue satin and chiffon dress with a low V-neck which had a paler blue insert. A white silk camellia rode on her right shoulder. The dress, fashionably trimmed with beading, possessed a flared skirt so that its scalloped hem was higher on one side than the other, revealing her shapely legs. Roger Gough had frequently told her that they were one of her best features, and should be seen more often. Her court shoes were made of matching blue kid with Louis heels—another fashion point.

Perhaps it was meeting Nicholas Allen, or Chrissie's rudeness when they had arrived home, which had made Verena determined to look her best in future. Her grandest evening dress she was saving for dinner on Saturday when Nicholas was a guest.

From Chrissie's exclamation, however, and the bustle in the entrance hall, it seemed that they were to have a guest for dinner that evening—and most likely for some time to come.

The unexpected visitor was her cousin, Piers Marlowe,

who must have arrived suddenly and without warning; a habit of his of which Sir Charles had recently complained. He had been Sir Charles's heir until Jamie had been born, the estate being entailed in the male line, so Jamie's birth had deprived him of both money and a title. Nevertheless, as Sir Charles had informed Verena and Chrissie when they had arrived back in England, he bore no grudge for his disinheritance.

'Win some, lose some,' he had told Sir Charles cheerfully when the news had arrived. Instead he had insisted on drinking the new heir's health in the best wine from Marlowe Court's cellars.

Verena ran downstairs quickly. She had not met Piers since she had been a shy little thing of thirteen when he had already been a handsome young man in his midtwenties, above taking much notice of girl cousins not yet ready for the Season, however big their eyes.

He had been so blondly handsome, so graceful both on a horse and off it, that for some years afterwards he had been the model for all the princes in the fairy tales she read. When she had grown up, he became all of the heroes in Miss Ethel M. Dell's romances, until passing time—and meeting other handsome young men—had blurred her memory of him.

What had ten years done to him? It had certainly changed her. Would he think that the change was for the better? A sudden thought struck Verena as she arrived in the entrance hall to find him as splendid as she had remembered him.

He was the exact opposite of Nicholas Allen! So why had she been so overwhelmed by Nicholas?

'Verena! Little Verena, it can't be! You've grown into a beauty fit to rival the famous Elizabeth Marlowe.' Piers was referring to a Marlowe ancestress of the early nineteenth century whose brilliant looks and vivacity had earned her a Duke for a husband.

Piers's greeting of her was as extravagantly admiring as Verena might have hoped for. So why was it that as he moved lightly forward to give her a chaste, cousinly kiss on her cheek, his blue eyes alight with pleasure, she felt none of the exhilaration that the first sight of Nicholas Allen had given her?

Oh, she was pleased to see him, to find him little changed from the golden idol of her adolescence, but the kiss, although welcome, did not stir her blood.

She had no time to be shocked by this unfortunate discovery. Unfortunate, because her grandfather had recently hinted that it might be a good idea for her to consider Piers as a possible husband.

'The estate isn't the gold mine it used to be, it's been hard hit by all these new taxes, but I could still manage to start you both off in married life with a useful dowry,' he had promised.

Remembering Piers, Verena had certainly not dismissed his suggestion out of hand, rather the contrary. But bitter experience had made her cautious. 'I'll think about it, Grandfather,' she had said, 'when I meet him again.'

Now she was meeting him again, and she had no intention of dismissing him out of hand because of one afternoon's odd encounter with a man whom she hardly knew, who was probably not of her class, and of whom, she felt sure, her grandfather would disapprove as a husband, for all that he was prepared to entertain him to dinner.

She stood back from the kiss. 'Oh, that is going the pace—to compare me with the fabulous Liz—but thank you for the compliment. At least, you haven't changed.'

'Ah, pretty cousin, I hope that's meant for a compliment.' The blue eyes twinkled at her admiringly. So much so that jealous Chrissie felt it necessary to intervene.

'When you two have finished admiring one another you ought to go and see your great-uncle, Piers. Knowing him, I'm sure that he would consider that your first duty when you arrive is to the master of the house.'

'Of course, Chrissie. I may call my new cousin Chrissie, I hope. But what is a poor fellow to do when confronted with a pair of raving beauties after he's spent a long day driving from London? Surely even great-uncle Charles wouldn't grudge me a few moments spent in admiration?'

This flattery struck Verena as a little ripe, but was meat and drink to Chrissie who felt that she had been starved of male attention for far too long.

But what riches she was now being offered! First Nicholas Allen, whose attraction, like Verena, she could not quite explain, and now this gorgeous creature—Nicholas's opposite—more gorgeous even than all of the matinee idols whom Chrissie had ever worshipped—Apollo in person, no less.

The look with which she honoured Piers was almost a simper. 'Put like that—no. All the same…'

'All the same he'd better go,' remarked Verena a trifle drily. 'Grandfather is a stickler for propriety.'

She was well aware that Chrissie was separating her from Piers in the hope that, later, she might get him to herself. Remembering that Chrissie had taken the trouble to visit Nicholas in person to give him his dinner invitation, it seemed to Verena that every handsome male in her vicinity was going to be required to do homage to her—with nothing left over for her. Chrissie would annex them all.

As she had annexed Roger.

Verena shivered a little as this unwanted memory surfaced for the second time.

Never again. If she found another man to love, and who seemed as though he might be reasonably faithful, this time she would fight for him with every weapon in her armoury.

Piers gone, Chrissie disappeared, too. 'Must make myself presentable,' she announced, although she had already changed for dinner and was wearing a fashionable little black dress which did the double duty of offering a concession to her widowed state and also displaying her body to its best advantage.

'I thought that you had already dressed for dinner,' Verena said, being catty for once.

'What! Wear this dreary rag now that cousin Piers is with us! No, indeed. I see *you*'re dressed to kill. Did you know that he was coming and didn't have the decency to tell me?'

These arrows were shot from Chrissie's ever-ready bow as she dashed out of the room.

A quarter of an hour later she arrived in the drawing-room in a stunning off-the-shoulder creation in scarlet and silver which had already mown down half the men at the hill station where the Marlowes had lived in India. She had been saving it to mow down Piers. Nicholas would now get the benefit of the green-and-gold ensemble with which she had captured Major Roger Gough.

Sir Charles, Piers and Vernon, Sir Charles's land agent, all rose to their feet on her entrance. 'I do hope that I haven't made dinner late,' she offered, false contrition written all over her pretty face.

'Fortunately, no,' returned Sir Charles, the only male in the room who was impervious to Chrissie's charms. 'I had dinner put back to allow Piers a little rest after his long journey. After all, unlike tomorrow's, this is a family dinner party so no harm done.'

Piers raised his eyebrows. 'Splendid. I'm pleased to learn

that since Chrissie and Verena came home you have ceased to be a recluse.'

Sir Charles grunted something which might be construed as assent. Piers lit a cigarette and continued with his friendly chatter, designed to put everyone at ease.

If he had a fault, Verena reflected, it was that he was too skilled in the minutiae of family diplomacy. Now he was asking with a great show of interest, 'May I enquire as to who your guests are tomorrow, Great-uncle?'

'Not many.' Sir Charles was curt. 'John Webster, Lord and Lady Axminster, and my old friend Anne Hopwood. Oh, and that man of John's he thinks so much of, young Allen. He says that he has become a most able lieutenant. Chrissie has been introduced to him, but I believe Verena hasn't met him yet.'

It would be odd not to report on her and Jamie's afternoon adventure, so Verena offered, 'Oh, but I have, Grandfather. When we were out walking this afternoon Jamie had a fall and cut his knee, so I took him to Jesse Pye's cottage for first aid. Of course, we soon discovered that Mr Allen lives there now. He kindly looked after Jamie's knee and later he gave us afternoon tea.'

'You never said anything about meeting Nick Allen when you came home,' burst from Chrissie.

'You never gave me the opportunity,' said Verena drily.

Piers, who had been watching the two women closely, drawled, 'Nicholas Allen, eh? I remember meeting him at cousin John's office on my last visit. I understand that he's a great man for the ladies, Vee, you'd better watch out for him!'

'Well, he wasn't a great man with me, Piers. He seemed more concerned with Jamie's knee than with my charms!'

'Oh, I wouldn't put it past him to have a go, Vee, when he gets to know you better. After all, you are a Marlowe

of Marlowe Court with a good dowry and all that. When
he first got here he made a dead set at Isobel Playfair—
you remember her, Vee, old Playfair's eldest?

'Anyway, she fancied him something rotten, and he even
had the gall to propose marriage to her. She soon gave him
the push. Wasn't going to marry a penniless nobody of an
office boy in a one-horse town.'

He puffed his cigarette reminiscently, and twinkled at
Verena. Here was a splendid opportunity to do a possible
rival down and he took it with both hands.

'And then he was after Daisy Goring. She fell flat on her
face before him, but she wasn't flat enough to marry him.'

He laughed uproariously. 'Joke there, Vee, pun on flat.
Have a good laugh, do.' He added the last sentence because, although Chrissie was apparently overwhelmed by
his racy wit, Verena's face was stony. Perhaps she wasn't
aware that a flat was slang for someone who was easily
cheated.

'Can't imagine what the ladies see in him: ugly brute,
what? Can't understand what cousin John sees in him, either.'

'He's a hard worker, John says,' commented Sir Charles
helpfully.

Verena said nothing. She was in a state of mild shock.
Was this mannerless and unkind creature the idol she had
worshipped from afar for so many years? Could he really
be the sort of man her grandfather wished her to marry—
this gossiping boor?

Nicholas Allen had made no kind of wrong move towards her when she was with him. Quite the contrary, he
had been gentlemanly courtesy itself. Men often said that
gossip was the monopoly of women, but Piers was proving
himself a master, not a mistress, of the art—if it could be
so called.

Chrissie said, 'I thought that he was great fun.'

'Oh, such fellows often are,' offered Piers carelessly. 'But we don't let our wives and daughters marry them! Why are we talking about him? Let's concentrate on something jollier.'

Verena could not stop herself. '*We* haven't been talking about him at all, Piers, *you* have.'

Piers cocked a shrewd eyebrow at her. 'So, he did make an impression on you, Vee; fancy that.'

'No, I don't, Piers: fancy him—or that. And any impression he made was on Jamie because he was so kind to him, not on me. But I agree with you, let's talk about something else.'

All present were staring at her hard enough to cause her some discomfort for she was seldom so downright, normally displaying instead the diplomatic arts which she had learned in Anglo-India's formal society. Fortunately for everyone's peace of mind, Gantry, the butler, put his head round the door and announced that dinner was served.

This effectively killed any further conversation about Nicholas Allen stone dead: not least because Piers had no wish to antagonise Verena before he had proposed to her.

Unaware that on the previous evening he had been the subject of conversation in the drawing-room of Marlowe Court, Nicholas Allen was standing before the small mirror in his cottage bedroom putting the finishing touches to the evening dress which he knew he would be required to wear for dinner there.

What he was wearing was neither new nor splendid. It was second-hand, having been bought in a London shop which specialised in stocking the cast-off clothing of those in society.

Since Nicholas had driven away from Padworth he had

never touched a penny of the Schuyler money which had been left to him by his grandfather, but he still possessed a tidy income bequeathed to him by a non-Schuyler aunt which he used to buy a very few luxuries which were not really luxuries at all—such as his typewriter and the books which lined his shelves.

Otherwise he tried to live off his pay from John Webster which John had increased over the three years which he had spent in West Bretton.

Not only was he practising a point of principle—having determined to take no profit whatsoever from being a member of the powerful Schuyler family—but he had no desire to be seen as moneyed. So, when he needed a dinner jacket and its matching braided trousers, he had not bought the new ones which he could have easily afforded, but those which betrayed their second-hand origins. The fit was tight and the trousers were shiny.

No matter, he had never been a dandy and was certainly not going to start being one in the wilds of Devonshire!

Mocking himself a little, he had said to his mirror when he had first worn them, 'Claus Schuyler is dead! Long live Nicholas Allen!'

Not that he wore them very often. Now, with all his buttons fastened, his cheap cufflinks firmly fixed in his shirt cuffs, and his hair brushed, he decided that he was splendid enough to go to dine at Marlowe Court and meet the lovely Chrissie again.

He had scarcely given another thought to Verena, although he had mused once or twice on young Jamie. John Webster had told him that morning when he had visited the office in West Bretton with some copy that Sir Charles was a little worried about the boy.

'He doesn't seem either very well, or very happy. He thinks that England doesn't agree with him.'

Being with the little boy and his half-sister had reminded Nicholas of how much he missed the younger members of his family. He wondered exactly how old the girl was. He had thought at first that she was barely out of her teens, still a flapper, but mental arithmetic when she had spoken of her time in India had told him that she must be older than that. She was probably in her very early twenties.

It was a bit of a pity that her stepmother was such a stunner: she was likely to be overshadowed by her and end up an also-ran in the marriage stakes.

Thinking of Chrissie had begun to rouse his too-long dormant senses. He had been celibate since that brief mad affair with Daisy Goring eighteen months ago. He wondered how she was enjoying married life. Not at all, perhaps, if her husband was the jealous sort who expected her to be faithful.

His watch told him that it was time to walk to Marlowe Court. The journey wasn't long enough to justify him using his little Morris—bought after he had sold his Bentley in Barnstaple for far less than it was worth. He had never driven it after his arrival in West Bretton; it hardly fitted the picture of a young man so much in need of a job that he was willing to be John Webster's dogsbody.

But he was far more than that now, and he had found that he enjoyed living within a small income and counting his pennies. His great-grandfather, the Captain, who had counted his cents daily—or so legend had it—would have been proud of him. He must be more like the old man than he, and everyone else, had thought.

He took this new piece of insight with him into Marlowe Court's drawing-room. Except for the Axminsters, who had a fair way to travel, he was the last to arrive. As he expected he had already met everyone there, even the superbly handsome rake who was leaning against the mantelpiece as though he owned it, and smoking an expensive Turkish cigarette in a tortoiseshell holder.

He gave Nicholas a hard stare before drawling, 'Met before, haven't we, Allen? At the Gorings' eighteen months ago. Seen Daisy lately, have you?'

'Not since she married,' he responded cheerfully. 'Have you?'

He knew that when Daisy had fallen for him he had cut Piers out, and that Piers had resented it bitterly. Office boys who wore second-hand dinner suits were not supposed to put down one of society's darlings.

Verena was not the only person present to notice that Piers's stare was a somewhat puzzled one. As on the last occasion on which they had met, Piers had the oddest feeling that he had met—or seen—young Allen before. But where? Surely he would have known that ghastly dinner jacket anywhere! And remembered it too!

He gave up. Not least because the Axminsters were announced and there was the usual round of male handshakes and ladies' kisses—which consisted of nothing more than the coming together of rouged cheeks—followed by the offering and accepting of a pre-dinner sherry. Chrissie was splendidly adept at performing such mild nothings.

She patted the place beside her on the *chaise-longue* where she had disposed herself in her green-and-gold glory, an offering which Nicholas promptly accepted. Like Piers she flaunted a giant cigarette holder, and held out to Nicholas an engraved silver cigarette case, a present from her late husband, for him to take a gasper from it—a voguish word for a cigarette which dated from the Great War.

'Oh, I forgot,' she exclaimed prettily. 'You don't indulge, do you?'

Nicholas shook his head. 'No. Don't like it and can't afford to.' He noticed that Verena was not smoking either, although everyone else was, even elderly Miss Anne Hopwood of whom Sir Charles was making a fuss. He, John Webster and Lord Axminster were puffing on excellent Havana cigars.

Moved by he knew not what, Nicholas leaned forward and said, 'You don't smoke, Verena?'

She shook her head. 'No, like you, I dislike it. I tried to smoke in India because I felt very much an odd woman out, but it was useless. I simply felt sick, so I gave up.'

Verena was looking much better tonight than she had done on the previous afternoon, Nicholas thought approvingly. Her dress, although not as stunning as her stepmother's, was attractive and suited her very different looks. It was a delicate lemon in colour, trimmed with cream flowers at the hem and waist. It ended just below the knees to show a pair of shapely legs ending in feet in cream kid slippers with tiny silver rosettes on them. Her dark hair was confined in a lemon silk bandeau which ended in a large bow just under one ear.

To his surprise Nicholas decided that she made her stepmother look more than a trifle overblown and garish. Modish simplicity had its points after all.

'You don't look an odd woman out to me,' he told her, 'quite the contrary. Very much an even woman in!'

'Thank you.' Verena smiled back at him, showing him for the first time an attractive dimple about an inch from the left side of her rosy lips. 'I've waited a long time to hear someone say that.'

She was remembering that Roger had always been impatient with her because she didn't smoke, and that the phrase, 'odd woman out' had been his. It had taken a provincial nobody, the object of her cousin Piers's scorn, to compliment her on what was usually seen as eccentricity.

Chrissie, furious that Verena was monopolising Nick again, blew smoke—and a dart—in his direction.

'Piers tells me that you had a thing for Isobel Playfair. You do surprise me. I don't remember her as particularly attractive.'

'No? Perhaps she improved while you were in India. Some women are late developers. John told me that she has just had her first child, a boy.'

Chrissie didn't quite know how to respond to this cheerful reply. Nick didn't look or sound like a man depressed at the memory of having failed to net a considerable heiress. She was saved from any further comment by the interesting, but depressing turn which the general conversation had taken.

Lord Axminster was explaining his relatively late arrival which had caused dinner to be put back for the second night in succession.

'Percy Bidworth rang me just as we were leaving. He had tried to contact me earlier in the day. It seems that the gang who have been looting country houses locally have made Bidworth Hall their latest target. He came back from a week spent with his cousin near Exeter to discover the place upside down.

'Not only had his collection of miniatures worth a small fortune been taken, but his big Van Dyck and some of the smaller oils, as well as a quantity of eighteenth-century porcelain. You remember it, Charles? Stood in some fine cabinets on the long passageway on the first floor between the picture gallery and the big reception room. The glass fronts of the cabinets had been smashed to pieces to get at it. Some silver had gone as well. Whoever took it knew, as usual, what they were doing. The flashy, but worthless, stuff had all been left behind. He wanted to warn me, and also to advise me to do everything possible to try to prevent our place from suffering a similar disaster.

'Fortunately I had the Leonardo drawings put in the vaults of my London bank, but that still leaves Grandfather's collection of Renaissance paintings at risk. The Chief Constable says that Scotland Yard think that some society toff—their words—must be running things. If the locals don't catch this gang, they'll be down here soon, you mark my words.'

Shocked exclamations ran round the room. John Webster said reflectively, 'Obviously the same gang which has been operating around the West Country for the last three years. Whoever it is knows the district and the houses and what they contain. Society thieves—such as Raffles—carrying on like this in popular novels may be romantic to read about, but they're pretty vile in real life.'

'They must have at the very least a pantechnicon or a large van with them,' said Nicholas thoughtfully, 'to take all that away at once. Strange that no one has ever seen it.'

'But didn't the servants hear anything?' Verena asked sensibly. So far she had not joined in the useless lamentations, Nicholas noticed, but was looking, instead, at the practical aspects of the whole distressing business.

'It seems that the thieves, as usual, knew that the Bidworths would be away, and also knew exactly where the servants' quarters were and entered the Hall as far away from them as possible. Not only that, they must have thrown down blankets to deaden the noise they were making.'

'Clever thieves, then,' was Nicholas's contribution. Both Piers and Verena looked as though they wished to say something further but the butler arriving to announce that dinner was served broke up the discussion.

Verena found herself sitting between Piers and

Nicholas—which seemed like a piece of symbolism which she could well have done without. She was still in the process of being surprised at how much Nicholas affected her—and how little Piers did. It really ought to have been the other way round.

'That's a splendid outfit you're wearing, Verena. Makes me realise more than ever how much you've grown up.'

'Slimy bounder,' was Nicholas's inward reaction as these kind words floated his way. He disliked Piers intensely, thought him an unpleasant snob, and John Webster's comment to him earlier in the day, that Sir Charles was hoping that Verena and Piers might marry, had shocked him. Surely she deserved better than that!

He was also a trifle disturbed by the knowledge that Piers must have seen him, albeit briefly, in the days when he had been Nicholas Schuyler. It was to be hoped that he didn't belatedly remember who he really was.

It wasn't likely, but it was a possibility which he had ceased to worry about—until tonight—in the three years which he had spent so happily and anonymously in West Bretton.

John Webster was telling Anne Hopwood that he was thinking of giving up publishing the *Clarion* some time soon, and concentrating on running the Redroofs estate instead of employing an agent to do it for him.

'But what will happen to the *Clarion*,' she asked him anxiously. 'Surely you aren't going to sell it!'

'I must. I've no heirs to leave it to,' John said sadly, 'and a new man will invigorate it. He'll have young Allen to help him—he's practically running it now, as it is. He's picked up the business so speedily, is already acting as a freelance with a paper in Exeter, and has even sold some articles on West Country life to the *Daily Telegraph*. He learned more in a year than I learned in ten, and best of all he has an old head on young shoulders which has saved me money more than once. I'm the fifth wheel these days.'

Piers looked up as his plate was removed. 'No longer an office boy, eh, Allen, but quite the paragon! You ought to be able to afford a decent dinner jacket now. Get John to advise you on what to buy.'

The sneer in his voice was palpable. Nicholas looked at him across Verena.

'Can't see what's wrong with my present one,' he offered mildly. 'Bit tight on the shoulders, perhaps, but I don't wear it often enough to splash out on a new one. Take care of the pennies, my great-grandfather always said, and the pounds will take care of themselves.'

In reality the old man had spoken of cents and dollars, but the principle remained the same.

Most of the dinner party, including Sir Charles, Lord Axminster, and Verena smiled approvingly at this modestly naïve speech from a young man who obviously knew his place.

Piers didn't. His sneer more pronounced than ever he drawled, 'And I suppose great-grandad had a few bob, had he?' in a manner which implied that he hadn't.

'A few,' said Nicholas with his most charming white grin, thinking of his great-grandfather, Ghysbrecht Schuyler, the scheming Dutch-American peasant who had made himself the richest man on earth by his cunning and his determination never to waste as little as a cent of his vast fortune.

The smile exasperated Piers. 'And none of it came to you?'

'Oh, a few bob, nothing fancy,' returned Nicholas, speaking of the inherited millions which he had left untouched in Coutts Bank since he had walked out of Padworth on a hot summer's afternoon.

Verena, who had seen not only Sir Charles's distaste for Piers's baiting of a guest at his table, but also Lord Axminster's, said, 'I hope that you are proud of your ancestor, Nicholas, because he was careful enough to leave you something, however small.'

In view of the truth of his financial situation Nicholas felt a bit of a cur on hearing this kind defence, but could only mutter, 'Thank you, Verena, of course I am.'

'Good,' she said, and smiling at Piers, added, 'I think that we can leave it at that, don't you?'

Chrissie, not to be outdone, added her gloss to the discussion by saying, 'It's not Nick's fault that he's poor. I'm sure he works hard to make up for his family's lack of wealth.'

Oh, God, thought Nicholas frantically, what on earth have I started? He was saved by Piers suddenly realising that he was not adding to his reputation by baiting a poor young man so publicly.

Worse, there was also the chance that Sir Charles's support for his bid for Verena's hand—and her dowry—might disappear if he continued to allow his jealousy of a rival to provoke him into too much open spite.

He announced hastily, 'I was only trying to advise someone whom I thought might welcome a little help. Forgive me, Allen, if I gave you the wrong impression by trying to do so.'

'Of course, Marlowe. Always willing to accept help whenever it's offered. Living a quiet life in West Bretton doesn't really prepare one to enter the great world—which I hope to do one day.'

The last sentence was, Nicholas knew, yet another thundering lie. He had lived in the great world and had no particular wish to return to it, but a provincial peasant was traditionally supposed to have only one ambition and that was to succeed in the capital. Countless novels had been written on that theme. He was busy writing one himself.

The next course's arrival, a baron of beef, ended discussion as the guests, including Nicholas, set to heartily, and the meal ended, under Sir Charles's direction, in inconsequential chitchat, consequential chitchat having proved rather embarrassing.

He even managed to keep the conversation uncontroversial after the ladies retired, leaving the men to drink Sir Charles's excellent port. Piers did himself proud, but his host was not the only one to notice that young Allen quietly passed the decanter on without using it when it arrived before him for the second time.

One of the vows Nicholas had made on arriving in West Bretton was that of relative abstinence. His days of wild drinking, with its inevitable sad consequences, were over.

He took little part in the discussion about the chances of the runners in the Derby, to be held in the following week, and only surfaced when he heard Sir Charles speaking of young Jamie.

'He suffers from a poor constitution, I'm afraid. He needs hardening. Boarding school for him as soon as he's fit to go. Bit of a mollycoddle. Been too much with the women, I'm afraid.'

'Oh, quite,' agreed Lord Axminster, 'fatal for a young feller, that. Needs a tough regime to straighten him out.'

Every head but Nicholas's nodded agreement. He could not refrain from saying, as tentatively as he could, 'Didn't seem much wrong with him to me, the other day. Miss Verena brought him to my cottage for some first aid and he took his medicine like a man. Never flinched when I cleaned a rather nasty wound and treated it with iodine. Seemed a jolly little chap.'

'Even so,' added Piers, eager to be in Sir Charles's good

books again, 'don't alter the general principle.' To Nicholas he said, 'Pass the port, old fellow, don't hang on to it, if you don't want it. No stomach for alcohol, eh?'

'In moderation,' said Nicholas coolly, pushing the decanter towards Piers. He was relieved when Sir Charles finally led them back into the drawing-room where Chrissie was having trouble in deciding which of her two possible beaux she would annex first.

She plumped for Piers. After all, Nicholas was stuck in West Bretton and would always be on hand, whilst Piers's comings and goings, according to his great-uncle, were invariably erratic.

This left Nicholas at a loose end. Sir Charles, John Webster, Anne Hopwood and the Axminsters began reminiscing about the happy days of their youth. He looked around for Verena, but could not find her. He decided instead on a breath of fresh air. French windows opened on to the garden, and as discreetly as he could, he let himself out.

The ladies, waiting for the men, had occupied their time by drinking Harrod's best coffee brought from London, and talking gossip about various friends and relations and the Royal family. The Prince of Wales was always a reliable— or rather unreliable—subject for a happy twenty-five minutes' headshaking.

'Still going round with the Dudley Ward woman,' lamented Lady Axminster, 'spent some time in Nottinghamshire with her, I'm told. I find neither her, nor the county, attractive.'

And that's Nottinghamshire disposed of, thought Verena, amused. Aloud she said, 'I suppose that what we all want is for him to provide us with a Princess of Wales.'

'Very true,' said Anne Hopwood. 'Now the person I am sorry for is his poor mama.'

Everyone said Amen to that. Chrissie's contribution was, 'So long as she's pretty. I mean the Princess he picks.'

A spirited discussion on whom he might choose followed. Bored, Verena rose and wandered off towards the French windows. She wondered what was wrong with her that she soon tired of the staple of gossip which made up the world of the women around her.

Outside, the evening was beautiful. She strolled along the paths of her grandfather's neglected garden. Neglected, although it was carefully weeded and tended, because her grandmother's interesting lay-out of plants *à la* Gertrude Jekyll had been allowed to decline into a more conventional prettiness after her death.

I wonder if Grandfather would allow me to revive it, she mused as she sat down on a rustic bench to listen to the water from a small fountain drop gently into the pool beneath.

In the distance a bird began to sing. The contrast between the fulfilled peace of the night outside the house and the noisy emptiness of the petty world inside, struck Verena forcibly.

Alas, she heard footsteps approaching. Someone was coming to disturb her heavenly calm. It was one of the men. And then as he drew near to pause at the bench and to put out a hand to stop her rising, she saw that it was Nicholas Allen, he of the ill-fitting dinner jacket—and the strange influence on her.

'No,' he said quietly, 'don't get up. I'll go back in again. I didn't mean to disturb you.'

Verena said, equally quietly, 'By no means. I expect that you came out to enjoy the peaceful night as I did. It would be cruel to deprive you of its beauty. Perhaps you might like to share it with me,' and she pointed to the empty place on the seat beside her.

She thought for a moment that he was going to refuse—and was surprised at how disappointed she felt, and how happy it made her when he accepted her invitation. The strange affinity which she was beginning to feel with him grew stronger each time that they met.

She wondered briefly whether he felt the same—but surely not. After Isobel Playfair, Daisy Goring and now Chrissie, she must seem like a small brown sparrow among birds of paradise.

Neither of them spoke for a little time. The moon rose above a low bank of clouds and threw a silver tinge on everything. The bird began to sing again. When it stopped, Nicholas spoke at last—to quote Shakespeare.

'"It was the nightingale and not the lark…"'

'*Romeo and Juliet*, of course.'

He smiled at her, transforming his face which was stern in repose. 'No "of course" about it. You know the play?'

'Only from reading it. I've never seen it acted. Have you?'

'Once, at Stratford, I had the privilege of seeing the Bard's star-crossed lovers. It was quite magical. Shakespeare's better on the stage than on the page for all the beauty of his written words.'

Nicholas Allen had a way with words, too, no doubt about it, and deserved a reward. She gave it to him.

'And no "of course" for you for knowing that it was the nightingale.'

'I might have guessed.'

'But you didn't.' Now how was I sure of that?

He smiled his transforming smile again. 'No, I have a clever relative, I'm not quite sure whether he's my uncle or my cousin. What is certain is that his knowledge is enormous. He taught me to listen to birdsong and identify it when I was a sprat and he was a mackerel—if you take my meaning.'

'That your uncertainly named relative is older than you are.'

This, together with her appreciation of his mild joke, both pleased and amused him. It was one which he could never have made to Chrissie and the others, nor would they have responded as she had done.

'Oh, he would like that. "Uncertainly named." If I ever meet him again, I shall pass it on.'

That was an odd thing for him to say. Perhaps the relative had gone abroad. That would explain it. Another odd thing was that although to be alone with him stirred her as being with Major Roger Gough had never done, she was quite content just to sit by him and enjoy the silence which followed their brief exchange of words.

And then the nightingale sang again. Liquid notes which poured into the waiting air. Pure sound which owed nothing to artifice. The night was alive with beauty.

When the lovely noise stopped, Nicholas, moved by something which he had never felt before, and which he would have found it difficult to describe, turned towards Verena to take her hand in his. As he touched her he was overcome by the oddest sensation. For a fraction of a second the night disappeared. He was seated on a river bank in dappled shade, still holding her hand—and he was filled with such happiness that his senses reeled.

And then he was back in the present, holding Verena's hand.

Why? What did he mean to do with it? each of them silently asked. It was the first time he had touched her and, if her reaction to his mere presence had been strong, his touch was overwhelming.

Verena's eyes dilated, and she stared at him entranced. Nicholas, the more experienced of the two, though greatly surprised by his own strange and brief vision, knew what to do with her hand.

He turned it over and kissed the palm. Verena shivered, her body alive with wonder. Nicholas knew at once, without being told, that she was finding herself in unknown territory. Chrissie had hinted to him in passing on the night when they had first met that her stepdaughter had once been engaged, 'but it didn't take'. He now knew that, despite that engagement, she was a novice in a game in which he had once been an adept. The game of love.

Was it that? Was it her innocence which was attracting him so suddenly and so strongly? When he had first met her she had made little impression on him, so why was he so powerfully attracted now?

Was it, perhaps, the night? Did she really possess a subtle, delicate beauty and an amused, clever mind, or was the magic of the moon deceiving him? Whatever, he could not resist leaning forward to progress from kissing her palm to kissing her tender, slightly parted lips.

It was a gentle kiss, as innocent as she was. Not at all like the ones with which he had favoured Chrissie when she had visited him in his cottage—and which he now regretted. He was also relieved that he had taken their intimacy that morning no further than kissing—much to Chrissie's disappointment.

To Verena the kiss was a part of the magic night which had brought him to her—to prove that the affinity which she felt for him was no illusion, no daydream. The kiss also told her that whatever she had felt for Roger Gough it was not love, and that she owed Chrissie a favour for having seduced him away from her.

The only question was, did Nicholas feel the same for

her? Or was this tender lovemaking something which he offered any young woman who temporarily attracted him? Or, as Piers had suggested, did he see her as a worthwhile catch like Isobel and the others? She was no heiress, but she would have a reasonable dowry when she married.

Regardless of that she made no effort to end the kiss, and it was Nicholas, now almost fully roused, who did so. He heard her give a little sigh—was it of regret?

'I'm sorry' he said. 'I shouldn't have done that—and without any warning, too.'

To his surprise she smiled and asked him gently, 'Why, didn't you like doing it? I did.'

'Too much,' he said as frank as she. 'I should have led up to it gently, tested the waters, as it were, not almost jumped on you.'

'Jumped on me! That was the gentlest jump a girl was ever subjected to!'

Roger had always been a little rough with her, as though he were stealing something. Nicholas had treated her as gently as a bee sips at a flower. Perhaps he thought that she was too fragile for a real kiss. She wasn't quite sure what she thought a real kiss entailed.

Something between Roger's plundering and Nicholas's gentleness, perhaps. He was laughing now. Not at her, but with her.

'You would like me to kiss you again, perhaps?'

'If you like. It's better than listening to Chrissie and the rest gossiping about the Prince of Wales!'

Now this was impudent, she knew, and was rewarded for it. 'Minx,' he muttered, his own eyes alight, 'you shall pay for that.' This time she found both his arms were around her and his kiss, though not rough, was powerful and seducing. As her lips opened under his he inserted just the tip of his tongue into her mouth before withdrawing it.

The effect was electrifying. Verena jumped as though galvanised, and Nicholas, surprised by his own immediate response to hers, drew back.

'No, not now. It's too soon. We're neither of us ready for more than light flirting yet. Besides, we shall have to return indoors soon and you mustn't be subjected to unpleasant criticism.' He hesitated before he added, 'And don't let Chrissie bully you.'

There was no mockery in his voice when he spoke of Chrissie. Verena, who was overcome by the new sensations which she had just experienced, moved away from him and said sadly, for she had been enjoying herself, 'Very true—and I mustn't expose you to my cousin's nasty tongue. As for Chrissie—she doesn't bully me. Please understand that anything I do for Jamie is freely done.'

He did not answer her directly, just nodded his head. Encouraged, she continued, 'Will you think me an experienced conspirator if I suggest that we return separately, and not together?'

'No, but I shall think that you have a great deal of common sense. You go first. I suggest that you think of a few censorious remarks about the Prince of Wales on your way back and work them into the conversation. It should put paid to any suspicion that you and I have been imitating him.'

This set Verena giggling. She rose to go. 'You're not very serious, are you, Nicholas Allen? I thought that you were when I first met you. I'd wager that you have done a little conspiring of your own in the past.'

'For my sins,' he offered ruefully and truthfully. 'But not lately. Visit me soon. Bring Jamie, and I promise to spring a nice surprise on you both. I'm free next Wednesday.'

'What a surprise,' she said softly, 'for so am I.'

He watched her disappear into the dark—to leave him

alone for a short time with the moon, the nightingale, and the falling water. Her charming innocence had moved him in a way which heated experience never could, and left him feeling that the world was a better place than he had always believed it to be.

Chapter Three

'Wherever have you been?' Chrissie hissed under her breath at Verena when she walked through the French windows into the drawing room. 'Jamie woke up, and I had to go upstairs to look after him, since Priddie couldn't cope and you were missing.'

Verena felt like telling her stepmother that she was not Jamie's nursemaid, but knowing that anything she said might rebound on him, she held her tongue. She was pleased that Nicholas had not been present to hear Chrissie's tart rebuke, because he might have felt that it confirmed his belief that Chrissie bullied her.

'I'm sure that he was pleased to see his mother.'

'Well, he wasn't. He was screaming for you. I really don't know what I have to do to win a little affection from him. He really is the oddest child.'

Seeing Piers coming towards her she raised her voice. 'And was it pleasant in the garden, my dear?'

'Very.' Verena's voice was smooth. 'I enjoyed myself greatly. I had not thought a moonlight night could be so romantic until I returned to Devon.'

'Didn't happen to see Allen outside, did you, Vee?' asked Piers suspiciously. 'He's disappeared, and John

Webster wanted to ask him about some learned nonsense of which he thought Allen might know the origin. It seems that cousin John's paragon could tour the music halls as a memory man. He's as good as an encyclopedia, John says.'

Oh dear, whatever had got into Piers? Had he always been so nasty—or was it simply Nicholas who was provoking him into such spite? And if so, why?

She was saved from answering, and having to lie—for she wanted neither Chrissie nor Piers to know of her happy interlude with Nicholas—by his arrival, not through the French windows, but through a side door.

Piers immediately leaped on him. 'Thank God you've come. Perhaps you can end a silly argument between Axminster and cousin John. And where had you skived off to?'

'To the library. You do know what a library is, Marlowe? Even if you don't know where it is.'

This piece of insolence was so coolly delivered that for a moment Piers was unaware that he had been insulted. When he did he gave a roar and leaned forward to thrust his face into Nicholas's and grasp him by the shoulder.

'Now, what the devil do you mean by that, Allen? You should know enough not to sauce your betters when they are silly enough to invite you among them!'

Nicholas, who had suddenly tired of being the target for Piers's venom, used his left hand to catch Piers's hand in order to remove it from his shoulder.

As once before that evening, the touch of another set off an odd and immediate response. But unlike that which Verena had provoked, this one was hateful in the extreme. He was not in the light, but in the dark. Something horrible was about to attack him. The sensation of evil was so strong that he almost flung Piers's hand from him—but some vestige of caution told him to hold on.

He managed, with difficulty, to say something which did not give away his extreme distress.

'I may only be John Webster's dogsbody, Marlowe, but common decency should demand that you treat me with a little courtesy when your great-uncle invites me into his home. If you apologise for your insulting remarks to me, I shall apologise for mine to you. That will save both our faces and prevent a nasty brawl which can bring credit on neither of us.'

'Let go of my hand first,' ground out Piers, who had suddenly realised that Nick Allen was a good deal stronger and fitter than he was, and that a ding dong with him might not be a good idea.

Nicholas prepared to do as he was asked, but in grasping Piers's wrist, both the sleeve of his dinner jacket and his shirt cuff had ridden up to reveal his watch. It had been a present from his father on his twenty-first birthday, and was the only thing in his Schuyler life which he had not discarded. It was one of the most expensive on the market, a Patek Philippe.

He had started to take it off to put it away for good shortly after he had decided to settle in West Bretton, but as he began to unfasten it, he had a sudden memory of his twenty-first birthday party, the last happy occasion in his life as Nicholas Allen Schuyler.

He slowly fastened it up again. No one he was likely to meet would know how rare it was. Even John Webster, who had seen it when he had worked in his shirt sleeves, had not realised its value. Most people would take it for granted that it was not really gold but was simply a cheap copy of the real thing.

Piers looked down at the hand—and the watch. His stupidity was not so much intellectual as moral. One of his talents was that he knew the trappings of his world; those objects which the great and fortunate possessed. He boasted that he could always tell the real thing from the dross.

He also possessed a certain low cunning. He knew at once that the watch that the office boy before him was sporting on his wrist was something of greater value than any office boy would ever own—and he took care not to let the man he despised know what he had seen.

And, being cunning he wondered whether Nicholas Allen needed investigating—and what other use he could make of this odd piece of knowledge.

If Nicholas had not been so shocked by his second strange experience of the night, he might have seen Piers recognise what he would have preferred him not to. He regained his hand, and went through the motions of empty reconciliation while he came to terms with what he had learned of himself.

Twice, at times of great emotion, he had experienced something similar to the flashes of intuition with which his cousin, Gis Havilland, was blessed or cursed. Whether he had seen a real future, or a symbolic one, he did not know. Only afterwards, Gis had once told him, was it possible to know what the flashes were trying to tell you.

He also remembered the one which Gis had experienced just before he had left Padworth and which he had forgotten until now. His cousin had called him Nicholas Allen, as though he had known that that was the name he would adopt when he had renounced being Nicholas Schuyler.

Well, one thing was certain. This weird talent was never going to tell him what would be sure to win the Derby! Nothing so useful—and Gis had once said something like that to him long ago.

How odd that of all the people whom he had missed in the last three years it should be Gis whom he missed the most—Gis, whom he had thought that he disliked. And another piece of intuition told him that he and Gis were very similar—but by no means the same.

All of this ran through his head as he and Piers made reluctant peace; he told John Webster what he wished to know; chatted agreeably with Sir Charles and Lord Axminster; and heard from a distance Verena, calm and apparently serious, making barbed and witty comments about the Prince of Wales as he had recommended her to do!

After that the evening was relatively uneventful. He made up a bridge four with Sir Charles, John Webster and Lord Axminster; Lord Axminster being his partner. Piers cried off on the grounds that it was not his game. He preferred instead to escort the ladies off to the billiard room where the women, being novices, had a jolly time trying not to tear the cloth, and Piers was able to display his prowess in making cannons and potting the ball, secure in the knowledge that no one present could give him a good game.

An added advantage was that in showing them all, particularly Verena, how to handle the cue correctly and make the shots, he was able to get his arms around them without incurring their displeasure. After all, he was only helping them.

Verena found his attentions distasteful. Pleading a slight headache, she sat down to watch the game. Her growing dislike for Piers was a continuing source of surprise to her—especially since she had looked forward so much to meeting him again. His reality, though, was a very different thing from her dreams of him.

Nicholas, on the other hand, unlike Piers, was hiding his light under a bushel. Gifted with the Schuyler talent for mathematics—although he had rarely used it profitably in his career at the merchant bank—and possessing an excel-

lent memory, he played below his paper and still helped
his partner to win the game. He was careful to use his skills
in such a way as to avoid comment.

Once or twice he even exclaimed at his good fortune,
and Lord Axminster, who usually lost any card game which
he played against Sir Charles, praised young Allen's be-
ginner's luck.

Only John Webster, who was beginning to grasp that his
one-time office boy—now almost partner—possessed,
when he decided to use it, a mind as sharp as a knife,
wondered whether it was Nicholas's skill which gave him
his victory rather than the vagaries of chance.

All in all, both those at Marlowe Court, and their visitors,
went to bed happy. Verena, drawing the curtains to look at
the moon before she prepared for bed, wondered at her
pleasure in what had been an uneventful evening. She tried
to avoid reaching the conclusion that the presence of
Nicholas Allen had been a major factor in its success.

Certainly she could not argue that Piers had any responsibility in the matter. Quite the contrary—he certainly did
not improve on further acquaintance.

She was still in the same happy mood when, after breakfast, Sir Charles sent word that he would like to speak to
her in his study. Chrissie, who had come down very late,
wearing a negligée, as though she had been driven from
bed at dawn, said nastily, 'Oh, a royal summons! I wonder
what he wants with you to be so formal. One might imagine
we still lived in the nineteenth century.'

Her expression, though, was a sly one. She thought that
she knew what Sir Charles was about, and was not sure
that she approved. Verena also suspected why her grandfather wished to see her, and was even more unhappy.

He was sitting at his desk in front of the window when

she entered. He rose and motioned her to an armchair before the empty hearth, sitting down himself in another opposite to her.

'My dear child, I trust that I did not discommode you by sending for you so early?'

She shook her head. 'No, Grandfather, I had already finished my breakfast.'

'Good, good, I like an early riser.' He paused and she gained the impression that he did not quite know how to begin saying whatever he wished to say to her.

'You must know, Verena, that I always have your best interests at heart. I have watched you with young Jamie, and I am sure that you would make an excellent wife and mother. Yesterday afternoon your cousin Piers came to see me in my capacity as head of the family. Quite properly he sought my consent before he asked you for your hand in marriage. I told him that I would be delighted to see the junior branch of the family continue the line seeing that, after Jamie, he is the only Marlowe male left to inherit the baronetcy.

'I also told him, however, that the final decision must be yours—but that my best wishes would go with him. He agreed with me that I should speak to you before he proposed, seeing that, in some sense, I stand as your guardian. He asked me to inform you that he would wish to pay his addresses to you at three o'clock this afternoon in the small drawing-room.

'Now, my dear, the final decision must be yours, but I would like to think that you will bear my wishes in mind while you debate how best to reply to him.'

He fell silent, and if the smile which he gave her was a little nervous, Verena could understand why. They were, after all, living in the 1920s when the position of women—

and of granddaughters—was very different from that which it had been in her grandfather's youth.

Had he asked her before she had met Piers again, her reply might have been different. But the man she had seen and heard since his arrival two days ago was very different from the one whose memory she had treasured since she was a small girl.

His speech and behaviour to those he considered his inferiors shocked her. She wondered how, after the first days of marriage, he would treat her? For all his easy charm there was a coarseness of fibre about him which contrasted strongly with the delicacy which Nicholas Allen, the man whom he considered to be his inferior, showed to her and to others.

Sir Charles saw her hesitation and sighed. He wanted the marriage because he thought that it would be a steadying influence on Piers, given the kind of girl Verena was.

'The decision is mine, Grandfather?'

It was as much a statement as a question. Her grandfather said, 'Even if I could compel you to marry Piers—as I might have been able to do in the past—I would not do so; it is your life and therefore you must make this decision, not I. I merely remind you that there are compelling reasons why this marriage would be a good one.'

Verena decided to be daring. 'Can he afford to marry, Grandfather? I was of the belief that Piers does not have a large income.'

'Should you agree to marry him, I would be prepared to add to your dowry sufficiently to give you an income to live in comfort.'

Which told Verena how much he wished her to accept Piers. And all for the sake of the Marlowe name!

Ah, but was she prepared to marry for the sake of the name? She thought not. She had recently been deciding whether or not to leave home and go to live in London. She would need to find work, for what her father had left her was little enough to live on. Like many girls of her class she had not been given formal training of any kind, but her old school friend, Deirdre Hamilton, was about to open a dress shop in Chelsea, using a recent legacy to finance it, and had asked Verena if she would like to be her assistant.

'Your downright common sense would be invaluable,' she had written. 'You needn't give me an answer yet, but I would like to have a Yes or No by the autumn.'

Downright common sense, indeed! Was that how people saw her? Was that why Chrissie tried to exploit her over Jamie and why Sir Charles wished her to marry the flighty Piers—to steady him? Worse and worse. Did Nicholas Allen see her as the epitome of common sense?

Well, common sense told her not to marry Piers, not only because he had none, but because she did not love him, and it seemed very possible that the more she knew him the less she would like him—let alone love him.

After more thought, and very little lunch, for she did not look forward to refusing him, Verena made her way to the small drawing-room where Piers was waiting for her. He had not come down for lunch which was tactful of him, preferring to have it in his room.

He was standing before the French windows, but walked towards her as she entered. She was struck all over again by his extreme good looks and his perfect physique. More, without being a dandy, he had the art of wearing his splendid clothes to their best advantage. He would never turn up to dinner wearing an ill-fitting dress suit like Nicholas, or be seen in the pullover and flannels she had seen Nicholas in at Jesse Pye's cottage.

'Dear Verena,' he said, smiling. He leaned forward to kiss her gently on the cheek. 'You look splendid, as usual.'

Now this was flattery, for Verena had deliberately not changed her perfectly ordinary, and somewhat dated, yellow linen dress with its square neck, low waistline and skirt ending just below the knee, for anything at all modish.

'Grandfather said that you wished to speak to me,' she returned, disengaging herself from a kiss which had done nothing to her pulse rate but lower it.

'And he told you why?'

'Yes.' This might be brusque but Verena felt that the less said the better—it gave him nothing to hold on to.

'I hope that you do not find my proposal over-hasty. I remember you as a charming child and you have grown into an even more charming woman—a woman to love and a woman I would wish to make my wife.'

He paused and bowed. 'I hope, my dear Verena, that you will do me the honour of accepting my proposal of marriage. We call one another cousin, but the relationship is a distant one and dates back into the middle of the last century. Our marriage would, indeed, have the advantage of reuniting two separate and distant branches of the Marlowe family—as Sir Charles agreed.'

To Verena's astonishment he went down on one knee, taking her hand as he did so and kissing it—another wasted kiss since, yet again, it did nothing for her.

Verena could not prevent herself from saying, 'I would scarcely have thought that our family was grand enough to go in for dynastic marriages.'

Piers chose to interpret this as a joke, and made one in return. 'We could always set the fashion. Say you will marry me, Verena, and make us both happy.'

To refuse him was going to be harder—and more painful—than she might have thought.

She retrieved her hand, and said as quietly and calmly as she could, 'I am sorry to disappoint, or hurt you, Piers, but I do not think that marriage between the two of us would answer. I can see some of its worldly advantages for both of us, but in the end it comes down to the fact that I do not love you, and have always thought of you as a friend, not a husband.'

Even the last part of the sentence was not true, for since she had met him again she could not care for him as a friend, either, but she did not wish to hurt him, and so she could not be completely frank.

Piers's smile disappeared. He did not relish being refused anything.

'Come, my dear, reconsider. Sir Charles…'

Verena interrupted him. 'What Sir Charles wishes deserves to be considered, and I have thought carefully about my answer since he spoke to me this morning, but that answer must be No. I cannot marry you simply to make Sir Charles happy. I would be your cousin and your friend, but I cannot be your wife.'

'That is your final word?'

'Yes, Piers, sadly, that is what it is.'

She might have known that he would not take refusal lightly. He caught her hand, roughly this time. 'So, that's the way of it! I saw you making eyes at that commoner, young Allen, last night, and I know that you had a moonlight tryst with him whilst you both pretended to be otherwise engaged. What would Sir Charles have to say to that, I wonder? That you were making love on a bench in the moonlight with a local yokel!'

Verena stared at his face, twisted so that all his good looks had disappeared. Despite herself she stammered, 'How—?'

'How did I know? My man, Fenton, was in the garden

on my orders. Not that I thought that you and Allen would make love so soon after meeting, but just to keep an eye on things. You see, my dear lying cousin, it pays to know what others are up to. I've a mind to tell my great-uncle what I know of his sweet, innocent Verena, but not yet. Just remember that I can blow your reputation whenever I choose. Like to change your mind, marry me and be safe?'

Verena stood up. 'Never. Never, for I would not marry a man who claims to be a gentleman, but speaks to me in such a vulgar manner. Nicholas Allen may not be of what you call good birth, but nevertheless he is twice the gentleman you are. Now, allow me to leave you, before either of us says anything truly unforgivable. I shall not tell Grandfather of what has passed between us, for it does neither of us credit.'

She was shaking as she spoke. Later she was to realise that Piers would not fulfil his threats to blacken her character to her grandfather—it would be too dangerous. Sir Charles had already shown in his quiet way that he did not care for Piers's arrogant and dismissive remarks about those he disliked, or did not consider to be his equals, and he would not take kindly to an attack on a young woman who had refused him.

But at the time she was overwhelmed by the sheer weight of Piers's nastiness and had only one wish: to be as far away from him as possible.

To her great relief Piers stood back to allow her to leave the room, taking with her the good income which Sir Charles had promised him if he married her. One thing was sure. He would make John Webster's office boy pay for this day's disappointment if it were the last thing he did.

Chapter Four

Nicholas was surprised by how much he was looking forward to seeing Verena and young Jamie again: it was not that living in sleepy West Bretton bored him, quite the contrary. But before he had renounced his name and family he had enjoyed the company of pretty young women and the Schuyler and Havilland grandchildren, and there had been little in West Bretton to replace them.

Instead he had filled his days with joining in the amusements of the little town, and pursuing those other interests which, being a Schuyler, he had been discouraged from practising.

So far as women were concerned his brief affairs with Isobel Playfair and Daisy Goring had been disappointing, and after them he had lived a celibate life—something which would have surprised his father.

He ate his breakfast and lunch on Wednesday with even more zest than usual. Verena had told him, before he had left Marlowe Court on the night of the dinner, that she and Jamie would arrive at two o'clock, and he was sure that they would be punctual, so it would be as well to be ready on the dot.

When the expected knock came on his front door

Nicholas was ready and raring to go, as his Yankee cousins said. It had taken him some time and thought to decide which tie to wear with his Viyella shirt, to put on a newly cleaned pair of flannels, and his best, if somewhat worn and anonymous, navy blue blazer—also a second-hand acquisition—so that he might be properly dressed for a jaunt on a bright summer's day.

On opening his front door, however, he found only Verena standing on the step, looking apologetic. 'Come in, come in,' he said, looking around him. 'Jamie not with you?'

Verena hesitated in the doorway. 'I'm afraid not. He had a very severe bout of asthma last night, and we had to send for the doctor. He gave orders for him to rest as much as possible, and Priddie—Miss Pridham, that is—insists on nursing him. She says that it is her duty. But if you want to cry off and take us out another time…' Her voice died away.

She had seen his disappointment at Jamie's absence, and chided herself savagely and silently for not understanding that it was to entertain him, and not herself, that he had invited them out.

Nicholas was having contrary feelings. He was assuming that she had only agreed to come because of her half-brother, and would, by what she had said, prefer not to spend the afternoon with him.

But the cliché had it—and Nicholas was not one to ignore a piece of common sense because it was a cliché—'that faint heart never won fair lady.' He wasn't sure that he wanted to win Verena, but the memory of their encounter in the moonlight and the prospect of being with her again had buoyed him up all week.

Here goes, he thought, and said aloud, 'You couldn't bring yourself to keep me company on your own, then?'

The smile which accompanied this offer had Verena weak at the knees again. What was it about him that had such an effect on her?

'If you wouldn't be bored?' she ventured, hoping that it wasn't mere kindness which had him making the offer.

But kindness was never mere, was it? The memory of Piers's lack of it, had her valuing the man before her all over again.

Nicholas was giving her a mock bow. 'I promise not to be bored if you won't be. I understand that you haven't lived in the West Country for nearly ten years, so it won't be difficult to entertain you, I'm sure—so much will have changed.

'How about taking a spin over to Lynmouth in my little Morris? There's not much room in it, but it covers the miles nicely, if somewhat slowly. We could paddle in the sea, pretending that we have a couple of kiddies with us and make believe that we're doing it for them, and not for ourselves.'

Verena began to laugh. She never knew what he was going to say next—which was quite a change from the conversation which she had endured, rather than enjoyed, in India.

'I can't remember when I last paddled in the sea. Is it compulsory for me to tie a knotted handkerchief around my head before they let me in? If so, I shall be disappointed. My handkerchief is a small lacy one, fit only to be worn by a pigmy.'

Nicholas, shook his head gravely, joining in the game. 'Oh, no, it's the men who wear the handkerchiefs. I shall also have to roll up my flannels—which will do nothing for their cut. You must carry a parasol and try to look as though you're walking down Bond Street, instead of along the beach in the waves.'

'I haven't got a parasol with me,' Verena told him mournfully.

'Never mind. I shall allow you to have a ride on a donkey to make up for not being up to the mark in the paddling stakes. Now, we must be off if we are to fit in everything which I want us to do.'

Nicholas's Morris was parked in the open at the side of the cottage in front of a tumbledown shed which was too rickety and too small to hold the Morris.

'Jesse used to keep pigeons in it, I believe,' he told her as he handed her into the little car, so different from his long-gone Bentley and the expensive monsters he had driven to victory at Brooklands race track.

'I could discourse to you in true journalistic fashion, on the beauties of Exmoor and the Somerset coast,' he said as they began to drive across it in the bright afternoon sunshine, 'but I suppose that you know more about it than I do.'

Verena shook her head. 'Not at all. I was only thirteen when we left, and all I know is what I have read in *Lorna Doone*, which is hardly a guide to the West Country of the nineteen twenties.'

'Indeed not,' agreed Nicholas who was skilfully and carefully negotiating the narrow lanes they were travelling through, barely one-car wide with high hedges on each side, and many twists and turns. 'Don't expect Carver Doone to leap at you from behind a tree—but you might see a deer and you will certainly see a lot of sheep when we're on the open moor proper.'

And so they did. The sheep were everywhere, across the road as well as across the moor, staring rudely at the car and trotting haughtily away as Nicholas changed down and slowed the Morris to a walking pace—'We don't want roast mutton for dinner tonight, do we?'

It was such fun being with him, Verena found. He made everything entertaining and informative without in any way being boring or pedantic. He joked about the missing deer, making up a comic story about rustlers having strayed from America's Wild West in order to make off with deer instead of cattle.

'I've thought about breeding deer for food,' he told her, and now she wasn't sure whether he was joking or not. 'Properly cooked, venison is delicious. Trouble is, everyone treats it as though it's beef, and then it's like eating shoe leather—no, I'm being rude to shoe leather, it's worse than that,' he finished gravely.

'Oh, I do wish Jamie was with us,' Verena said impulsively. 'He was so sorry to miss his treat with the Dragon man—that's his name for you. He would have loved to hear your stories. You ought to write them down.'

Nicholas gave her an odd look. 'Too busy writing for and helping to run the *Clarion*. You know, when we reach Lynmouth and have had our paddle I'll take you up to Lynton in the cliff railway. I could write a little piece for the paper about that and the other summer delights of the North Devon coast.'

Verena had never been up in the cliff railway. Miss Pridham had always refused to allow her to travel on it. 'You never know who you might be sitting next to,' she had said gravely. 'Perhaps some urchin from goodness knows where full of mumps and measles or some other horrid illness. You might pick something up!'

She regarded every child who was not fortunate enough to have been born a Marlowe of Marlowe Court as a walking reservoir of infectious diseases.

Nicholas drove them to Lynmouth by way of Porlock, missing out Minehead, a small and select resort full of elderly ladies and retired colonels who never paddle, he told her. 'We shouldn't be able to let our hair down there.'

This meant that Verena had the somewhat frightening experience of approaching Lynmouth by way first of Porlock, and then of Countesbury Hill, both of which were full of notices warning the motorist to take care, and requiring, Nicholas informed her, 'as much skill to negotiate as would be required at Brooklands.'

'Piers had a go at racing at Brooklands,' Verena said, in order to take her mind off the dangers of the hills, 'but it wasn't his sort of thing at all.'

'Did he now,' said Nicholas drily, neglecting to inform Verena that in his ill-spent youth, before he had settled down to become a virtuous apprentice at West Bretton, he had been considered one of England's most daring young racing drivers. Perhaps that had been where Piers had seen him.

'Yes,' said Verena. 'He prefers polo, although he hasn't played much lately.'

'Probably can't afford to,' offered Nicholas.

Verena shook her head. 'Oh, I don't think that he's short of money.'

This was not what John Webster had told Nicholas, but he was not prepared to enlighten Verena about Piers's shaky finances.

By now they were driving into Lynmouth past the cottage where the poet Shelley had briefly lived, to park in front of 'The Rising Sun,' which looked out over the basin where small yachts and dinghies were moored. Lynmouth itself was a quiet place where the more genteel forgathered although it did, as Nicholas promised, have a number of attractions for those less decorous souls who wanted to do more than to stroll in their best clothes along the front.

The tide was in and the donkeys were out. 'All the fun

of the fair,' Nicholas exclaimed, sitting down on the pebbly beach, beginning to remove his shoes and socks and, as promised, roll up his trouser legs. He had brought two large towels with him so that Verena could wrap one round her and chastely remove her stockings in the lee of the cliffs.

And then, hand in hand, they walked gingerly across the stony beach into the sea, with the gulls wheeling and screaming above them.

Verena was always to remember that golden afternoon with Nicholas. They paddled, she rode on a donkey, and then they played catch with a ball Nicholas fetched from the car, and a variation of cricket with an old tennis racquet. It was all the kind of unladylike fun which Miss Pridham had never allowed her to indulge in when she had been a little girl.

She could no more imagine enjoying herself in this fashion with Piers than, as she put it to herself, flying to the moon. 'Trippers!' he would have exclaimed scornfully. 'You're behaving just like day trippers!'

What he would have said to Nicholas going to a small kiosk to buy ice creams and coming back with two over-filled cones to lick as they walked along by the river, Verena could hardly imagine.

'I found out when I first came here, three years ago, that ice cream tastes better this way,' Nicholas said when he handed Verena hers. He looked sideways at her happy, flushed face after he had taken a giant lick at his dripping cone, and asked, 'Enjoying yourself?'

Verena, busy licking madly at her yellow ice cream to prevent it from dripping away before she could eat it, said, 'Oh, yes. I can't remember when I have enjoyed myself more. I only wish that Jamie could have been with us.'

'So do I. One really needs a few children to enjoy the

seaside properly. Not that we haven't been making a good fist of behaving like children ourselves.'

'I never behaved like this when I was a child,' confessed Verena. 'I wasn't allowed to. My governess would have had fits.'

'Well, she's not here now so her health is quite safe.' Nicholas looked at his watch. 'May I suggest that as it is the magic hour of four o'clock we take the cliff railway to Lynton, which is the even more ladylike part of the resort, and partake of afternoon tea in a manner which would please Miss Pridham—that is her name, is it not?'

'I should like nothing more. The view must be nearly as splendid as the one from the car on Countesbury Hill and far less worrying.'

'True,' agreed Nicholas. 'This way, then.'

They found that one of the cars was just arriving at the bottom of the cliff and that a small queue was waiting to board it once its passengers had disembarked.

'How does it work?' she asked.

Nicholas, making mental notes for an article as he spoke, explained to her that the little railway was powered by water.

'Hydraulics,' he began, 'the car at the top is full of water in a special tank and ours is empty, so when the brakes are off the car at the top falls down and ours rises.' Much to her surprise Verena found that she enjoyed him being serious as much as she enjoyed him being comical.

She watched him covertly, wondering as she did so why a man of such a lively mind and of such talents should have ended up in West Bretton. He was well read, and John Webster's praise of his abilities to her grandfather had been heartfelt.

No matter. He handed her into car and recommended her to stand at the back in order to get the best view of

Lynmouth as they ascended. He was right, of course. When the car began to rise he pointed out to her—far below them—the River Lyn, from whence the little resort took its name, winding down from the surrounding hills.

'It's really quite the prettiest river you are ever likely to see,' he told her, 'and because its descent to the sea is so steep it has the advantage of never being likely to flood.'

Halfway up the hill the descending car passed them. Verena, her eyes still on the view, was surprised when it did so, and gave a little squeak. Nicholas gallantly put an arm around her to reassure her, and kissed her on her warm cheek.

'Oh, nice,' he exclaimed naughtily, and did it again. 'That's the car going down, loaded with water, which pulled our car up. That explanation,' he said, 'was designed so that I might combine instruction with pleasure. The pleasure being this...' and he kissed her cheek for the third time.

'Priddie would say that we are behaving like servants on holiday,' she told him as she turned her head to kiss his protecting hand—something which she had never thought that she would do in public. The gesture was irresistible, meant to reward him for her afternoon's pleasure.

'So she would—but why should they be the only ones to have fun? Think what we miss with our strange notions of etiquette, and doing the right thing—and all that.'

There was something odd about his reply: an oddness which Verena only identified later. He had said 'we,' associating himself unconsciously with her class.

At the time she laughed as the car arrived at the top, and slipped her hand in his while they walked along. Another common thing to do in public, Priddie would have said.

There was more than one tearoom on the little road, all with chaste net curtains behind plate-glass windows.

Nicholas steered her into one called Peg's Pantry which he had visited before, where they ordered Earl Grey tea and ate scones and Cornish clotted cream and jam and talked happily about the books they had read or were reading.

'That's what I like about living in the country, plenty of time to read,' Nicholas said after calling for the teapot to be refilled, and for another helping of scones. 'I really have a shameful appetite,' he confessed. 'My mother said it was because I was so large. My father preferred to think me greedy.'

'And which of them was correct?' asked Verena solemnly, a twinkle in her eye. She thought that there was something so sad about the way in which he had spoken of his father that it made her want to cheer him up.

'Both, I suppose. I find that if I get too hungry I start having a bad headache. The quack at West Bretton was more sympathetic than my London doctor. He said that it might be something to do with blood sugar. And there's a great excuse for over-eating if I ever needed one!'

He wasn't fat, though, Verena thought. Quite the contrary. There was a hard strength about him which, if he were not so cheerful, would have been intimidating. She also noted that he had lived in London before he came to West Bretton.

Their second order of scones arrived and was duly despatched, Verena doing her share of the eating. She hadn't had such an appetite for years and told Nicholas so.

'Sun, sea, open air and being happy works wonders,' he told her.

He paid the bill and tipped the pretty waitress generously. It was plain that he bowled her over with his magnetism and charm, as he did most women—for you couldn't attribute his success with them to his handsome face. But handsome faces, Verena was beginning to find, were not a certain guide to a good character, or a good mind for that matter.

As they walked along the road they passed a shop selling both new and second-hand books. 'Let's go in,' Nicholas said, 'we might find a treasure.'

Treasure or not, the shop was crammed to the bulwarks with books. Nicholas found a first edition of an early novel by John Galsworthy, and Verena picked up a copy of *Little Women* which she had loved as a child but which had been lost in one of her father's many moves. 'I haven't read it for years, I wonder how well it will wear?'

Nicholas had also unearthed an early Rafael Sabatini, *Bardelys the Magnificent*, and added that to the pile which they had already collected.

In one corner Verena discovered a small table loaded with children's books—and there she found something to take home to console Jamie for having lost his afternoon's fun with the Dragon man. For the book was by the new and successful children's writer known simply as Merlin, and was the sequel to Jamie's favourite picture book *The Cowardly Dragon*. This one's title was *The Dragon's Hoard* and had a coloured picture on the cover of a huge dragon with its wings spread wide and a ring in its claws.

'Oh, look,' she exclaimed, holding it up. 'I must buy this for Jamie!'

Nicholas came over and took the book from her. 'Are you sure that he'll like it?'

'Like it? He'll love it! *The Cowardly Dragon* is quite his favourite book. He loves the bit where the poor dragon went home with its tail between its legs when it failed in its quest and decided to write about quests instead of living them.'

Nicholas handed the book back to her, a quizzical expression on his face. 'That being so, you must add it to *our* hoard,' for between them they had accumulated enough books to qualify as a hoard. 'Any more, and the Morris won't be able to accommodate them!'

It was time to go back to Lynmouth so they paid the gratified bookshop owner, took their parcels and made their way back to the cliff railway where they stood at the front of the car in order to get the best view of the village below them.

Verena puzzled over why their car dropped and the other rose. It must have risen with an empty tank so where had the water come from? She pondered on this all the way down and when they got to the bottom decided that since she had, that afternoon, abandoned all the principles of proper public behaviour which Priddie had instilled in her, she might as well go the whole hog.

They were watching their car being loaded again and mischievously she said, 'If you can explain to me why—our car on the way up being empty of water, and the one which passed us being full—we were able to descend when we went down, I shall give you a kiss.'

So he explained—and kissed her.

Which set the seal on the afternoon, for deciding that simply kissing Verena's cheek was not enough, Nicholas set down his parcel, put his arms around her and gave her a proper kiss—to the amusement of all the spectators but one, who stared jealously at them.

Why should the Marlowe chit have Nicholas Allen if she couldn't—and be kissed by him in public, too!

Chapter Five

That same afternoon Torry Longthorne had been thinking about her missing son. It would soon be three years since Nicholas had disappeared. At first both she and Gerard had expected that he would return, penitent, and promising to mend his ways. He had never stayed away for very long before, and they had expected that it would not be long before they saw him again.

But the days, and then the months and years, had passed and still no Nicholas had arrived asking for forgiveness. Gerard, overcome with regret, for he had had no desire to drive his youngest son away permanently, hired a detective to try to find him.

But after several months the man had reported back that he would be wasting Lord Longthorne's money if he carried on with the search. The only thing which he had been able to trace was Nicholas's Bentley. Unfortunately when its new owner, who lived in Chelsea, referred him to the second-hand dealer from whom he had bought it, he had been told that the car had been a near wreck when he had acquired it, with several others, from a shady individual with a Midlands base who had himself recently disappeared.

The date of its purchase had been some fourteen months after Nicholas had left Padworth. Nicholas might, or might not, have sold or wrecked it during that time. He might, or might not, be living in the Midlands. It could have changed hands several times.

His friends in London had not seen hide nor hair of him, either, and the landlord who owned his rented flat in Half Moon Street knew only that a plain van had removed Nicholas's possessions a fortnight after he had left Padworth, but the man who drove it had been given instructions not to reveal its destination.

At Coutts Bank Gerard, as a great favour, had been confidentially informed that since his disappearance Mr Nicholas Allen Schuyler had drawn no money from his main account there—his inheritance of his share of the Schuyler millions. He had, however, withdrawn a small sum from his other, lesser, account on the day after he had left Padworth, and they had heard nothing from him since.

Whichever way the detective and Gerard turned they found a dead end, as Gerard gently told an unhappy Torry. 'He has probably changed his name, and I can only hope that he has found work, for the money he took with him from Coutts Bank would not have kept him for very long. But what work? He was trained for nothing.'

'So that's it,' said Nicholas's mother numbly. 'He is dead to us—as he promised.'

'I cannot forgive him for treating you so cruelly by disappearing in this manner,' exclaimed Gerard. 'I know that I was hard on him, but it was no more than he deserved.'

'I was wrong, Gerard. I should have stood up for him more than I did—and he must have known that I didn't.'

She hesitated. 'I believe that he has a much stronger character than either of us gave him credit for. I said at the time that he is very like you.'

She sighed. 'I would just like to know that he is safe and well.'

For some reason she had been thinking constantly of him ever since she had risen on that glorious summer's day when Nicholas had taken Verena to Lynton and Lynmouth. Perhaps it was being at Padworth, which reminded her that the annual get-together of the clan would soon come round again, that had brought him to her mind so vividly.

It was useless to repine, to wish the world would turn back, and that somehow he would never have left, but would have made his peace with his father.

Miss Thorne, Gerard's secretary, came in. 'Lord Longthorne would like you to know that the box of books you were expecting from Harrods has arrived. They are in his study.'

'Oh, excellent.' Nothing, Torry thought, could be better; unpacking the books might take her mind away from her wilful youngest child. 'Tell Mr and Mrs Gis Havilland when they arrive that I shall be with them soon.' Gis lived not far from Padworth and he and his family were always welcome visitors for a long, or short, weekend.

Miss Thorne had obligingly opened the box for her. At the bottom of it was a small cache of children's books, which she had ordered from the catalogue that Harrods had earlier sent to her. Among them was one entitled *The Cowardly Dragon* by Merlin—a book which young Brant had demanded for his coming birthday.

Torry smiled painfully. The title of the book brought back memories of Nicholas again, happy among his nieces and nephews. She picked it up and opened it. The pictures were charmingly simple, done by someone who loved his subject, but it was the text which held her.

She remembered Nicholas's jokes that last afternoon as he told the little ones the story of the cowardly dragon; and here, in front of her, were the words he had used, the jokes he had made...!

No, it could not be, she must be dreaming. And then she remembered something else. She went upstairs to the little drawing-room next to her bedroom and fetched from a tallboy's drawer a folder, not looked at these many years. On the cover was Nicholas's name in an adolescent's still-not-fully adult writing.

She opened it, and fetched out some pen-and-ink drawings of plants, trees and animals. True, they were amateurish, but they had a certain power similar to those in the book which she had carried upstairs with her.

Now she was remembering that Nicholas had wanted to go to art school—'I can't make up my mind,' he had told her at thirteen, 'whether I want to be a great writer or a great painter—perhaps I could be both.'

What had happened to those ambitions? Crushed beneath the weight of the traditions which demanded that a Schuyler male should be something quite different. Was it possible that Merlin was her errant, wayward son?

Torry, sitting there with the book and the folder of drawings on her knee, looked at the name and address of the publisher on the back of the title page and made a trunk call to London.

Nothing would be lost and much might be gained if she asked who Merlin really was. What was the name of the man—or woman—behind the pseudonym?

Another dead end! She was passed from hand to hand to the publisher himself, once she used the magic name of Lady Longthorne. Only to be informed, with great regret, that the publisher could tell her nothing. Neither Merlin's name nor his address were available. Not only was it the publisher's policy never to pass on names and addresses, but the author had given strict orders that nothing about him—or her—was to be revealed. Not even Merlin's sex.

Torry did not wish to disclose immediately why she was ringing so urgently. In any case, she might be deceiving herself by assuming that Nicholas could have written and illustrated the book, driven by her desire to believe that he was safe and well somewhere.

She put the receiver back on its hook and walked downstairs. In the entrance hall she found Gis Havilland who had arrived while she was upstairs, had installed his family on the lawn, and had come in to pay her his respects. His manners were always perfect.

He knew immediately that something was wrong. 'What is it, Aunt Torry?'

She could not tell him the full truth since she feared that Gis might suppose that she was being foolish, seeing connections to Nicholas which did not exist. Instead, her eyes filling with tears, she said, 'I have been thinking about Nicholas. Tell me, Gis, did he ever say anything which might have given you any idea as to where he might go?'

Gis shook his handsome head. 'No, Aunt Torry, no idea at all. I doubt whether he knew himself.'

'Oh, Gis, if only I could be sure that he is safe and sound. Have you no idea where he might be or what he is doing?'

He hesitated. 'Aunt Torry, I really have no notion of where he is, nor of what he might be doing. All I can say is that I feel very strongly that at the moment he is well and happy—for what that is worth.'

So his intuition had told him something, but Torry knew that it worked only in the most vague and indirect manner.

Gis was speaking again. 'From what I know of him— and this has nothing to do with my intuition—I am sure of one thing, at least. It is this. Nicholas hated consequentiality and wherever he is, whatever he is doing, he is doing it without reference to being a Schuyler, or having been a Schuyler. He will be true to his inmost self—and that is probably why he has disappeared so completely.'

'You are saying that he does not want to be found?'

'Exactly—and this is a guess, you understand. I think that he will come home when he is ready to do so.'

Torry clutched the book and the folder to her. 'Are we not to look for him, then?'

'That is for you to decide. We all have to make our own decisions, dear Aunt.'

I shan't tell Gerard of my suspicions, Torry thought, after she had thanked Gis for his kindness, he would think me foolish. Instead I shall ask him to have a new search made, something might turn up which was missed before. If Gis is to be believed, I need not fear the worst. And if Nicholas is truly Merlin who wrote and illustrated this book then I may even hope for the best.

As Gis had intuited, Nicholas was happy that afternoon—and so was Verena. After leaving the bookshop and stowing their treasures away in the Morris, he suggested that they visit one of Lynmouth's most famous sights, Watersmeet.

Verena looked anxiously at her watch. 'Do we have time to go there? Oughtn't we to be setting off for West Bretton soon?'

'You have an engagement waiting?' Nicholas asked politely.

'Not exactly…' Verena began.

'Good, then you might like to prolong this happy afternoon into the evening. I propose that we leave Lynmouth about half-past five and stop at one of the little country pubs on the way home and treat ourselves to cider and a pasty. How about it?'

Cider and a pasty in the evening at a country pub with a young man whom she scarcely knew! What on earth would Priddie say to such outrageous behaviour by Miss Marlowe of Marlowe Court?

'They will be expecting me to dinner,' she offered, and was immediately aware of how feeble she sounded. 'They don't even know where I have gone—I never told anyone because I thought that I was going straight back home after telling you Jamie was ill.'

'Well, thank goodness you didn't,' said Nicholas fervently, 'you've quite made my day by coming out with me. You could always ring Marlowe Court from here, you know, and tell them that you won't be in for dinner. Etiquette will then be satisfied.'

He was aware that his tone in the last sentence was a little satirical.

Verena flushed. 'You must think me a bit of a fool...'

'No, but I think—forgive me for saying so—that you ought to do something *you* want to do for a change, not always sacrifice yourself in order to look after others.'

Verena could not stop herself. 'I did do something I wanted to do the day after the dinner party. I turned down Piers's proposal of marriage, even though Grandfather and everyone else wanted me to accept him.'

'Well, that's a good start, I must say. Improve on it! Have a pasty with me to celebrate it! Congratulations on turning the prancing popinjay down. By all the signs he'd make a rotten husband for a decent girl like you. There's a telephone box over there.'

His exuberance was infectious. 'What shall I tell them? How shall I explain—'

'Explain nothing. You're not a child.' He grinned at her. He couldn't tell her how different this was from taking Isobel Playfair and Daisy Goring around. He had almost

had to fight Daisy off the first time they had been alone.
There was something refreshing in Verena's charming innocence; her determination always to do the right thing.

Explaining nothing was a bit difficult. Chrissie answered
the phone and began questioning her as though she were a
leading member of the Spanish Inquisition. 'Why won't
you be home for dinner? Where are you? What are you
doing? I was depending on you to look after Jamie this
evening so that I could go round to the Playfairs. Priddie
is quite worn out. She was depending on you too.'

Verena almost gave way. Only the sight of Nicholas
mouthing at her outside the telephone box and giving her
the thumbs-up sign kept her from instant capitulation.

'Sorry, Chrissie,' she lied desperately. 'Can't hear you
properly, something wrong with the line at this end. Ooh,
and I've run out of money.' So saying, she cut her stepmother off in mid-flow.

Nicholas rewarded her with another kiss on the cheek
when she emerged from the box, a trifle red in the face. 'I
could tell you were having a hard time in there. Who did
you get? The rampant stepmother champing at the bit?'

'Yes, and I cut her off, too, after telling her a thundering
lie. You know what, Nicholas Allen, you're corrupting me.'

'Oh, splendid. A bit of corruption never hurt anyone. It's
overdoing it that causes trouble. Now for Watersmeet.'

She shouldn't have laughed but she did. A pair of amber
eyes, a superb physique and a comical tongue were proving
her undoing. Oh, he was so...so... Verena couldn't think
of a suitable word so settled on naughty, which seemed to
fit the bill.

The rest of her day out passed like an excited dream.
Watersmeet was as beautiful as he had said it would be.
Alone, in the shade of the trees, watching the waterfall,
they sat among the rocks, and if his arm stole about her

waist and she rested her head on his shoulder, and he kissed her, and then she kissed him back...so what.

He was much more fun than Major Roger Gough had ever been, and she ought to thank Chrissie for having seduced him away from her. And was that what Nicholas was doing to her, seducing her? And if so, oughtn't she to stop him? Only she didn't want to.

It was Nicholas who stopped himself with a little groan. She offered herself to him so ardently and so simply that the temptation to carry on to the ultimate end of lovemaking was almost too much for him. But when he looked down at her soft face, her closed eyes and her sweetly inviting mouth he felt that he would be a cur to ravage such gentle honesty.

'No,' he said, disengaging himself, 'that's enough for now. We must leave something for another day as my old nurse used to say when she took my sweeties away. You're a witch, Verena. Have you no idea of the magic you weave and how it undoes a poor mortal like me?'

'Now you're teasing me. Roger said...' She stopped.

'Roger? Roger who? Or perhaps I ought to ask, what did Roger say? No, don't answer me if you don't wish to.'

'Oh, I do wish.' The desperate honesty with which Verena faced life compelled her to answer his question.

'Roger was...a man I used to know. He said that I was frigid, so you must be teasing me to suggest that I...' Embarrassment had her falling silent.

'Forgive me again, my shy witch, but you do seem to have been surrounded by the most ineffable asses God ever sent down on earth. Not only the prancing popinjay, but also Roger the ruthless. I'll bet he was as coarse a lover as the man who kept his chain mail on whilst he was indulging himself if he was unable to appreciate your magic.'

Verena began to laugh. She was remembering Roger, a

man armoured by the certainty of his attractions. Why had his kisses had so little effect on her when Nicholas's had so much? Chain mail and Roger had been made for each other—but how did Nicholas know that?

She asked him.

His eyes were wicked when he answered her. 'Oh, I was just trying to picture the kind of unimaginative fool who would say such a thing to you! Did I hit the mark?'

'Yes, very much so, and if I'm a witch, then you're a wizard—or should I say warlock?'

'Made for each other, then,' and he kissed her again.

'Do you flirt like this with all the girls?' she asked him breathlessly when the kiss was over.

'Not these past three years,' Nicholas replied obscurely. 'You see how honoured you are.'

He rose and held out his hand to her. 'Time to go. Your chariot awaits—if a witch will condescend to use it instead of a broomstick.'

'Oh, I'm disappointed. I thought you were going to wave your magic wand, say abracadabra, and we should instantly arrive at your little pub on the moor.'

'Would that life were so easy. But at least the Morris awaits us and not a horse and cart which would have been our transport a hundred years ago.'

The pub turned out to be as charming as Nicholas had suggested, and the Cornish pasty as flavourful. Nicholas urged her to go easy on the cider.

'It's not the stuff they sell in bottles,' he told her. 'It's the real thing. The locals call it scrumpy; it's lethal to drink too much, thinking that it's rather tasty lemonade. One of their tricks is to give it to unsuspecting tourists who've only drunk the soft stuff in their local back home—and then watch the mayhem which follows!'

It didn't taste lethal, though, and so Verena told him.

'Oh, I can see that I've got hold of a real toper! But you must believe me for my sake. Bad enough that I should keep you out late, even worse if you rolled home tight. I can't have the prancing popinjay coming after me with a horsewhip.'

No one had ever made her laugh so much before. Only his eyes gave him away when he was teasing her. Roger had been solemn and a trifle dismissive with her, Piers had been unctuous with a slight suggestion in his manner that he was doing her a favour.

After they had finished their supper Nicholas introduced her to a game called Devil Among the Tailors, a form of table skittles at which she soon proved adept.

There was a darts match going on in one corner, and Nicholas promised to teach her how to play the next time they came. The landlord knew Nicholas, called him Nick, and offered him a free pasty. It was all very jolly and very innocent. She noticed that Nicholas only had one glass of cider and didn't drink all of that. She couldn't help comparing him with Piers, who was quite a heavy drinker.

Afterwards they drove back to Marlowe Court through the gathering dark. The little car's headlights lit up the high hedgerows on the narrow lanes and Verena was reminded how, in one of Dornford Yates's exciting and romantic novels, he had described the headlights of Berry's powerful car doing the same thing in the French byways as it tore along at all of sixty miles an hour.

She told Nicholas so. He laughed. 'Oh, I might have guessed that you'd enjoy reading him. So improbable—but Berry's a real character, isn't he?'

'You're a bit like him,' said Verena daringly.

'Oh dear, no. I can't equate all that daring heroism he goes in for, involving jewel thieves, smugglers and intercontinental crooks, with being John Webster's dogsbody.

Come to think of it, the only excitement we get in West Bretton is when someone steals a dog!'

'But we have had jewel thieves—and worse, lately,' Verena reminded him.

'So we have. My first lurid headlines since I reached the West Country. But it's the exception, not the rule, that we're talking about.'

After that they sat in companionable silence. Nicholas quietly sang one of Noel Coward's songs and Verena joined in and helped him when he forgot the words and started to go, 'da, da, da.' All in all it was the happiest day that both of them had enjoyed for a long time.

And so Verena told him in her frank way when they reached Marlowe Court and he had stopped in front of its tall Corinthian columns, and handed her out.

'Do come in,' she said. 'You deserve a nightcap after driving me all that way this afternoon and evening.'

He shook his head. 'Thanks, but I'll take a rain check. The prancing popinjay doesn't want to see me, and I certainly don't want to see him.'

The real reason was that he didn't want his presence to create an unhappy scene which might mar their perfect day. After being with her, he thought that she was strong enough to fight her own battles, contrary to the earlier opinion he had formed that she was a doormat for Chrissie and the others to trample on.

Verena had thought that he might make quite a thing of saying goodnight to her. She was used to men who thought that taking a girl out meant that they might take a few liberties with her as well.

But he didn't. He simply leaned forward and kissed her gently on the tip of the nose, saying as he withdrew, 'Goodnight, sweet witch, and sleep tight. Remember me in your dreams.' And then he got into the car and drove off towards the gates which led on to the road.

Verena watched him until his car's lights disappeared before she took out her key and entered the house. Normally she would have rung the bell, but she wished to arrive without ceremony and disappear up to her room before Chrissie had the opportunity to begin cross-questioning her fiercely.

No such luck! She was tiptoeing across the entrance hall when the door of the large drawing-room opened and Chrissie stood there, staring at her like the basilisk in the ancient legends who could turn someone to stone simply by looking at them.

'So there you are! We wondered whether you intended to come home at all! Sir Charles has been asking after you. He was most worried when you failed to return in time for dinner. You had better come in and reassure him.'

It was the last thing which Verena wanted to do. A confrontation with the arbiters of her world would sully the memories of her happy day. But good form and the lessons instilled in her by grandparents, parents and governesses meant that she had a duty to respond to the wishes of her elders and betters. She could ignore Chrissie, but not Sir Charles.

She followed Chrissie into the drawing-room to discover that there had been guests for dinner. Piers, leaning as usual against the mantelpiece, was talking to Daisy Goring, now Daisy Champernown, and her husband, Giles. They all raised their eyebrows when she entered. At her informal clothing and her old cardigan, doubtless.

'Dear child,' said Sir Charles, 'we were most worried when Chrissie told us that you were not returning in time for dinner. Have you had something to eat? Do you want me to ring for the butler?'

'No, thank you, Grandfather. I have already eaten.'

Chrissie put her oar in. 'Have you, indeed, and where was that? Daisy told me after dinner that she visited Lynton this afternoon and saw you there with Nick Allen.' She looked slyly across at her father-in-law and decided to tell him of Daisy's juiciest bit of gossip.

'She said that she was most surprised to see him kissing you in the public street as though you were a pair of servants on holiday. I told her that you had probably sneaked off with him for the day rather than help me to look after poor Jamie. One wonders what you were doing with him this evening!'

This hand grenade thrown down in front of the assembled company had the desired effect. Sir Charles, after harrumphing, looked reproachfully at his errant granddaughter. Piers drawled, 'What, has the counterjumper notched up another conquest?' Miss Pridham exclaimed, 'Oh, Verena, how could you?' and Daisy and her husband shook their heads knowingly.

The worm turned at last. 'You don't need to wonder what I was doing tonight, Chrissie. I shall tell you. I was having supper with Nicholas Allen in a little pub on the edge of the moor, and very nice it was, too. I can recommend the Cornish pasties to you all, and the scrumpy was an experience in itself. And now, seeing that I have entertained you enough, you will, I hope, allow me to excuse myself and retire to my room.'

She turned at the door to add, 'Oh, and for your information, Chrissie, Nicholas behaved like a perfect gentleman all day, quite unlike Major Roger Gough and some other so-called gentlemen I have known. Goodnight.'

She had to say one thing for Piers, his mouth had twitched a little early on in her harangue, but at the end he had managed to make himself look as solemn as the rest of the company.

Oh, Nicholas had well and truly corrupted her! Don't explain yourself, he had told her, or apologise, and so she hadn't. She was sorry that she had had to be impertinent to Sir Charles, but the rest could go hang.

And as Nicholas had hoped he would, he popped up in her dreams that night. They were soaring high over Exmoor, rising into the clouds rather than prosaically trundling along bad roads in his little Morris. He might be an impudent seducer, he was a hired hand at John Webster's newspaper, and certainly not a fit person for Miss Marlowe of Marlowe Court to consort with, but oh, how much she had enjoyed being with him!

Chapter Six

'What do you know about this young fellow, Allen, John?' Sir Charles asked John Webster, who was not only his cousin but had been his best friend since childhood.

They were sitting on the terrace at the back of Marlowe Court in the golden June afternoon. They had just been talking together about Margaret Bondfield, whom Ramsay Macdonald, Britain's new Prime Minister, had appointed to be Minister of Labour in Britain's first Labour government.

'Well, as I said the other night, he's clever, a hard worker and a quick learner. He's quite transforming the old *Clarion* without destroying its essential character as a country newspaper. I'm a little worried that I could lose him. He might want to spread his wings and try his hand in London.'

This was not quite the answer which Sir Charles wanted. He said so in his courteous fashion.

'Oh, you mean his social background, what sort of family he comes from. I know nothing of that; he's been remarkably close-mouthed about anything to do with his personal life before he arrived in West Bretton. I do know one thing, though. He's an Oxford graduate. He didn't tell me that. It slipped out one day when he wasn't being quite as wary as usual. It bore out my growing belief that he has had a public school and University education. He has a remarkable fund of all-round knowledge.'

'Hmmph,' grunted Sir Charles. 'A scholarship lad, perhaps?'

John shook his head. 'I don't think so. Every now and then, not often and quite unconsciously, he says or does something which betrays a privileged background. It's not arrogance—he singularly lacks that—in fact, I don't quite know how I know, if you follow me. Why do you ask?'

'Verena,' said Sir Charles succinctly. 'She seems very taken with him. I had hoped that she and Piers might hit it off. He's willing, but she isn't. You see why I'm worried. And Piers said something the other night when she came home late after being out with Allen all afternoon and evening which worried me rather.'

'Oh, yes? What was that?' John Webster didn't like Piers, but would never tell Sir Charles so.

'We were talking about the thefts from local country houses—did you know that the Axminsters were broken into the other night?—and Piers pointed out that all the robberies had taken place during the last three years. They began at almost exactly the same time that young Allen arrived in West Bretton. What, Piers wanted to know, was a feller like Allen doing in West Bretton anyway—not exactly your usual country type?'

'Oh, that's preposterous,' exclaimed John angrily. 'Nick is the last person I'd suspect of being the mastermind organising or helping to commit such crimes. He's the most open young chap I know.'

'But you know so little of him,' argued Sir Charles reasonably, 'for all his supposed openness. And you must admit what a splendid disguise working as a journalist in West Bretton would be, if he is involved in the robberies. It gives him a perfect reason for being here. You did say, too, that he pops up to London occasionally without giving any hint of what he's about when he gets there.'

'Well, if popping up to London occasionally without saying why is the mark of a devious young master criminal then half the young and youngish gentlemen round here—including Piers—must fall under suspicion!'

'Piers told me privately that he wears a damned expensive watch, and seems to have rather more money to throw about than he could earn as your assistant.'

John was now rather angry. 'I don't know about the watch but he lives a damned simple life. He's rented Jesse Pye's cottage, it's meagrely furnished and his life here is that of someone who needs to watch the pennies. He joined the Amateur Dramatic Society and has taken part in their last two winter productions. He plays cricket with the town team in summer when they're short of a man, gives a hand with British Legion functions—as you know—although he was too young to fight in the War. He's also helping to organise the summer Flannel Dance.

'In fact, he doesn't show any signs of either high, or suspicious, living—quite the contrary.'

'Well, you know best,' sighed Sir Charles. 'But I do wish we knew more about his background. I wrote to my old friend Jack Allen who lives in Northumberland to ask if he had any relatives who had a son called Nicholas of about young Allen's age. He said no. He rang the Nottinghamshire branch of the family with whom he'd lost touch over the years, and they knew nothing of a Nicholas, either. Dead ends everywhere,' he said glumly.

John, who was rather more rattled by Piers's unpleasant supposition than his manner to Sir Charles betrayed, changed the subject rapidly. He had defended Nicholas nobly, but nevertheless a worm of suspicion had been set free to gnaw away at his brain in the night hours precisely because he *had* sometimes asked himself who exactly Nicholas Allen was, who appeared to have no known relatives.

Piers, who had wandered on to the terrace to hear the end of the two old men's conversation, grinned with pleasure at the success of his untruthful and unpleasant piece of gossip.

No one would have been more surprised than Nicholas himself to learn of the fairy stories which Piers was spreading about him. In the fortnight since he had taken Verena to Lynton and Lynmouth his life had been completely innocent, as it had been ever since he had arrived in West Bretton.

He smiled ruefully to himself as he wondered what his father would make of his complete transformation if he ever learned of it. Even his relationship with Verena was quite unlike those which he had shared with women in his old life. The affair with that actress, for instance…

How could he have been such a fool—and why did he see so plainly now how empty and stupid that life had been when he couldn't see it then?

Young Jamie had recovered quite quickly from his attack of asthma and he had driven him, Verena, and Hercules, a few miles out of West Bretton towards its fellow village, North Bretton, to play French cricket and picnic by the River Bret in the shade of its willows.

Verena, Nicholas thought, was looking enchanting in an informal little sundress of lemon linen, white sandals and a white cotton cardigan. Jamie, as usual, poor little chap, was overdressed in heavy grey flannel shorts, a long-sleeved shirt, a tie, and a woollen pullover—his mother and grandfather's choice, no doubt.

Nicholas had taken along with him a copy of Kenneth

Grahame's *The Wind in the Willows* and read the first chapters from it to Verena and Jamie after they had eaten sandwiches and iced buns and drunk strong tea from a thermos flask—all of which, plus attendant crockery and cutlery, Nicholas had prepared for them after a hard morning at the *Clarion*.

'You must let me arrange for Cook to pack a meal for us the next time we come out,' Verena had exclaimed when he had produced a battered picnic basket from the Morris's back seat. 'It's a shame that you had to do all that after spending the morning at work.'

Nicholas, his mouth full of a doorstep cheese-and-pickle sandwich, disagreed with her. 'No, the great fun of a picnic is this sort of food. You can eat dainty sandwiches and flyaway cakes and drink Earl Grey tea indoors. What do you say to that, Jamie?' he asked.

He had insisted on the little boy taking off his pullover and rolling up his sleeves so that he might enjoy the sun without dying of heat stroke.

Jamie gave his opinion vigorously. 'Oh, I hate the sort of tea they serve in the drawing-room at home. I much prefer nursery tea—and this.'

'And there I was feeling sorry for him having to eat nursery tea,' said Verena mournfully. 'Never again.'

'Oh, I loved nursery tea, too,' said Nicholas, forgetting his role of poor young man from a dubious background. 'Marmite and soldiers with boiled eggs, pound cake, jam tarts and a roaring fire and Nanny bullying you while it rained stair-rods outside and you were warm and dry indoors!'

Verena and Jamie were both laughing so much at this picturesque description of the joys of nursery life that Verena forgot to notice what Nicholas had given away. He knew immediately what he had done, but was relieved to see that his hearers were too busy enjoying themselves to pick up his gaffe about having had a nanny.

The joys of the first few chapters of *The Wind in the Willows* held them entranced since it suited their rural setting so much. Jamie said blissfully when Nicholas had finished, 'Oh, I liked that, sir. Not perhaps quite so much as the dragon book Vee bought me from Lynton—that was just the ticket—but it was jolly all the same. May Vee borrow your book to read to me at bedtime?'

'I rather think that Vee—if I may so call her—has a copy of her own, but if not, I shall be pleased to lend her mine.'

As soon as he had spoken he realised that he had blundered again. For on the flyleaf of his copy his mother had written, 'To Nicholas Allen Schuyler, with love from his Mama.'

Fortunately, Verena said, 'That's a kind thought, but I do have a copy of my own. And it will be a relief to read about Ratty, Toad and Mole for a change and not blood-thirsty dragons.'

'Merlin's dragons aren't blood—what you said,' reprimanded Jamie. 'They're kind dragons.'

He could not understand why his half-sister and the Dragon man laughed gently at him when he said this.

'Well, they are,' he told them reproachfully. 'Do you think that Merlin will write another story about them, sir?'

'Perhaps,' Nicholas replied. 'But I couldn't guarantee it. He might have to wait until the dragons tell him what to write.'

'Oh, he doesn't need a dragon to do that!' Jamie was scornful. 'I can tell him. Wouldn't it be fun for him to write about dragon races—with men riding them!'

Nicholas looked thoughtful. 'You mean like the Schneider Trophy?' He was referring to the races between seaplanes which occurred periodically and in which Great Britain took part.

Jamie wriggled excitedly. 'Yes. Oh, Vee, do you think that we could write to Merlin and ask him? Do say yes, Vee, do say yes.'

Before Verena could answer, Nicholas said, his eyes wicked, 'Why not, Jamie? Or you could wish upon a star tonight and, being Merlin, he might be able to hear you.'

'Wish first and write to him later,' said Jamie practically. He rose to his feet and ran towards the river, Hercules tearing after him, waving his extended arms up and down, and shouting, 'Look at me, I'm a dragon! I'm going to win the dragon Schneider Trophy.'

The Dragon man and his princess—as he was beginning to think of Nicholas and his sister—looked at one another, amused. Verena said quietly. 'You are kind, Nicholas, not to discourage him and his enthusiasms. Living in a houseful of grownups is a bit hard on him sometimes. He finds it difficult to live up to their expectations.'

'I know.' Nicholas's reply was more heartfelt than he knew. 'Let him write his letter, Vee. He'll have to grow up all too soon.'

'And this picnic will have to end all too soon,' sighed Verena wistfully as she began to pack up the plates, cups and the remnants of their meal, after looking at her watch. 'I have to be back. We have guests for dinner tonight. They're due to arrive by five o'clock, and by then I must be properly dressed and in my right mind, as Priddie used to say when I was a child.'

'Forgive me,' said Nicholas naughtily, as he leaned forward to kiss her as he helped her in her task, 'but I really prefer you improperly dressed and in your wrong mind!'

'You mean as I am now?'

'Exactly, and before you rightly reprimand me for my

impertinence allow me to tell you how much I have enjoyed this afternoon. We must do it again soon. Unfortunately, I can't manage next Wednesday—other commitments—but let's make it a firm date for the one after. Fortunately we shall see one another before then at the British Legion hop at the Town Hall on Saturday. Save me a dance, do. Don't prance all night with the ineffable popinjay.'

'Now you're being unkind.'

'I know. If you promise to dance with me, I'll promise never to be naughty again.'

'Goodness,' and Verena began to laugh because he had put on an expression exactly like that of William in Richmal Crompton's book—another of Jamie's favourites. 'How could I ask you to do anything so impossible.'

'Or so undesirable? Say that you like me being naughty.'

He was irresistible in this mood—and Verena didn't resist him. 'You know I do—but I shouldn't.'

'If Jamie weren't with us I would reward you for that—improperly.'

'Then remind me always to bring Jamie with me when we go out together.'

'Oh, cruel witch, you can't mean it!'

He leaned forward to kiss her again, but just as his lips reached hers he was interrupted by Jamie's return, still in his dragon mode.

'Oh, we're not going home so soon, are we? What are you doing, sir? Has Vee got something in her eye?'

'I believe she has. Do let me have a look,' and Nicholas made a great pantomime of examining her eye, whilst Verena tried not to laugh.

'No, nothing there.' Nicholas sat back on his heels. 'Home, Jamie. Your sister has duties to perform, and you must support her by ceasing to be a dragon, resuming all that clobber you came in, and being a good boy.'

'Must I, sir? Oh, I suppose I must. Mama will be cross if I don't, and Sir Charles will say that I look like a street Arab if I'm not wearing my tie and pullover. You never wear a tie and a pullover, sir, so why should I?'

'I do in winter, sometimes in summer, but never on a picnic. Can you swim, Jamie?'

He shook his head. 'Mama says I'm too delicate, but I would like to.'

'Right, then if you put your clothes on now without arguing with me, I promise to take you down to Parson's Pool and teach you—but mum's the word on that, do you understand me?'

Jamie nodded again, happily this time.

'Good, now round up Hercules, and put him on your knee and hold him tight when we drive back. Can't have him jumping all over the driver, can we?'

This being agreed, they all drove back to Marlowe Court, where Nicholas dropped them off before the big front doors. Jamie insisted on waving goodbye to him until the little Morris disappeared through the gates at the end of the avenue.

Before he was out of sight they were joined by Piers, who surveyed their flushed, happy faces with sophisticated disapproval.

'Been out with the local yokel again, I suppose? Strange tastes you've got, Verena. No cider and pasties this time, I suppose, but you both look as though you've been rolling in the grass.'

'No, we don't, cousin Piers, because we haven't. We had a really jolly time. We had a picnic, Mr Allen read *The Wind in the Willows* to us, and I pretended to be a dragon—so there. Much you know about it.'

'Jamie!' exclaimed Verena, blushing. 'You mustn't talk to cousin Piers like that.'

'I won't if he won't tell whoppers about us and Mr Allen.'

'I suppose that Mr Allen never tells whoppers when you're having this educational beanfeast in the open. I must say that he hasn't improved your manners, James Marlowe, quite the contrary. You'd better go straight up to Miss Pridham in the nursery before I improve them for you.'

Jamie went bright red and formed his small hands into fists. Verena, shocked, said as kindly as she could, 'Do as Piers says, Jamie. You've had a splendid afternoon, don't spoil it.'

'For you, Vee,' said Jamie, choking back tears. 'I'll do what he says for you.' He's no business talking about the Dragon man like that, he muttered to himself as he ran into the house.

Verena turned on Piers and unwittingly echoed her half-brother. 'You've no business talking about Nicholas Allen like that, Piers. You know nothing of him.'

Piers raised one perfectly arched eyebrow. 'No? I know that an impudent nobody has no right to escort Miss Marlowe of Marlowe Court, and Marlowe Court's heir, around the countryside without proper chaperonage… In fact, he shouldn't be escorting you at all.'

'Oh, Piers! Listen to yourself. This is 1929. I'm of age, and may do as I please. You are neither my guardian nor my husband…'

'More's the pity,' he interjected. 'Chrissie is quite shocked by your behaviour and intends to forbid Jamie to have anything more to do with Allen. She is waiting with Priddie to tell him that.'

Verena went quite white. 'How can you both be so cruel! Can't you see how much better Jamie is since Nicholas took an interest in him? We've been out with him several times now, on walks, as well as on today's picnic, and he's never once had an asthma attack when Nicholas has been with him. Not once.'

'That's because he spoils him rotten—as you do. A good prep school followed by boarding school will soon stop all that nonsense. And do come into the house—we're arguing on the steps like a pair of servants. I suppose that it's associating with him that has you behaving like one.'

Verena rounded on him. 'Tell me, Piers, what is this obsession with servants that everyone at Marlowe Court suffers from? It shows a horrible lack of confidence constantly to be comparing our behaviour with those you despise. They're men and women, just like us, no more and no less.'

'Turning Socialist, are you, Vee? Is that his doing, too?'

'Oh, you're impossible…'

They had reached the entrance hall where Verena was interrupted in mid-sentence by one of the maids running downstairs and, all etiquette forgotten, was shouting her name.

'Oh, Miss Verena, thank God I've found you. Master Jamie has been taken so poorly again, he can scarcely breathe. Neither Madam nor Miss Pridham can do anything with him. They want you to go up to the nursery immediately to look after him, whilst the butler sends for the doctor. They fear for him.'

'No!' Piers and his nastiness forgotten, Verena ran upstairs. She knew immediately what had happened. Chrissie had forbidden him to see Nicholas again and by doing so had triggered off an asthma attack—and by what the maid had said, a severe one.

Tears running down her face, she could not help remembering his joy by the river, his pleasure in listening to Nicholas read to him, of how he had bounded and swooped

round the field pretending to be a dragon, Hercules running
happily behind him.

What was the poor little dragonet doing now? She shot
into his bedroom, pushing Chrissie and Miss Pridham savagely on one side. Jamie lay there gasping and panting. He
tried to sit up when she arrived, but fell back, wheezing
harder than ever.

'Oh, Vee, oh, Vee, she says, she says…' He could not
go on.

'Shush, I know, Piers told me. Don't worry.'

His eyes were agonised. 'I'm not to see the Dragon man
again,' he managed, 'and Hercules is to be given away!
She says he's a nuisance.'

'Well, he is,' announced Chrissie harshly, 'and so is
Nicholas Allen. This is his fault. He excited Jamie—and
this is the result.' She pointed dramatically at the bed.

Verena said furiously, 'What utter nonsense! Not long
ago you thought Nicholas Allen was a divine man. What
happened to change that? And how dare you say that this
is Nicholas's fault? Jamie never has an attack when he's
with Nicholas, never, do you hear me? This one started
after you had forbidden him to see Nick, and told him that
you were going to get rid of Hercules—didn't it?'

'How dare you speak to me like that!'

'Oh, I dare. I shall speak to my grandfather about this.'

'And so shall I. I am his mother.'

'And a damned poor one at that,' said Verena, who had
never sworn in her life before. 'I shall speak to the doctor
as well.'

Miss Pridham faltered, 'Jamie did start to be ill immediately after you forbade him to see Mr Allen again, and
ordered Hercules to be put down, Mrs Marlowe.'

'And he wasn't ill all afternoon—until he came home,'
put in Verena.

Chrissie turned angrily on Miss Pridham. 'How dare you interfere? You know nothing about it.'

Verena, who was growing more and more surprised by her own determination, intervened as Miss Pridham flushed red and began to stammer.

'How dare *you* say that, Chrissie? Priddie has spent the last forty years caring successfully for Marlowe children. And may I suggest that you leave me with Jamie until the doctor comes. I can usually manage to comfort him, whereas you merely manage to upset him.'

Chrissie opened her mouth to protest, but changed her mind when Jamie called weakly from his bed, 'Vee, oh, Vee, I want you.'

Ignoring everything, and everybody, Verena went over to him and took his hand. He lifted himself to lie against her breast, trying not to wheeze and saying, 'Read to me from the dragon book, Vee.'

Before Verena could rise, Priddie went over to the bookcase and came back with *The Cowardly Dragon*. Verena opened it and began to read, Chrissie staring balefully at her from an old basket chair into which she had sagged.

Jamie clutched at Verena's hand as though it were a lifeline, but as she began to read to him from a book which he knew by heart, his breathing improved and changed until his hand dropped away. He had fallen asleep.

Verena read on for a few minutes, before she closed the book and stopped. She did not move, but allowed him to sleep on, his small head now on her lap.

Chrissie rose, said loudly and inconsiderately, 'What a commotion! I sometimes wonder if he behaves like this on purpose in order to get attention.'

Both Verena and Miss Pridham were shocked by this callous remark. Miss Pridham flushed; Verena almost began to speak but, fearing that she might awaken the sleeping child, held her tongue. Nothing more could be gained by fighting with Chrissie before the doctor arrived.

After that—well, after that would depend on what he decided.

Sir Charles said to Verena, 'My dear, what is this that your mother has been telling me about your interference in her care of young James?'

'She is not my mother,' Verena returned, 'but she is Jamie's and a poor fist she is making of it.'

Sir Charles sighed. He seemed to be sighing rather a lot since his son's wife had returned to the ancestral home. 'Nevertheless…'

Daringly, Verena intervened, all her good manners disappearing in her desire to protect her half-brother from his selfish mother.

'Nevertheless, Grandfather, the doctor agreed with me that it was unlikely that going out with Mr Allen this afternoon was the cause of Jamie's attack. He thought that distress at losing both a friend and his dog might be the true reason. He suggested a compromise: that Jamie should be allowed to see Mr Allen occasionally, but that if Chrissie thought that Hercules might be partly to blame for Jamie's attacks, then it would not hurt for him to be sold or given away. Jamie would naturally be greatly distressed if he thought that his pet was going to be put down.'

'Sensible, sensible,' agreed Sir Charles, in approval of this face-saving arrangement. 'Sorry about the dog, but his mother knows best, I'm sure.'

'So,' Verena continued, 'since I have a friend whom I am sure would like to give Hercules a home, I wonder if I might be allowed to try to arrange the matter immediately?'

'If your, er, stepmother agrees, yes.'

Chrissie arriving in the drawing room at this point, was asked her opinion on the matter.

'Oh, do what you like with the wretched animal. I want it out of the house as soon as possible. I'm sure that, whatever you and the doctor think, all that running round Jamie does with him is partly the cause of his asthma.'

Having won her point, and knowing as she did so that she was to some extent going to deceive Sir Charles and Chrissie, Verena made no reply.

'Good. Then you will forgive me, Grandfather, if I skip dinner with the Eversons this evening in order to find Hercules a new home. You will present them with my apologies. I can ask Cook to make me up a light supper when I return home.'

Sir Charles nodded somewhat glumly. His peaceful life had virtually been destroyed by his late son's family, but it was his duty to look after them, however much he was inconvenienced.

He told Piers so when he strolled in, before the Eversons came down for dinner.

Piers's answer was as might have been expected. 'Sorry to hear that the quack hasn't banned Jamie from running around with Allen. Pity about the dog, though. Should have been the other way round.'

It was fortunate that Verena had already left so did not hear this unkind verdict on the doctor's judgement of Solomon. She had run upstairs, put on a warm woolly, for the evening had turned cool, collected Hercules from the stables to which he had been sent in disgrace, fastened on his lead—and walked rapidly in the direction of Nicholas's cottage.

Nicholas, who was in the process of cooking his supper, frowned when the knock on the door interrupted him. The frown turned to a smile when he found Verena on his door-step, and an enthusiastic Hercules barking a greeting.

'Hello, Verena, come in, do. What brings you here at this hour? I thought that dinner at Marlowe Court always began at half past seven on the dot.'

Once indoors, Verena looked earnestly at him. 'Oh, Nicholas, I've come to ask a favour of you. If you feel that it's too much I shall quite understand.'

Nicholas had seen immediately that she was greatly dis-tressed. He took her gently by the hand and made her sit down.

'What is it, Verena? Who and what has upset you?'

It all came pouring out. Jamie's asthma attack, Chrissie's cruel response, and finally the decision to banish Hercules.

'I thought,' she finished, 'that if it wasn't asking too much of you, you might see your way to giving Hercules a home where Jamie could come to visit him. We could take him out with us, too. That way, he wouldn't lose Hercules completely. I'm afraid that if he does, it will make him ill again.'

Nicholas's anger at this sad tale was not written on his face, but inside he seethed. 'Poor little chap,' was all he said. 'Of course, I'll take him. I was thinking of buying a watchdog, so Hercules has come along at the right time.'

Verena looked dubiously at small Hercules who was now lying trustingly at Nicholas's feet. 'Are you sure? He doesn't look like much of a watchdog to me.'

'Perhaps not, but he's better than nothing. Oh, Vee, don't look at me like that—' for her face had lit up '—you don't know what you do to me.'

What could she say? That he had no idea what *he* did to *her*. That every time that she met him the feeling of ex-citement which overcame her grew stronger and stronger. And that this last act of kindness to Jamie had in some way set the seal on these feelings so that she no longer felt compelled to deny them.

Could it be love which was causing them? They were so different from anything which she had felt for Roger, so strong and powerful that they revealed to her how tepid their affair had been. And if she were honest, Roger had been to some degree in the right in their last quarrel after she had discovered him in bed with Chrissie when he had called her frigid, and she had thrown her engagement ring at him.

She didn't feel frigid when she was with Nicholas. On the contrary, she burned for him. She yearned to touch him, and for him to touch her. As she yearned now.

Unknowingly her yearning was written on her face. Her eyes were alight, her mouth had softened, and opened slightly. She licked her lips with a soft pink tongue and Nicholas almost groaned aloud at the sight. He knelt by her on the floor so that their eyes were on a level. He did not touch her.

'You haven't answered me,' he said softly. 'Do you know?'

She shook her head. 'No. I only know what you do to me.'

'And what is that?' he asked her.

She turned her face away from him. 'Don't make me say.'

'Is it this, Verena, is it this? You want me to do this when we are together,' and he leaned forward to claim her mouth, and at the same time he cupped the back of her head in his big hand, her eyes closing as he did so.

Oh, how sweet his mouth was on hers! How sweet to be kissed gently and then more strongly, his tongue forcing her lips apart so that it might caress hers—but still gently.

The effect on Verena was electric. She gave a little cry

at the back of her throat and sagged against him, only his hand at the back of her head holding her up. She made no effort to withdraw from his intimate caress, simply allowed herself to enjoy it.

Nicholas was equally strongly affected. Not for a long time had he been aroused so quickly. The knowledge of the powerful effect he had on her was partly responsible for that. They had come so far so quickly that he was almost frightened. He knew that she was innocent, and was sure that she was inexperienced, and that therefore he must not take advantage of her.

She was no Daisy Goring, no Chrissie, both of whom were experts in the jousts of love. He must try to go slowly with her—or not at all. He must certainly not push her to the limit on the first occasion that she had visited him alone.

He pulled away. She murmured, 'No,' and tried, her eyes still closed, to reclaim his mouth.

'Yes,' he said. 'Oh, Verena, it is because we are so strongly attracted to each other that we must go slowly—otherwise we shall go up in flames.'

She opened her eyes wide, said simply, 'You too?' And how he loved her for that.

'Yes, and since I am the experienced one, and you are the novice, then it is I who must take the lead, and I who must call a halt. Besides, from what you say—and what you don't say—I am sure that there are those at Marlowe Court who would expect me to try to seduce you if we were ever alone. I would not like to live down to their low opinion of me—and of you—by our being parties in a seduction!'

This last sentence brought forth a ghostly chuckle from Verena. 'But I want to go on,' she almost wailed. 'You aren't seducing me—if anything, it's the other way round!'

'Not tonight,' he told her.

'Then when?'

Nicholas threw his head back and laughed at this frank question. 'You darling, when the time is right, not before.'

'But how shall we know when it is?'

'We shall know when you are sure it is I whom you want, that you were not simply blinded by the delight of your first grown-up kiss. Now,' and he rose from his kneeling position, 'we must behave ourselves. When you arrived I was preparing my supper. If I invited you to share it with me, do you think that we can control our unruly passions long enough to allow us to eat it and part without disgracing ourselves?'

'Yes,' said Verena quickly before he could change his mind.

'It's only tinned salmon and salad and a custard tart from the pastry cook in West Bretton. Sure you wouldn't rather go home to the fleshpots of Marlowe Court?'

'Quite sure. I've never had tinned salmon before. Come to think of it I've never been kissed properly before. Two firsts in one night might seem a bit excessive, but I think I can stand the excitement.'

'And tea,' added Nicholas, 'to drink with the meal, not wine. And Hercules won't be anything like so pampered here as he was at the Court.'

'He might be happier.'

'True. Are you happy to be with me, Verena?'

'You know I am. Will you allow me to slice the tomatoes and the cucumber? I see that you were only halfway through preparing the salad.'

'And the dressing is out of a bottle, I fear.'

'Nicholas, it is you I am growing to love, not your salad cream.'

There, she had said it.

They stared at one another. He said, 'No, it is not in the

rules to tell me that tonight. We must behave ourselves, and if you confess to that, then I must cap it by confessing my feelings for you—and where would that end?'

'Well, we probably wouldn't get any supper.'

'Oh, you tempt me,' he said softly. 'You really do. *Vade retro, Sathanas*. Do you know what that means, Verena?'

'Yes,' she told him. ''Get thee behind me, Satan'', which means, do not tempt me, Satan—but I never knew that the devil was a woman.'

She had surprised him. Almost, he made to kiss her again for capping his quotation, but he checked himself. 'No, I must keep my word, and you must help me to make the salad.'

'If you say so,' Verena replied mournfully.

'Well, it breaks my heart, too, to say nothing of what it does to the rest of me, but there are many reasons why we must be good.'

So Nicholas opened a tin of pink salmon, sliced a crusty loaf and spread it with good farm butter, whilst Verena made a mixed salad from lettuce, tomatoes, cucumber, hard-boiled eggs, and radishes. They ate it dressed with salad cream from a bottle and it all tasted like manna. After they had polished off the custard they toasted themselves with tea, before Nicholas walked her back to the Court gates, where she said farewell to him and to Hercules, valiantly refraining from kissing them both goodbye.

'See you at the hop on Saturday,' were his last words to her, 'and don't forget to save me a dance.'

Chapter Seven

'Before we go in to dinner tonight,' said Sir Charles to the party assembled in the drawing-room on the following evening, 'I feel I ought to have a word with you all about Saturday evening.'

'Oh, you mean this—what is it?—so-called Flannel Dance, at the Town Hall run by the British Legion. I suppose it *is* incumbent on us to attend?' Piers sounded dismissive.

'Indeed.' Sir Charles was grave. 'It is our duty, it is the duty of all the family at Marlowe Court, seeing that I am Chairman of the West Bretton branch, and we are in a sense honouring the men who died for us in the War.'

Silence followed. They all knew that Sir Charles had lost two sons, and John Webster, who was also present, had lost his only son.

'The thing is,' drawled Piers, 'that I understand that, by calling it a Flannel Dance, those who attend ought to be dressed informally—in flannels and sports jackets, of all things. But surely that does not extend to our party—it must be meant for the locals only.'

Another awkward silence followed. Sir Charles said stiffly, 'The decision to make it one arose from the fact that if we made dress formal most of the branch's membership would not be able to attend—thus leaving out many who served most gallantly in the late War. I feel that we should honour this decision by dressing accordingly.'

Piers shrugged. 'That seems a little extreme, sir. We attend the Christmas dance in our usual evening dress—why should this be any different?'

'Because, as I said, we are honouring all our members by obeying the rules agreed by them. I fear that you are forgetting the principle of *noblesse oblige*, Piers—and that will never do.'

This was as near to a rebuke as Sir Charles ever got, and silenced Piers.

Next it was Chrissie's turn to ask in a suffering voice, 'Do I also understand that we are not to wear evening dresses, but must turn up in afternoon frocks?'

'I believe so.' Sir Charles looked across at Mrs Everson, who nodded agreement.

'Indeed, evening dress would look rather odd with flannels,' she assured Chrissie. 'And, after all, it is only for one evening.'

Piers did not need to say 'Thank God': his expression said it for him.

He was still wearing it when the party from the Court arrived at the Town Hall after dinner to find the dance in full swing.

'There's your bucolic suitor,' he said disagreeably to Verena when he saw Nicholas walk off the floor at the end of a waltz with Edith Ashby, the daughter of the headmaster of the local school. 'I must say that I find flannel bags absolutely the thing for him to wear. Imagine him in evening dress!'

Verena could. She thought that he would look absolutely

splendid in it. His strange golden eyes lit up when he caught sight of her, but good manners had him escorting Miss Ashby back to her parents and her seat before he made his way over to Sir Charles's party.

'Good evening, sir,' he said cheerfully. 'I'm sure we're all greatly honoured by your visit. May I ask you to allow me to lead your granddaughter on to the floor for the next dance?'

This deference had Sir Charles beaming. 'Certainly, young man. I'm happy to see that some of the younger generation still retain a semblance of good form. Enjoy yourself, my dear. That is why you came, after all.'

'You couldn't have said anything better,' Verena whispered to Nicholas as he swept her into the quickstep. 'He has just been arguing with Piers, who thinks it frightfully bad form to attend a dance wearing informal clothing. Grandfather told him that good manners matter more than empty ritual—and came out with *noblesse oblige* for about the fifth time this week.'

'Well, *I* enjoy a dance more when I'm not buttoned up to the neck in stiff clothing,' replied Nicholas, 'and I think that you look stunning in your afternoon frock. At least I shan't be tripping over the hem of a long evening dress— I'm not exactly the world's most graceful dancer.'

He was not lying. Verena did look stunning. She was wearing a delicate rose-pink silk dress with a lace overskirt gathered at the waist into a large artificial rose. It ended just below the knee—hence his comment about long evening dresses. Her shoes and stockings were of the same colour and she had had the tactful good sense to wear no expensive jewellery.

Verena thought that Nicholas was a better dancer than he claimed to be, and as she was swung about the floor in his arms the hot excitement which she felt whenever she was with him increased until she began to wonder if she was contracting a fever.

She was not the only person to be strongly affected. Nicholas, closer to her than he had ever been before, had to begin thinking about cool mountain streams and arctic wastes to prevent himself from becoming aroused. Looking down into her delicate face, flushed by the delights of the dance, wasn't helping him to stay calm, either.

Both Chrissie and Piers were unwilling and unhappy spectators of what both could plainly see was a mutual passion. Chrissie had never thought that her gentle and despised stepdaughter would be able to take a man away from her—in the past the reverse had always been true. As for Piers, he had no real feeling for Verena: his hatred of Nicholas was caused by the knowledge that he was attracting the girl whom Piers had seen as his financial saviour.

The lovers, unaware that they had betrayed themselves to jealous eyes, sighed together as the dance ended.

'I don't know what the etiquette of these things is,' said Nicholas as they applauded the little band which did duty for all such evenings in that part of Devonshire, 'but I must ask you to save some more dances for me. I've never before managed to dance with a girl and not tread on her toes at least three times. I haven't trodden on yours once—quite a record for me.'

'The girls must have been very clumsy then,' she told him, 'because we seem to go together beautifully.'

'I could kiss you for that,' he said, as he walked her back to her party, 'if we weren't in such a public place—later, perhaps.'

Why did the mere thought of a kiss from him set Verena's heart hammering and her breath shortening? Like Nicholas, she controlled her errant body with difficulty. She must not give herself away too much. She was acutely aware of Chrissie's displeasure and of Piers's mocking face.

'Enjoy dancing with the local yokel?' was his offering after Nicholas had walked away.

Verena resented this description of Nicholas so much that she said, her voice as coldly controlled as she could make it, 'Piers, why do you think that being brutally rude about Nicholas Allen should make me be attracted to you? On the contrary, I find that your constant display of bad manners so far as he is concerned fully justifies my refusal of your proposal.'

Well, that might be pompous, but it had to be said. And oddly, the more unkind Piers grew the more he strengthened her feelings for Nicholas.

She hadn't upset Piers. He offered her a patronising smile. 'My, my, little cousin, you are bewitched by him. Who would have thought it?'

Verena's face grew hot. She turned away from him before she said something unforgivable. Alas, she found herself facing Chrissie, whom she was sure was about to improve the shining hour by following Piers's example and sneering at Nicholas.

She forestalled any such attempt by running her flag up the mast, as it were, and walking over to where Nicholas stood talking to John Webster and to West Bretton's Mayor.

'Hullo, Uncle John. I wonder if you'd consent to lend Nicholas to me for a short time. I'm feeling thirsty and I understand that there are refreshments in the Mayor's Parlour, and I could do with an escort.'

'Oh, he's all yours tonight, my dear. He's a free man once he leaves the *Clarion*'s offices.'

'Don't you believe him, Vee,' Nicholas said. 'He's a

slave driver in and out of the office, but if he says I'm free tonight, then here is my arm,' and he held it out to her.

'What is it, Vee?' he asked her quietly when they were on the way to the refreshments. 'You're trembling. Has someone upset you?'

How perceptive he was, quite unlike some she knew. 'Yes…no,' she managed to reply. 'Everything and nothing. I'm rambling, stop me.'

'Ah, which of the unholy duo is it who is sticking pins into you?' He saw her lips quiver and added quickly, 'Both of them, I see. Here—' and he handed her a glass of lemonade '—drink this and damnation to all unpleasant gossips as you do. Don't let them spoil your evening.'

'I won't,' Verena announced, drinking down the lemonade in one defiant swallow. 'That's why I came over to you. Which is unfair to you, I know, because it will only result in them tearing you to pieces all over again.'

'Much that will trouble me,' he said with a strange laugh. 'I've been ripped apart by fiercer critics than the pair of paper tigers who've just come in to see what we're up to.'

He had picked up a glass of red wine and held it mockingly towards Piers, bending his head in parody of a toast. Piers had Chrissie on his arm, and was staring rudely at the long table laid out with a variety of simple fare and not-too-expensive drinks.

'I suppose one must show willing,' he remarked to her in an undertone which was meant to be heard, 'but I can think of better ways to spend a Saturday night. That's wine you're waving about, Allen. If you want my advice, don't gulp it down as though it's lemonade or coarse ale.'

'Really,' said Nicholas, examining his glass carefully. 'You do surprise me, I thought that it was lemonade. Could you, from the depths of your vast knowledge, enlighten me as to its vintage and year? You might also add as a rider what, in your opinion, does constitute the best way to spend a Saturday night. I'm always ready to be educated by those in the know.'

Piers glared at him. Verena stifled a giggle. Chrissie said angrily, 'I suppose you think that's funny.'

'Asking to be educated is never funny, Chrissie. On the contrary, most informed opinion thinks that it's serious and to be admired.' He twirled his glass, put it to his nose and sniffed at the wine's non-existent bouquet as seriously as though he were a *sommelier*, or a master of the vintage.

'You're right, Marlowe, it *is* red wine. I should never have guessed.' He drank a little delicately before saying, 'You haven't enlightened me about Saturday nights, Marlowe. Do tell, I could do with a good one. Vee, too.'

'Nicholas!' Verena's tone was reproving, even though it was amusing to see Piers being taunted for a change. She thought that he was about to burst, and that it was just as well that the age of duelling was over. In any case it would not be proper for the four of them to be the centre of a scene at the Flannel Dance. Grandfather wouldn't like it.

'Now you're being really naughty,' she told him.

'Am I?' His tone and face were suddenly serious. 'I suppose I am. It all depends on who is doing the baiting, doesn't it, Marlowe, whether it's witty or tedious and insulting. Even yokels like me have feelings, believe it or not.'

He put down his glass of wine with extreme care, although he had only taken one swallow from it. 'Trouble is, Marlowe, I'm virtually a teetotaller these days—another count against me, I suppose. You will excuse us both now, I'm sure. I can hear a slow foxtrot starting up outside and I wouldn't like Vee to miss my imitation of Fred Astaire.'

He held out his arm to her, and she took it, trembling

with suppressed amusement rather than the anger she had felt earlier.

'Is it true?' she asked him. 'Are you really almost a tee-totaller? You had a glass of cider with me on the night we came home from Lynmouth.'

'Since I came to West Bretton, yes,' he told her as he manoeuvred her gently on to the dance floor. 'I rarely ever drink—and when I do I ration myself to a little. Just before I arrived here I suddenly decided that the road to Hell was paved with barrels of beer and casks of wine and that if I were not careful I might become an alcoholic and not be able to resist it. The only way to get off it was to renounce alcohol, if not completely, as much as possible.'

He looked earnestly at her. 'I think I only drank because I was unhappy—and now I'm not. I saw how unhappy you were when you came over to me—which was the reason why I couldn't stop myself from baiting Piers. Forgive me for doing so, I was a bit insufferable—I suppose that I was reverting to my old habits which I renounced when I came to the West Country. I promise not to be naughty again.'

'No, Nicholas, you are not to apologise to me; I know why you were rude to Piers and Chrissie—it was out of kindness to me. But believe me when I say that, although they both have the power to upset me briefly, neither of them ever say or do anything which can cause me long-term distress. And I wouldn't like you to suffer in any way through defending me. I don't want you to end up losing your job and becoming one of England's millions of un-employed because you felt the need to be chivalrous. That would distress me even more than Piers's taunts.'

They were heart to heart, breast to breast in the slow rhythms of the foxtrot. Nicholas did not have to bend his head much to kiss her gently on her damask cheek. 'Yes, you are a darling to worry about me—and the unemployed.'

'I do worry about them,' she told him earnestly, 'because of my own idle life. Oh, I know that we Marlowes are not all that rich and privileged, but we are so much better off than the great mass of people that I sometimes feel ashamed.'

He did not answer her. He was thinking of his own privileged background. Of the vast sum of money which stood to his name in Coutts Bank. Oh, yes, he was only living on what he earned from his writing and from the *Clarion*, but all the same he was still immensely rich Nicholas Allen Schuyler who had no pit of total ruin to fall into.

Speaking of the unfortunate had sobered them both. Nicholas loved Verena for her compassion, and she loved him because he was so busy trying, as she thought, not to end up in a dole queue.

There were times when the knowledge that he was deceiving those around him depressed Nicholas rather than amused him, and this was becoming one of them.

Which was not fair to Verena… He pulled himself together for he did not want to spoil her pleasure in the evening. As a result they ended the foxtrot in happy agreement that, even though this was not one of Piers's famed Saturday nights, they were having a good time.

Piers was not. He squired Chrissie for part of the evening, before attaching himself to John Webster's party. Something which Verena had let fall earlier about young Allen had interested him.

'What's this I hear about Allen having a holiday this week?' he remarked idly. 'Bit early in the year, isn't it?'

If John Webster wondered why Piers Marlowe of all people should be interested in young Allen's leisure arrangements he did not say so.

'Oh, he's not had a real holiday since I took him on. He said that he wished to take three days off to visit London to clear up some family business, so I was only too willing to let him go from Tuesday to Friday this coming week.'

'Via Exeter or Bridgewater, I suppose. Does he have a motor?'

'A little Morris, and yes, he mentioned Exeter. Why the interest?'

'Oh, I still think that there's something odd about him. These robberies…'

'No, Piers, you go too far.' John Webster was angry. 'You have not the lightest reason to believe any such thing—or to speak to Sir Charles about it.'

Piers smiled. 'But it troubles both of you, doesn't it? Such a queer fish to choose to live in West Bretton. Oh, very well, I'll say no more,' he finished hastily, on seeing John's rising anger.

He sauntered away. So Allen was going to Exeter—and then London, if it could be believed. What if he could persuade people to believe something else? It would mean killing two birds with one stone—always a useful occupation. He was so pleased with himself that he could even watch Nicholas and Verena laughing together because, he told himself gleefully, young Allen wouldn't be laughing long.

Nicholas had been entertaining Verena with tales of his experiences as a cub reporter following village flower shows, weddings and school concerts.

'I hadn't the slightest notion of the amount of tact required,' he told her frankly. 'But I learned quickly. John Webster soon had me running along the right lines. You're not some campaigning chap on the *Mirror* or the *Daily Herald* setting the world to rights, he told me. You're giving a lot of simple people pleasure and while I don't want you to lie I want you to tell the truth "with advantages" as Shakespeare once said.'

Verena was appreciative. 'With advantages. I like that.'

Nicholas leaned forward and said confidentially, 'I tell you what I would like, Vee. You know I'm going to London on Tuesday for three nights?'

Yes, she knew.

'Well, it would make me very happy if you would agree to have a Cornish cream tea with me on Monday afternoon at four. I'm sure John would let me off for a tea break. I almost think that I could bear to visit the Great Sewer if I had the memory of that to take with me. Do say yes, Vee.'

There was not the slightest chance that she would say anything else, and so she told him.

'Bromley's tearoom, then. Do you know, that was the first place I visited when I came to West Bretton, and I was so enchanted by that, and everything else I saw in North Devon that I decided to put down roots here.'

For the first time Verena wondered where Nicholas's roots had been before then. Some unknown place where he had not been happy. As their love for one another grew he was telling her so much about himself that perhaps he would, one day soon, tell her that.

''Til Monday, sweet witch,' he breathed in her ear as they danced the last waltz together. He would have liked to have shared every dance with her, but he had his duty to the other young women of West Bretton since here as everywhere due to the slaughter in the last war, women still outnumbered men.

And Verena had to do her duty as the granddaughter of the Squire and was pushed around the floor by the doctor, the bank manager, and the captain of the cricket team, with a quarter of her mind on them and the rest on Nicholas. Not until the last waltz was played could she be in his arms again—and then only briefly.

She was so excited that when she finally fell into bed at Marlowe Court she could not sleep. Her awakening senses,

senses which her selfish fiancé had not taken the trouble to bring to life, kept her body from resigning itself to unconsciousness. Over and over again she was in Nicholas's arms, becoming aware at last that she wanted much more in the way of lovemaking from him than she had ever previously experienced. More than that, she wanted to give him pleasure, to see his amber eyes glitter, to…

Verena sat bolt upright in bed, all her senses on fire. She switched on the small electric lamp by her bed, picked up her watch—and groaned. It was only half-past three and she felt that she had been trying to go to sleep for an eternity.

There was only one thing for it. She would go downstairs to the library, find a book to read, and then visit the kitchen to make herself a drink. Perhaps such mundane tasks might quieten down her errant body.

She slipped on her dressing gown and, creeping past Piers's room, she made for the stairs. She was almost there when she heard, behind her, his bedroom door open. Perhaps like her, he was unable to sleep. She had not, however, the slightest wish to encounter him in the small hours, clad only her nightwear, so she flattened herself into the shadows of a large niche in the corridor wall well away from the overhead light, and hoped that Piers would walk by it without seeing her.

Only, when the footsteps reached and passed her, they belonged not to Piers, but to Chrissie. Chrissie, who was clad in a scanty nightie and was fastening up her dressing gown. Verena was not so innocent that she did not know that her stepmother's face was swollen and rosy, not with sleep, but with lovemaking.

Nor was she shocked by what she saw. It was simply Chrissie at her tricks again; but, at least this time she did not care that it was Piers whom she had annexed—as she had cared when Chrissie had annexed Roger Gough. She was welcome to him—and he to her—but all the same she felt a great sadness overwhelm her at the memory of her dead father who had loved Chrissie—but whom Chrissie had never loved—and whom she had frequently cheated. Verena was not even sure that Jamie was her father's son. But she loved him all the same.

What Chrissie had loved was the prospect of becoming Lady Marlowe, something which was now forever lost to her.

Verena returned to her bed. Seeing the evidence of her stepmother's new liaison had had the odd effect of quietening her down. She drifted into sleep, the strains of the last waltz in her head, soothing, rather than exciting her.

Nicholas arrived in London carrying with him the happy memory of his cream tea at Bromleys's with Verena, exactly as he had promised her. He had discovered that the nicest thing about his love affair with her was that he liked the quiet times they shared when they laughed and talked about the many interests which they discovered they had in common. It was almost like discovering his other half.

Yesterday she had told him what she had planned: that as soon as Chrissie took Jamie to live in London, she would contact one of her old friends and take up the offer of helping her in her dress shop in Chelsea.

'The only thing is,' she had told him earnestly, 'I don't want to leave West Bretton now.'

'Because?' he asked her.

'You know,' she said and blushed rosy red.

'Do I, Vee, do I?'

He was teasing her, and oh, the simple pleasure it gave him.

It gave Verena a simple pleasure to tease him back. 'I like it here.'

'It? You said it? Is there no he?'

Verena liked it when he played with words. She had tried to do so with Roger and he had stared at her uncomprehendingly.

'There might be,' she said primly—and laughed into her teacup. Yes, the meal had been a success, a definite success from the view point of both parties for they began to laugh together and Nicholas held Verena's hand under the table.

The only drawback from Nicholas's point of view came when he returned to the *Clarion*'s offices, and was greeted by John Webster.

'You met Verena Marlowe for tea?' he asked.

Nicholas thought that he knew what might be coming. 'You know I did. I told you so.' His voice was cold after a fashion which John Webster had never heard before, and it surprised him—almost shocked him by its severity.

He put down the sheaf of papers he was holding and said, 'You know that I value you, Nick, both as a colleague and a friend, which is why I ought to warn you. It won't do, you know.'

'What won't do?'

Again there was the touch of steel from a man whose gentleness was proverbial in West Bretton. Something which Piers Marlowe had said on the night of the Flannel Dance told John that he, too, had been given a taste of the steel.

What he could not know was that when Nicholas Allen felt himself threatened he reverted to being pure Schuyler, the true descendant of the ruthless Captain who brooked no denying of his will. It was not a conscious thing, but came from the depths of his being, there not only because of his conditioning, but because of the power of the genes he carried.

'Trying to court Verena Marlowe. She is Sir Charles's granddaughter, the Squire's grand-daughter, and he would never agree to her marrying you.'

Nicholas smiled—it was not a true smile, but rather a baring of teeth, and it was again unconscious.

'Two points, John. One, I am not trying to court Verena, I *am* courting her, and two, she is of age, and her own mistress.'

'But stands to lose her dowry—it is to be given at Sir Charles's pleasure. That I do know.'

'And being her dowry—not mine—that is for Verena to consider, not me. I would advise her to consider that carefully if I asked her to marry me—but the choice remains hers. Anything else?'

Unknowingly Nicholas was using the exact tone of voice of the father he had rejected when he was rebuking an impertinent member of a committee he was chairing. His mother had not been wrong when she had told Gerard that his son was more like him than either of them knew.

John said, a trifle desperately, 'I thought that I ought to warn you.'

'And now you have warned me. That article you asked me to finish by today is in the papers you are holding, ready to be edited. I have also completed the list of coming events for the next week and that is there also. And John…' he paused.

John Webster, looking at the papers in his hand, said, 'Yes, Nick?'

'You had the right to speak to me as you did, and I had the right to answer you—as I did. May we leave it at that? I should not like the matter to come between us.'

Again, it was Gerard Schuyler speaking, peacemaking

after trouble. Nicholas's hearer replied conciliatingly, as many had replied to Gerard, 'Of course. It was my duty, you understand. It is over.'

'Good.'

Nicholas walked into the room where the printing presses were housed. John Webster stared after him. He had employed young Allen for three years and thought that he knew him well. He was suddenly aware that he did not know him at all! He found himself thinking of Piers's insinuations and they no longer seemed as unlikely as they had previously done. There was a power and severity about young Allen which he had never suspected.

Remembering this scene on the train which carried him to London, Nicholas sighed. As with Piers the other night, he had been challenged and his response had surprised even him. He laughed to himself as he created a variant of an old joke: You can take the boy away from the Schuylers, but can you take the Schuylers away from the boy!

Forget that, he told himself, concentrate on why you are going to London. He fetched a letter from the small attaché case he was carrying and read it. It was from his publisher who knew him as Merlin, the author of the dragon books.

He had begun to write them to pass the time in his long lonely nights in Jesse Pye's cottage shortly after he had arrived at West Bretton. He had always wanted to write but the hectic life he had lived in London had left him little time to pursue his childhood's ambitions. He had illustrated them with pen-and-wash sketches whose simplicity had delighted the children who read them.

He had sent them off to a publisher who had seen their potential and so his career had begun. He had told no one in West Bretton of his success. It was for him to know, as only he knew who he really was. He wanted to remain simple Nick Allen and did not care for the idea of the great world dabbling its dirty fingers in his life. He was sadly sure that, sooner or later, his true identity would be revealed, but until then he wished to remain anonymous. He was grateful for the money he received—it was useful—but the idea of fame was hateful to him.

But this letter was not about dragons.

Six months ago he had sent to his publishers the manuscript of a comically satiric novel about London society, based partly on his knowledge of it through his membership of the Schuyler family, and partly on his own experiences. It told the tale of an innocent young man, a slightly brighter Bertie Wooster, a novice MP, who was caught up in the corrupt world of high society and politics.

His publisher, who knew him only as a writer of children's books, had been dismissive when, over a year ago, Nicholas had written to him saying that there would be no more dragon stories for the time being, since he had begun to write a satiric novel with the title of *Put money in thy purse*, a quotation from Shakespeare's *Othello* referring to corruption.

'After all,' he had said to his partner, 'he may be a wizard at writing kids' stuff, the new Beatrix Potter, but what can a young fellow who lives in an obscure backwater like North Devon know about the corridors of power!'

Nevertheless Nicholas, despite a discouraging letter, had persevered, and his publisher, who had been so sceptical at first, became ecstatic when, after Nicholas had sent the finished manuscript in, his reader had recommended him to read it for himself—'It's dynamite, and comic with it,' he had said. Both the publisher and his partner had agreed with him.

'Now how the devil does he know *that*!' being their constant cry. Nicholas had asked that, if the novel were accepted, his pseudonym should be changed to Arthur Merlin.

Accepted! The publisher, Stanton Harcourt of Harcourt and Maine, had been so delighted by it that the book was being rushed into publication, was already being trailed in the newspapers and on hoardings in the Underground, as the coming best-seller of the year, the successor to Michael Arlen's *Green Hat*.

Today he was going to be lunched at l'Escargot in Soho—he had refused the Ritz, the Dorchester, the Savoy and the Ivy in case there was someone present who might recognise him. He was to be given a copy of his book, and a fat cheque—an advance on publication—for the orders were coming in thick and fast as word had got out that reading it was a must.

The firm had asked him to allow himself to be photographed, to agree to be interviewed by the Press and the radio, but he had refused all their offers, and had insisted that a clause guaranteeing him no personal publicity should be written into his contract. His publisher had been annoyed until he had decided to tout his new find as 'the man of mystery'—something which raised the publicity temperature even higher.

Those who had read it in advance of publication were taking bets as to who the author might be. 'The reviews,' Harcourt said, 'looked like being ecstatic, too.'

'I can't believe it,' Nicholas told Harcourt after they had been shown to their table at l'Escargot. 'It's like a dream.'

'So long as it's not a nightmare,' chuckled Harcourt, shovelling food into his mouth, 'and it's far from being that.'

He was always surprised when he met his man. Nicholas had told him that his name was Arthur Merlin and that he lived not far from Exeter. His manuscripts were sent from an accommodation address there, and the dragon books had been published under his surname.

Nicholas's comparative youth and the puzzle of his knowledge of the great world piqued a man who thought that he knew most of those who lived in it. There was, though, something vaguely familiar in the craggy face and powerful body of the man before him, but it was a familiarity which he could not pin down.

Nicholas could almost feel Harcourt's curiosity about him, it was so strong, as they swallowed oysters—obviously no novelty to Merlin—drank consommé, wolfed down *sole en paupiettes*, *coq au vin* and *crème caramel*. Nicholas refused wine and drank sparkling water. His only reservation about the whole exciting business of being a coming success lay in trying to preserve his hard-won anonymity.

Fortunately the notion of the publicity to be gained by a mystery man who had already excited the national press was going, Harourt said delightedly, to raise sales enormously.

'And the next?' he asked Nicholas. 'What are you going to write next?'

'Another dragon book,' Nicholas announced in a voice which brooked no denial.

Harcourt pulled a face.

'I'll see how this one does first, before writing another,' Nicholas said, astonished to discover that he was turning into a true hard-headed Schuyler. 'Besides, I've a new idea for the dragons,' and he told Harcourt of Jamie's suggestion of a dragon Schneider Trophy race.

'Oh, splendid!' exclaimed Harcourt. 'But you must promise me you'll think about writing another comic satire.'

'Perhaps,' was all he got, and had to be satisfied with that. Privately he thought that if *Put money in thy purse* were the success it promised to be, young Mr Arthur

Merlin—and what an unlikely name that was—might change his mind.

They parted in the sunlight of a late June afternoon with mutual assertions of friendship and the promise of future profitable deals, Harcourt to return to his office, Nicholas to walk to Hatchards in Piccadilly to buy books before returning to his room in a small private hotel in Gower Street.

Hatchards, stuffed with books, was always a delight to visit, and was particularly so today with his large cheque in his wallet and the sight when he reached there, of a small display of his dragon books in the children's department.

There was also a prominent poster advertising *Put money in thy purse* as a masterly satire on our present condition, to be published on Friday by Harcourt and Maine.

All in all, Nicholas was feeling well satisfied with himself and life when he walked out of Hatchards with a carrier bag full of books, among them a present for Verena and another for Jamie. He was so lost in the delightful prospect of handing them over that a hard hand clamped on his shoulder surprised him so much that he jumped away, threw it off and turned to face his accoster—his cousin, Gis Havilland, who had followed him out of Hatchards.

'So it is you,' Gis said evenly. 'I thought that I saw you inside, but decided that I must be dreaming.'

Gis was, Nicholas thought, as splendidly glorious as ever in a beautifully cut dark suit quite unlike his own shabby flannels and well-worn tweed jacket. For the first time he was able to admire his cousin without envy or rancour. He was what Piers Marlowe aspired to be—but wasn't.

For his part Gis was surprised by Nicholas. He ignored his shabby clothing, that didn't matter. What did matter was the new maturity of his face and posture. He looked like a contented man at ease with himself, quite unlike the sulky boy who had stormed out of Padworth.

'I'm not going to badger you, Claus, with questions about where you are living now,' Gis began without preamble. 'It could, I suppose, be London.'

'So it could,' Nicholas said in a voice which John Webster had first heard on the previous afternoon. But he smiled as he said it. 'And my name is Nicholas, or Nick. There has been no Claus Schuyler for three years.'

'And you're happy, Nicholas? I was right to sense that recently, I think.'

'Yes.'

'And successful?'

'In my own terms, yes.'

'I can see that. I would guess that you are your own master now—in charge of yourself—not troubled by the demands of others.'

'Very much so.'

There was a terseness about this new Nicholas very different from the defensive volubility of the old one. His likeness to his father was astonishing, both physically and in the dismissive manner which Gerard adopted when he wanted to give nothing away.

'We can't talk here,' Gis said, looking around the busy street. 'How about having tea with me at Fortnum's? It's only a step away, and I could do with a few moments rest. I've been at the Air Ministry all morning, talking shop.'

Nicholas shook his head. 'No tea for me. I've just had a rather large lunch.'

'Just one cup, then. For old times' sake.'

He knew that, for once, he had said the wrong thing, when Nicholas replied coldly, 'I prefer never to think about old times.'

'New times, then?'

For some reason this amused Nicholas. For a moment he and Gis stood silent, face to face.

'Very well. One cup—and then I must be off. I can't imagine what we shall have to talk about.'

'Oh, I can,' returned Gis gaily, 'but we'll leave all that until we're comfortable in Fortnum's.'

As always Gis was true to his word. It was not until they had sailed aloft in Fortnum's lift and were seated at a table in the corner of the restaurant away from others, and he had ordered, that he spoke again.

'Are you strong enough to be kind?' he began as he poured Lapsang Souchong into Nicholas's cup before passing him the dish of lemon slices which went with it.

'Kind?' Nicholas left his cup untouched. 'To whom am I to be kind?'

'To your mother, for one. You know, Nicholas, we are very unlike, but we both did the same thing—rejected our family and disappeared. You must know that I ran away from mine to go to war—which was a worse thing than you have done by running away in peacetime.'

'Yes, I do know that, Gis.'

'It was only afterwards,' Gis said earnestly, 'that I understood how much I had hurt my parents, particularly my mother. Your mother grieves for you, Nicholas. She spoke to me of you recently—wanted me to find you, if I could. Your father employed a detective to try to trace you over two years ago when he realised that you were not coming back, but the man drew a blank. I don't want you to give away where you live or what you are doing, but I would like to think that you might at least let your mother—and your father—know that you are alive and well.'

'Well, that's simple enough,' Nicholas said grimly. 'You have seen me and you may tell them what they wish to hear.'

'No more than that?'

Nicholas drank down his tea and stood up. 'I'm happy,

Gis, for the first time in my life, and have been so ever since I drove away from Padworth and privilege. I have set down roots and live among those who are willing to judge me for what I am, not for what they hope I might be and am not. Why should I jeopardise my happiness?

'I have been baptised anew and do not wish to return to the world in which you—and the Schuylers—are content to live. I don't want either wealth or position. I haven't touched a penny of Schuyler money for three years. I have lived on my own earnings and I feel all the happier for it. Now, if you will forgive me, I must leave. I should like to visit the theatre this evening—it's one of the few things I miss about my new life.'

'Still afraid?' asked Gis quietly.

Nicholas laughed, and it was a genuine laugh. 'No, you can't believe that, Gis. If I were afraid I'd return to the fleshpots to do nothing ungracefully, not continue to earn my own living by hard work and diligence.'

Gis nodded. 'I know the feeling. But, one day, and it will not be long, I hope, you will have the courage to return, knowing that you are so much your own man that nothing can touch or change what you have made of yourself.'

Nicholas offered him what he had offered Stanton Harcourt. 'Perhaps. But not now, not yet, perhaps never. Give my love to Thea and the children, Gis, and to Ralph when you see him.'

He left, striding down the room, more than a few heads turning to follow him. Not because he was handsome, as Gis was, but because he had assumed, without his knowing it, the appearance of a man of power so that people wondered who he might be.

Gis looked thoughtfully at the leaves at the bottom of his tea cup, swirled them round, and said to the pattern which they had made, 'It won't be long, I think, before Nicholas Allen Schuyler consents to be part of his family.'

Chapter Eight

'Vee?'

'Yes, Jamie?'

'Why didn't we visit the Dragon man this Wednesday?'

Vee patiently explained for the second time that the Dragon man had gone to London earlier in the week, 'but he said that he would be back by Saturday.'

'That's today, Vee. Why can't we visit him today?'

Jamie had had his breakfast and was sitting at the nursery table doing a child's wooden jigsaw under Priddie's benevolent eye.

Verena had come in to see how he was. He had suffered another asthmatic attack the previous day, and he was looking pale and harried.

Priddie put down the *Daily Mail* which she had been reading, and said briskly, 'You are not to trouble your sister, Jamie. She has more to do than run round looking after little boys, and it would tire you too much to visit Mr Allen today.'

'Oh, I don't mind running round after Jamie,' Verena said, sitting beside him, 'and despite what everyone says I have always found that a walk in the fresh air, if taken slowly, does him more good than harm. Later this morning we could visit Jesse Pye's cottage and see if the Dragon man's back.'

'Jamie's mama wouldn't like that,' returned Priddie repressively.

'Perhaps not, but as she's not here "what the eye doesn't see, the heart doesn't grieve over"—or so you used to tell me.'

This last had been a favourite saying of Priddie's in the days when she had been younger and more adventurous. She looked disapproving but said nothing more. She disliked Chrissie and her lack of interest in Jamie, and was pleased when Chrissie had accepted an invitation to visit an old friend in Exeter for a few days, and had been only too happy to leave Jamie behind.

Her absence had fortunately coincided with that of Piers, another of Jamie's tormentors, who was away in Cornwall staying with a colleague from his Army days.

'Do say yes, Vee,' Jamie wheedled as he fitted the last piece of jigsaw into its place so that he now had a finished and gaudy picture of Goldilocks and the three bears.

'Very well, but you are not to tease Nicholas.'

'I won't, but he did say that he would teach me to swim. He promised.'

Priddie let out a small squeal. 'Indeed, you're not to go near the water, young man. It would be your death—and besides, your mama would disapprove.'

'She disapproves of everything,' muttered Jamie darkly.

Vee kissed him on the top of his curly head. 'Be a good boy, don't ask for the impossible and Priddie will agree to have you ready by a quarter to eleven, won't you, Priddie?'

'Only if he minds what you say, Miss Verena.'

'Oh, I shall, shan't I, Vee.'

Priddie still looked unhappy about all this proposed activity for a child she regarded as an invalid, but returned to reading her *Daily Mail*, exclaiming as she did so, 'Goodness me, there's been another big robbery round here, at Westermere Hall. It's a bad one, they say. One of the servants caught them at it, and is in hospital, unconscious, for his pains. They're not sure whether he'll live.'

She put the paper down, her face troubled. 'I can hardly sleep in my bed for worrying whether we shall be the next on their list.'

'Well, I would hardly think so,' Verena said encouragingly. 'We've some nice silver and a few reasonable paintings, but nothing like the value of those at Westermere Hall and the Axminsters' place.'

'All the same,' said Priddie. 'I hope that the butler makes sure that we're locked up at night and all the windows are properly closed. I shouldn't like to wake up dead.'

'Could you do that?' asked curious Jamie, to be shushed by Verena who didn't want Priddie to cancel his visit to Nicholas because he had been unintentionally impudent.

'Be quiet and read one of your books until Priddie gets you ready for your walk.'

After that he behaved himself so that Priddie duly had him ready at the appointed hour, dressed, as Nicholas was later to say, as though he were off with Scott to the Pole rather than taking a short walk on a balmy afternoon in late June.

Nicholas, who had been drafting out a synopsis for his new dragon book, saw them coming through his living-room window, and his heart leaped at the sight. He had arrived back in West Bretton late the previous evening, and was not due to start work again until the Monday morning.

He opened the door before they reached it, and was waiting for them.

'Come in, come in,' he called cheerfully. He was shocked at the sight of Jamie's pallor, angry at the sight of his suffocating clothing. 'I've already collected Hercules from John Webster—he's been looking after him for me.'

This was a totally unnecessary piece of information for Hercules, who had been sitting by his feet, ran towards Jamie ecstatically, every hair on his body erect, to greet his late master.

Jamie was equally ecstatic. 'He hasn't forgotten me, then.'

'No, indeed, how could he? For goodness' sake, young man, take off that heavy coat.'

'I'm wearing it because I've been ill again,' announced Jamie importantly.

'And no wonder, muffled up like that.' Nicholas went to the cupboard by the hearth, flung open its green painted doors and produced three of Woolworth's best glasses, and a bottle of Tizer, an evil-looking orange drink beloved of small boys.

'A jorum each,' he said in a tone which brooked no denial. 'Puts hair on your chest,' he told Jamie, who replied dubiously,

'Do you think Vee wants hair on her chest?'

'Probably not,' said Nicholas, grinning, 'but it only has that effect on small boys and men.' He raised his glass, '*Was hael!*, young fellow.'

'What does that mean, sir?'

'It's a Viking toast—and the answer is *Drink hael*, which means drink up. Let's hear it,' and Verena and Jamie dutifully raised their glasses before drinking, repeating, *Drink hael*.

'Splendid, that really starts the day off properly. Now, Jamie, if you go over to the sideboard facing the window you'll find a couple of parcels there. Bring them here and then read to me what's written on their labels.'

'Presents,' shouted Jamie, who, like all children, had few

inhibitions when faced with such a pleasant surprise. He read the labels slowly. 'One says Verena, and the other says Jamie.'

'Quite correct. Hand Verena hers, and then you may open yours.'

'A dragon book?' queried Jamie, tearing at the wrapping paper.

'Sorry, no. Merlin has only written two, but they told me in London that he is going to write another. This one will do for now, I think.'

It proved to be A.A. Milne's Christopher Robin story, *The House at Pooh corner*. 'Oh, my favourite after the dragon books, thank you, sir. May I shake your hand?'

Sir Charles had recently informed Jamie that men did not kiss people when thanking them. 'A handshake is quite sufficient.'

Consequently Nicholas and Jamie shook hands gravely. Jamie spoiled the effect a bit by snatching his hand away and shouting at Verena, 'Now you.'

Verena, saying, 'Oh, Nicholas, you shouldn't,' whilst slowly opening her parcel, found that she had been gifted with P.G. Wodehouse's *Summer Lightning*.

Nicholas watched pleasure mantle her face—and wished that he could kiss her.

'Shake hands, Vee,' said Jamie, dancing up and down with delight.

Verena smiled at them both and said naughtily, 'Oh, no, it's only men and boys who shake hands. Ladies are allowed to do this,' and she stretched up on tiptoe, saying, 'Thank you, Nicholas,' and kissed him on the cheek.

Oh, the darling! The impudent darling! For with Jamie there, grinning at them, he could not respond to her as he would like to do.

'You are not to tease me, Vee,' he said, putting on a mournful face.

'Who, me? Tease you? Oh, no, I was simply thanking you.'

'I can see myself giving you a whole library of books if I get such a simple thank you for each one of them!'

'Kissing,' said Jamie scornfully. 'Girls' stuff, Grandfather said.'

'Not always,' was Nicholas's answer with a knowing wink at Verena.

Later, when they went for a walk, she said to him, 'Joking apart, Nicholas, you shouldn't spend your hard-earned money on Jamie and me.'

It was one of the things which people said to him which made him feel a cur—even though he never now used his Schuyler wealth, and so was comparatively poor—but the wealth was still there, like an albatross around his neck.

'I was in Hatchards,' he said slowly, 'and it gave me great pleasure to buy them in order to give you and Jamie pleasure.'

Jamie, hearing his name, shouted, 'You promised to teach me to swim, sir. It's a warm day. Will you teach me this afternoon?'

'If your mother agrees, yes.'

'Oh, she's not here. Can't Vee say yes?'

Apparently secure in the knowledge of Chrissie's absence, Verena gave her consent. Later that day she sat on the side of the pool and watched a patient Nicholas standing in the water and holding an excited Jamie by the back of his bathing suit.

Nicholas had already shown him on the bank how to do a stroke which he called the doggie paddle— 'You're going to swim just like Hercules,' Nicholas had told him. He was now being encouraged to blow into the water, and lie in it as low and flat as possible while he kicked his legs and imitated Hercules' expert front-leg movements with his arms.

He was too excited to be frightened, and, a little to both Nicholas and Verena's surprise, he suddenly began to swim a few strokes of his own accord when Nicholas let go of him for a moment.

Only for a moment. Nicholas was careful not to allow him to be in any danger while he took his first few joyous strokes. After he had swum on his own a little more, with Nicholas standing guard over him, they moved to the shallows and Jamie was encouraged to play there, Nicholas splashing water over him, and Jamie splashing him back.

They were both making such a noise enjoying themselves, and Verena was so rapt in watching them that none of them saw their Nemesis approaching.

Chrissie, back from her Exeter jaunt, and most inappropriately dressed in a ninon frock, silk stockings and white, high-heeled shoes, was making her unsteady way towards them through the undergrowth, her face like thunder.

Her angry voice broke in on their happy play.

'What in the world do you think that you're doing, Verena, allowing *him* to take Jamie into the water! You know that I don't approve of him having anything to do with Nicholas Allen. I suppose you were taking advantage of my absence. Well, it's a good thing I came back early and caught you at your tricks. Come out of the water immediately, Jamie, before you have another of your attacks.'

Jamie, red in the face, shouted back at her, 'Shan't. I like being in the water. Nicholas has taught me to swim. If you weren't so unkind I'd show you.'

Nicholas stood up straight and tall. In his black one-piece bathing costume he looked a tower of muscular strength. 'Now, Jamie,' he said coolly, ignoring Chrissie's rude and insulting tone. 'That's no way to speak to your mama. Do as she says.'

Before Jamie, a mutinous lower lip stuck out, could either answer him or climb out of the water, he addressed Chrissie. 'It won't hurt him, you know, Chrissie. On the contrary, it will help him to breathe properly. One of my nephews was asthmatic and learning to swim did him no end of good.'

'He's not one of your nephews—whoever and whatever they might be—he's the heir to Marlowe Court, and he shouldn't be disobeying me and larking about in the water with Cousin John's office boy. And don't call me Chrissie—Mrs Marlowe or madam will do.'

Verena, who had advanced on Jamie with a bath towel in her hand in order to wrap him in it, said, 'How can you be so unkind, Chrissie? I suppose I should have asked your permission, but no harm has come of allowing him to go into the water with Nicholas. He has learned how to swim which can only be a good thing.'

'Do you think that teaching him to disobey his mother is a good thing? I shall certainly tell Sir Charles of this. He won't be pleased, you know. One thing is certain. Jamie will not be allowed to have anything to do with Mr Allen again.'

Jamie's face crumpled. 'No, you're not to say that.'

'Be quiet, you naughty boy. Do hurry up, Verena. I want him dressed and ready to go home as soon as possible. You're not to come with us. I need to speak to Jamie alone. *You* may do as you please, but I'm not having you put Jamie at risk again.'

There was nothing either of them could do to help Jamie. Intervention would only make matters worse. Dressed again, white-faced and sullen, his head hanging, he allowed his mother to take his hand, drag him up the slope and walk him home. He made no effort to speak, but the last thing that Nicholas and Verena heard was a sudden bout of anguished coughing.

At the sound Verena started off after them, to be stopped by Nicholas—who had just waded out of the pool—putting his hand on her arm to detain her, saying, 'No, you can do him no good by trying to help him. She will only use what you say to hurt him.'

'He's going to have another attack, I know he is,' said Verena frantically. 'And she'll say it's our fault when it's really hers.'

'Exactly. And we're helpless. She's his mother and that's the end of it.'

'It shouldn't be.'

'But it is. You can't take the cares of the world on your shoulders. If you alienate her completely, you won't be able to help him at all.'

Verena unwillingly conceded that that made good sense,

'And now I must get dressed,' he told her, 'and then we'll go to the cottage and have a cup of tea—that eternal remedy for modern mankind's troubles.'

Near to tears, Verena offered him a watery smile. 'I suppose that we were unwise, but he did so want to learn to swim and she will never allow it, I know.'

'True,' and Nicholas, carrying his towel and clothing disappeared into the trees.

He had offered her no easy comfort, and far from depressing Verena, oddly, it had the opposite effect. He was always true to himself, and now he was being true to her and Jamie by not lying to her about how difficult Chrissie might make life for both Jamie and herself. How could Chrissie despise him so?

'You mustn't fret,' he told her gently, as, back in the cottage, they drank tea, a slumbering Hercules at their feet.

'And you must be ready for Sir Charles. Chrissie is sure to go to him as soon as she has finished punishing Jamie.'

'Yes. He will want me to stop seeing you, I know he will.'

'True. I'm a bad influence on you. Or so Chrissie will say.'

He was being honest with her, so she was honest with him. 'And Piers. For some reason he has his knife into you as well.'

'I know.'

'I can't imagine why.'

Nicholas could, but did not tell her. Chrissie was jealous of Verena because she had set her cap at him and he had preferred Verena to her. Piers hated him because he thought, correctly, that Verena, having refused his proposal, had transferred her affections to himself. Given Piers's assumption of his coming from a lower class, this was an insult of the first magnitude.

'I don't want to go home,' Verena said suddenly. 'I'm like Jamie. I'm so much happier here with you and Hercules.'

'I would like to keep you here,' he told her gravely. 'But I can't. I wouldn't do anything to hurt you, or destroy your reputation—particularly with Chrissie ready to do just that if she gets half a chance.'

'Oh, Nicholas, don't worry about my reputation. I don't.'

He slipped to the floor to sit beside her chair, taking her hand in his. 'But you should, my darling. If I were the rake that Piers and Chrissie think I am, I should be making violent love to you now. But I mustn't—for both our sakes. It would be the act of a cad for me to seduce you, however much I love you, so we must go carefully.'

He kissed the hand he held and said ruefully, 'Even to

make love to you as mildly as this sets me on fire. Think what real lovemaking would do!'

She looked down at him and the passion she felt for him was written on her face so plainly that Nicholas shuddered beneath it. How strange it was that in his wild days he had known and made love to women whose allure and beauty was famous, including actresses and society women whose names were household words, and he had never been affected so strongly as simply being with Verena affected him now.

'Some day soon,' he told her, trying to control his errant senses, 'I shall be able to declare my feelings for you openly, honourably and without reservation. Until then we may only meet if we can wait for that day to come without betraying ourselves. I must ask you to be patient until then—and to trust me for asking you to wait.'

Verena shivered. She thought she knew what he was telling her. He loved her and wished to marry her. If she wondered why it was necessary for him to wait to declare himself then she must, if she truly loved him, not question him as to why the delay was necessary.

She thought that it might be because of the social and financial disparity between them; he being a poor young man of relatively low station and she being a rich young woman from an old gentry family, but delicacy prevented her from assuring him that these differences—so important to Sir Charles and the rest—were of no great matter to her, and that therefore he should ignore them.

Not only that, he had said that he loved her, but he had not yet said that he wished to marry her. It was simply an assumption she was making, and it was an assumption that might not be correct.

Young women of her station were not taught to be so forward as virtually to propose to a man, even if they loved him. What she could do was raise Nicholas's hand and kiss it back, feeling him shudder as she did so.

'To be with you, Nicholas, I would promise anything.'

'Anything? Even virtual chastity—however painful?'

She gave him the benefit of her great grave eyes. 'I had not known that chastity could be painful until I met you.'

'Oh, and that is why I love you,' he exclaimed impulsively. He had hated having to ask her to wait, but there were so many serious questions to be answered before he asked her to marry him.

Was it the right thing for him to do so without having told her, Sir Charles and the rest exactly who he was? He knew that were he to reveal his membership of an immensely rich Anglo-American family which was one of the most influential social, political and financial powers in English society, all objections to her marrying him would disappear.

Their troubles would be over immediately. Sir Charles would give his instant approval.

Given, however, that he had cut himself adrift from his past and his family in order to make his own way in the world without them, he found it repugnant to call upon his membership of that family on the first occasion that he found himself in difficulties. He most desperately wanted to be accepted for himself, not because he had turned out to be Nicholas Schuyler.

Verena had known nothing of him, and yet she had accepted him—and that was the thing which mattered most. Somehow he must try to resolve the difficulties which his desire to marry her was creating without taking the easy way out, something he had always done until he had driven away from Padworth.

'My darling,' he said gravely. 'Promise me that you will always love me, whatever you might find out about me.'

At the back of his mind was the fear that she might not want a man who had deceived everyone so profoundly; particularly a man with a notorious past. And now there was also the matter of the dragon books, and the novel which would be arriving in the bookshops on Monday morning.

Puzzled, Verena said as lightly as she could, 'That sounds ominous, Nicholas. Did you cheat at school or something?'

He threw his head back and laughed. Oh, he had asked her to trust him and he had not had the common sense to trust her.

'No, not that, never that. Now if you had said draughts and ludo that would be a different matter.'

'Well, I'm relieved to hear it,' Verena retorted. 'I should hate to see your face on a Police Wanted poster!'

Nicholas's laughter had cleared the air for them. For a brief moment both passion and doubt had disappeared. They were friends again, love had retreated, but it was still present, its wings folded above them.

Recalled to the mundane world and its master, time, Verena looked at her watch. 'Goodness, how late it's grown. I must be off to face the music. I'm sure that after Chrissie has had her say Sir Charles is waiting anxiously to warn me not to have anything to do with you. He has no idea what a gallant knight you are. Sir Galahad, the pure in heart, no less.'

Nicholas pulled a face. How little that description would have fitted him three years ago!

'I'm glad someone thinks so. On the other hand I have to confess that I had a small passion for Mordred once. I thought that he had a worse press than he deserved. After all King Arthur was a deceived fool, Guinevere no better than she should be, Sir Lancelot and half the Round Table were careless seducers, and Sir Perceval and Galahad were prigs. Mordred, a man who had been done out of his inheritance, was only an honest traitor, which seemed to me to make him no worse than the rest of them!'

'Oh, shame,' said Verena reprovingly. 'I always loved the story of King Arthur and now you have ruined it for me! But, come to think of it, as usual, you do have a point.' She thought, also, how clever he was, after a fashion which Sir Charles and the others would never understand.

He kissed her lightly on the cheek for that, and watched her walk away towards Marlowe Court where, undoubtedly, trouble was waiting for her, before making his way to the cottage with the glow of the afternoon's happiness still with him.

'Sir Charles would like to see you, Miss Verena, as soon as you have had time to change. He will be in his study.'

So the butler had greeted her on her return. There was no sign of Chrissie or Jamie, nor did she go looking for either of them.

Sir Charles was waiting for her, a copy of *Wisden* open on the table before him. His face was sad as he began to speak. 'I suppose that you know why I have asked to see you, Granddaughter. Your stepmother has told me that you have ignored her expressly stated wish that James should not be allowed to swim. Instead you have encouraged that young man of John Webster's to take him to Parson's Pool and immerse him in cold water. The result of that, she tells me, was an asthma attack of such severity that our doctor has telephoned to a specialist from the hospital at Exeter who, on hearing of his distressed state, has arranged to come and see him this evening.'

'Jamie did not have an asthma attack because Nicholas taught him to swim,' Verena said as calmly as she could.

It would not do to behave like a virago. 'On the contrary he was breathing as easily as I have ever seen him until his mother arrived to distress him, by forbidding him either to swim or to have anything to do with Mr Allen again.'

'Nevertheless she is his mother, and I am asking you to respect her wishes in future. I said that I would raise the matter with you in an attempt to avoid trouble between you.'

He stopped. Verena said coldly, 'Is that all, sir? May I go now if I promise to do exactly as my stepmother wishes in future?'

Sir Charles, looking old, sighed wearily. 'I am afraid not, my dear. There is another matter. It won't do, you know, this association of yours with young Allen. He is not of your class. He could not give you the life to which you have been accustomed since birth.

'Marrying him would bring you nothing but trouble. Marriage is no bed of roses at the best of times, but these differences would grow more serious when difficulties arose. I need not say that any other kind of connection with him would be even more disastrous. It would be doing you both a kindness if you would cease your acquaintanceship with him at once. You have been encouraging him to have hopes which can never be fulfilled.

'Believe me, I am older and wiser than you are, and speak of what I know. Disparity of station in marriage can only result in disaster. Let me be blunt. To be seduced by such a man would be an even greater disaster.'

Verena's head spun. What do I say to him? That I love Nicholas, that he offers me something which no other man has ever done? When I compare him with Roger Gough and my cousin Piers—there is no comparison! There is a meeting of minds between us, as well, if I am honest, as a meeting of bodies.

Aloud she said simply, 'I can't give him up, Grandfather. I love him. I can talk to him as I have never before been able to talk to any other man.

'He is good and kind, and he has never yet said or done a wrong thing to me. Instead he has insisted that we go carefully with one another because he does not want us to let ourselves down in the world's eyes. John says that he is hard-working and the people in West Bretton like him—which is more than I can say of Cousin Piers on either count.

'May I go now, please?'

Sir Charles sighed. 'Your stepmother says...'

Verena committed the unforgivable, she interrupted him. 'Oh, please, sir, spare me from having to listen to Chrissie's misrepresentations. I will do as you wish over Jamie because she is his mother. But where Nicholas is concerned that is my life, and I will make my decisions, not allow them to be made by a woman I have reason to dislike and distrust.'

She was hamstrung, she knew, because she could not tell him the truth about Chrissie: that she had repeatedly been unfaithful to her father before he died, and was now carrying on a clandestine affair with Piers behind Sir Charles's back.

'Now you are being wilful,' said Sir Charles unhappily. 'You know that I had hoped that you would marry your cousin. I cannot forbid you to see this man—but I would like to.'

Verena bowed her head. 'So long as I live here I have tried to obey your wishes—but I cannot give way over Nicholas, I cannot.'

'Very well, you must go your own way. But remember what I have said to you. I shall try not to reproach you when things go wrong—as they will. You may leave me.'

Verena made her way to her room, deeply unhappy, and regretting that she could not obey her grandfather. She was halfway up the stairs when there was the usual commotion in the entrance hall which told that Piers had returned from his Cornish visit—another cross for her to bear.

Only the thought of seeing Nicholas again soon had the power to comfort her.

Chapter Nine

Nicholas and Verena did not meet again until the following Wednesday afternoon. He had been busy at the *Clarion*'s office, for John Webster was giving him more and more work and responsibility to do with the paper. He wondered a little wryly if his journeys to Exeter and Barnstaple in search of stories were wholly necessary, and not just excuses to keep him away from Verena.

John also asked him if he would, as a favour, work on Wednesday morning, and he rather thought that that might be yet another ploy to keep him away from Miss Marlowe of Marlowe Court.

He was soon to find that he had misjudged John there. Mid-morning saw them drinking tea in the little office. John had been distrait all morning. He was beginning to look his age these days, and his first words to Nicholas confirmed that he was also feeling it.

'I've something to tell you, Nick, which I have been putting off. I'm going to sell the *Clarion*. It was a boon to run it after my son was killed, it kept my mind off things, but lately it has begun to seem more like a burden. Only your hard work has kept me carrying on. But no longer, I have decided to put it up for sale and retire. I shouldn't think it will affect your position. I shall give you the best reference possible to the new owner when the sale goes through. He's not likely to find a better lieutenant.'

Nicholas, his brain whirling, put his cup down. 'I can't say that I am other than sorry to hear your news. I have enjoyed working with you and learning the business. Do you have a buyer in mind?'

'No. I've been trying to draft out a notice. I shall have to put it in the hands of estate agents locally. I might even advertise in London. Someone is bound to want it.'

Someone did.

For the rest of the morning Nicholas did sums in his head and came to a decision which he thought might help him in his wish to marry Verena.

John was tidying up his desk preparatory to leaving when Nicholas approached him warily.

'I have a proposition for you, John, which I would like you to consider seriously.'

He hesitated for a moment and what he said next was a lie in a good cause. 'When I went to London last week it was to clear up legal matters connected with a legacy which an old aunt left me.'

Well, at least the aunt bit was true!

'Using that and her small portfolio of stocks and shares as collateral, I could probably raise a bank loan and make you an offer which I hope you could not refuse. So if you would tell me what you are asking for the business I could decide whether I might be able to meet your price.'

This last was also a thumping lie. His non-Schuyler legacy was large enough, he thought, to buy the *Clarion* many times over.

John stared at him before, somewhat reluctantly, he named his price. It was plain that he found it difficult to believe that Nicholas could be making him a serious offer.

Nicholas said slowly, 'This is the true market price you are quoting, John? I would not like to think that you were offering it to me for less out of kindness.'

'I would not deceive you over that, Nick, for it would not be fair to either of us.'

'That seems right and proper. Allow me to consider it for a moment.'

Nicholas thought it judicious to take some little time to do so, looking away from John, his face serious and somewhat troubled, as though he were doing mental arithmetic.

It was only afterwards that he wryly conceded that there was more of the old Captain's creative trickery in him than he liked to acknowledge. He was the true great-grandson of the founder of the house of Schuyler.

The worst thing was that it seemed to come to him so naturally and without forethought! Still, was not his whole existence at West Bretton a form of deceit known to the more inventive criminals of the USA as a sting—an elaborate pretence set up to deceive the world!

He said at last, 'I think I might just be able to manage that. I'll ring my aunt's bank and see if they will oblige me.'

The bank was not his aunt's: it was his own—Coutts—which would certainly be able to arrange immediately for a banker's draft to be made out to Nicholas Allen, and cause it to be deposited in the West Bretton branch of the Westminster Bank where he had an account.

The only drawback was that he had undoubtedly sparked off John Webster's curiosity by making such an offer at all. What John—and the rest of West Bretton—must never know was that he was able to buy the *Clarion* outright and that there was no loan involved.

John said dubiously, 'You are sure about this, Nick? I

would not like to see you throw your little legacy away. The new owner would be mad not to keep you on.'

Nicholas winced internally at the prospect of having to deceive a good man like John again, and said aloud, 'I should like to be my own master, if possible, and so am prepared to take that risk. I'll try to hurry things up so that if the bank decides that it cannot help me you can put the *Clarion* on the market as soon as possible. In the meantime, I would prefer you to say nothing until the matter is settled one way or another.'

More and more chicanery! He was also more like his father than he had known in his ability to manipulate others. Reason told him that he had watched and listened all his life to what went on at Padworth—hence his ability to write a convincing novel about the world of power.

He must visit London again before he could tell John that he would be able to raise the money and arrange the transfer from Coutts. One thing was certain, if he asked for secrecy over the matter then West Bretton would never know how he had really bought the *Clarion*.

After that it was difficult for them both to settle down to work and they left off early by mutual agreement. Nicholas looking forward to his afternoon with Verena, John worrying a little about Nicholas's offer.

To Verena her coming afternoon with Nicholas was like a lifeline thrown to a drowning sailor. She was finding life not only slow and boring, but unpleasant now that she was forbidden to have much to do with Jamie both before and after the specialist from Exeter had visited Marlowe Court on Sunday.

She was not allowed to be present when the specialist examined him, but she knew that something had gone very wrong when he did, because Chrissie had come downstairs in a fine old taking soon after the specialist had gone. She was particularly rude to Verena, so much so, that Verena sought out Priddie after dinner and asked what had happened to upset her so.

'It was that man,' Priddie said. 'Mrs Marlowe told him that Master Jamie had had two violent attacks of asthma after he had been with Mr Allen and that the second had been the worst of the two because Mr Allen had taken him swimming.'

'I knew she would,' said Verena mournfully, 'but I truly don't think that they had anything to do with it. They only began after his mother had forbidden him to swim or to have much to do with Mr Allen.'

Priddie coughed behind her hand. 'And so Master Jamie up and told him. His mother shouted at him to keep quiet, that he was being a naughty boy again—encouraged, she said, by his stepsister—and Master Jamie immediately began to wheeze and pant something cruel. The doctor examined him and said that it was most unlikely that swimming could have caused the attack for he now recommended his asthma patients to swim because they had to breathe properly when they were in the water, and that helped them.

'Mrs Marlowe began to argue with him, but he was quite short with her. He said that she must be careful what she said to him because the attacks could be brought on by nervous excitement, and that if Mr Allen wished to calm him and take him swimming he ought to be encouraged. Master Jamie then told him that you had been forbidden to have much to do with him, but he said that that might be a mistake, too.

'Oh, I could see that she was right cross, but while he was there she agreed with him and pretended that she would do as he said. But after he had gone she shouted at

Jamie again, and told him that she would do as she saw fit—the doctor had got it all wrong. The poor little lad went blue in the face, and she told him to stop it at once, he was putting it on to provoke her.

'And that's the way it was, Miss Verena. The doctor only made things worse, not better.'

What had Nicholas said? That she was not to take on the cares of the world, but it was going to be difficult to ignore Chrissie's unkindness to Jamie—particularly after her father had asked her to look after him.

Common sense told her that she would probably hurt him more by trying to intervene, but to stand aside seemed such a cowardly thing to do. The trouble was that both Sir Charles and Piers agreed with Chrissie that Jamie's asthma was being caused by those around him not being strict enough with him!

Since Chrissie had become Piers's mistress, he had joined her in helping to make Verena's life miserable by being openly unkind. He had at last succeeded in causing Sir Charles to believe that not only was she creating trouble for Chrissie over Jamie, but that her friendship with Nicholas Allen was the cause of her recent mutinous behaviour in refusing to marry him.

'He's a bad influence on the pair of them,' he had finished. 'I still think that it's more than coincidence that the robberies in the West Country began only after he arrived here. Someone ought to keep an eye on him. He was away when Westermere Hall was robbed. Said he was in London—but who knows?'

Sir Charles had reluctantly agreed with him. Life at Marlowe Court had been disrupted since Chrissie, Jamie and Verena had arrived there—particularly since they had met young Allen.

'Can't do anything without proof, what?' he said. 'Until then we're hamstrung.'

'Oh, he'll do something stupid. That sort always do. You'll see.'

Unaware of the undercurrents in her world, Verena walked happily to Jesse Pye's cottage to find Nicholas and Hercules were waiting for her. Since the day was fine, Nicholas had packed his small and battered picnic hamper and suggested that they walk to the River Bret again, taking a ball and a selection of light novels with them, as well as Hercules.

Verena carried the books. Hercules ran in front of them, bringing back memories of their recent happy afternoon with Jamie.

'How is he?' Nicholas asked.

Verena told him the sad story of the specialist's visit.

'I thought so. Poor little fellow.'

Verena said no more until they reached the river, to sit on its bank, companionably side by side. 'I took your advice over Jamie, although it made me unhappy.'

'It makes me unhappy, too.' Nicholas took her hand—it was the only part of her which he could trust himself to touch. 'But we cannot make our life fit our wishes, we can only endure it when it does not conform to them.'

'What made you so wise, Nicholas?' Verena was genuinely curious.

'I'm not wise,' he told her, his face a little wry. 'On the contrary, but life has taught me a few useful lessons. One of them is to be true to yourself whenever you can, but sometimes one has to accept the unacceptable—and soldier on.'

'And you say you are not wise!'

Nicholas kissed her hand. 'Remember, that like all of us I rarely practise what I preach. It's too difficult. Now let's play catch with the ball and try not to fall into the river while we do so.'

Verena, under Nicholas's tuition on the beach at Lynmouth, had improved her catching ability so much that he didn't always throw the ball directly to her. One of his throws was, as he later ruefully admitted, 'a real boss shot,' and in running to catch it she tripped and fell, to lie still for a moment, all the breath knocked out of her body.

Her stillness shocked Nicholas. He ran across to where she lay, knelt down beside her, and said hoarsely, 'You're not hurt, Verena, say you're not hurt.'

Some devil who resided inside her and whom she had not known existed before this afternoon, caused her to moan slightly and roll away from him.

Desperate, Nicholas slipped a hand under her head, and gently turned her towards him, lifting her a little. Verena let her eyes flutter open, closed them again and gave another moan.

What was he to do? All the worst forebodings of those at Marlowe Court, particularly Chrissie, would be justified if she had been injured whilst she was out with him. He laid her down gently, and bent over her, when, to his surprise, and a little to Verena's, for it was the devil's doing, not hers, she slipped her arms around his neck and kissed him, full on the lips.

Nicholas was immediately on fire as he had known he would be if he touched her other than lightly. He kissed her back. Their minds and body as one, they came together, their tongues touching as his gently forced her lips apart so that they met. Verena, who had not consciously decided to do anything so daring, had let her body decide for her. His hands were gently stroking her breasts and the sensation was so wonderful that she pulled her mouth away from his, and murmured his name, 'Oh, Nicholas...'

The sound restored him to sanity. He pulled his whole body away from her, something which took all his mental, rather than his physical, strength, exclaiming, 'Witch! You naughty witch, you weren't hurt at all, were you?'

The devil had tempted Nicholas, too, but the care for others which had ruled his life for the past three years enabled him to resist the urge to carry his lovemaking on to its logical and inevitable conclusion. His dearest love was a virgin and he must not betray her, or himself, by seducing her.

The eyes which were laughing up at him were inviting, but they were innocent, too.

'No, I wasn't hurt,' Verena said, sitting up. And then she put a hand over her mouth. 'Oh, Nicholas, I only meant to tease you. Whatever made me kiss you like that?'

'Mother Eve,' he said, his face alight, 'that's what—or rather who. She took over the moment I held you in my arms, and tempted me sorely. You do know what might have happened if I hadn't called a halt?'

'Yes, I do. Oh, Nicholas, I never have felt like that before, not even with…' She stopped, blushing.

'With him? The priceless pongo? What a sad chap he must have been.' He stood up to laugh down at her.

'I know that now,' said Verena, standing up. 'But I didn't then. I'm sorry I tempted you.'

'I'm not. I know where I stand with my witch now, if I didn't before.'

'And what's a pongo? Don't tell me if I've asked about something which I ought not to know!'

He put out a finger to stroke her lips. 'Not at all. A pongo's a soldier. Don't ask me why. The answer might be censorable!'

'In that case, suppose we take a rest and read our books. That should cool us both down before we eat our picnic.'

'What a splendid idea. I've brought along P.G. Wodehouse's *Psmith*, a favourite of mine, and *Unnatural Death*, the new novel by Dorothy L. Sayers—not one of her best, I'm told, but it should be great fun.'

'Bags I *Unnatural Death*,' said Verena enthusiastically, 'I adore Lord Peter Wimsey.'

Nicholas made a face. 'You do? There goes all my hopes of impressing you, then. I'm not a bit like him.'

'Oh, I only adore him when he's in the pages of a book. He would be impossible in real life. I couldn't fancy a man who was right all the time.'

'Oh, so I'm wrong all the time! Now I do know where I stand with you. At the bottom of the class!'

'Wretch,' said Verena, who was fast learning the game of verbal lovemaking of which Nicholas was a master. 'If you think that then you should be at the bottom of the class.'

To prevent himself from taking his teasing witch in his arms, Nicholas bent down to lift the books out of his bag. He handed her *Unnatural Death* with something of a flourish, and sat down to read *Psmith* in the hope that it might prevent his mind—and another vital part of his body—from wondering what it might have been like if he had accepted her unspoken invitation to make love to her.

After they had read a little, put their books away, and had enjoyed their tea, they both lay back in the warmth of the late afternoon and talked lazily about life.

'I have to go to London again on business next Wednesday, for the day, this time,' Nicholas said, 'so we shan't be able to meet then. Saturday afternoon, this week and next, should be on, though.'

'Shan't I meet you at Uncle John's dinner party on Thursday?'

''Fraid not.' This was the first time in the last year that

John had not asked him, and he was uneasily certain that it was his association with Verena which had caused him to be left out. John was apparently not prepared to offend the family at Marlowe Court by having him present.

'Saturday, then. Oh, I can't wait for it to come around. Couldn't we meet one evening?'

Prudence had him refusing. 'We must be patient, my sweet love. Nothing will be gained by our looking as though we are tweaking your grandfather's tail.' He thought as he spoke that when he had bought the *Clarion* from John, Sir Charles might relent and allow him to offer for Verena.

If not—then he would think about what to do next if that time ever came.

'What are you reading, Gis? Something intriguing if your expression is any guide.'

Gis, sitting in a basket chair on Padworth's lawn, looked up from his book in order to answer his cousin, Gerry Senior. The annual summer get-together of the Schuylers had come round again. His wife Thea was with the other wives, watching the younger children play on a large rug on Padworth's greenest lawn.

'The new sensation, *Put money in thy purse.*'

'Oh, that. Only out a week and half London society seems to have read it to find out if they are in it. Am I?'

'Only by inference. Your father certainly is.'

'He is? Will he be pleased—or otherwise?'

'Knowing Uncle Gerard, I doubt it. Listen. ''Robert''— that's the innocent hero—''soon discovered that Lord Renishaw was far from being a member of the old nobility. He was, instead, a member of the new. He was the scion of a family of American robber barons who had conquered England and were now looting it to their greater enrichment rather like those Norman thugs who had come over with Duke William in 1066.

"His home at Graveney was the magnet for those who were aware that even when he was not a member of the government he was still one of the powers behind it. He resembled not so much a religious grey eminence as a Yankee boxing manager who had parlayed his way into prominence."

'Ouch!' exclaimed Gerry Senior. 'That hurt! Is it all like that?'

'Well, the author is kinder to Lord Renishaw later on. He concedes that his political decisions are invariably wise—even if they do tend to help along his career and that of his large family.'

'Us, then. Definitely us.'

'Afraid so. The truth always hurts, you know.'

'Fine for you,' said Gerry Senior, laughing. 'Your name's not Schuyler.'

'Ah, but I'm in the book, too. It's a real *roman à clef*. Everyone's in it including Margot Asquith, Balfour and Lloyd George. He's Glyn Gower, known to one and all as—wait for it—"the old goat".'

'And who, cousin Gis, are you?'

'Oh, I'm the smoothly handsome universal expert, Jack Beauchamp, the war hero who won his medal at the Front—not in the air, you notice—and is famous for being able to solve everybody's problems, including his own. Oh, and he designs cars, not planes.'

'Have Harcourt and Maine gone mad?' Gerry enquired. 'Whatever happened to the law of libel? And who wrote the damned thing?'

'One Arthur Merlin, or so the blurb says. He also wrote those children's books about dragons, it says. Then he was simply Merlin.'

'He isn't anyone simple, that's for sure.'

'No, indeed. It's confoundedly well written—and entertaining, too. As for libel—who's going to sue and have their dirty linen aired in the courts?'

'They say the greater the truth the greater the libel. From what you tell me the writer is a member of the society he's lampooning. Any clues in the book?'

Gis decided not to share his suspicions with Gerry. Too near the bone.

'Read it yourself and see. I've finished with it. Here,' and he handed the book over, before strolling off in the direction of the house.

He had barely reached it when he met Lady Longthorne, his aunt Torry. She was carrying a book. He wondered uneasily whether it was *Put money in thy purse*, which his cousin Gerry was now reading avidly, occasionally laughing aloud at the naughtier passages.

'Oh, Gis, I'm glad I've met you while we are alone. May I ask you a question? Have you come across any clue as to where Nicholas might be?'

Fortunately he could answer that truthfully. He had certainly met Nicholas, but he had no idea where he lived.

'I'm sorry, Aunt, no clue at all. Why?'

'It's this book.' She waved it at him. 'It's a children's book by an author called Merlin. Its title is *The Cowardly Dragon*. I read it after I had spoken to you recently about trying to trace Nicholas and you had told me that you intuited that he was happy.

'Do you remember the day when he left Padworth for good? Earlier in the afternoon he had been telling the little ones a story about a cowardly dragon. By chance I listened to him—and so, I think, did you. Could it possibly be a coincidence that this book, written by someone who has adopted a pseudonym, tells exactly the same tale? And

Nicholas can't have read it because it wasn't published until after he had left us. And the drawings are exactly like those he did before Gerard ordered him to go to Oxford and not to art school.'

Gis examined the book. 'Aunt Torry,' he asked earnestly, 'have you spoken to Uncle Gerard about this?'

'No, why? But I think that I ought to, don't you?'

'No, I don't. Not yet, anyway. You see, this man, Merlin, who I agree with you is most probably Nicholas, is the author of the new satiric novel which is currently exciting London.'

Gis thought ruefully that he was behaving exactly as Merlin had portrayed him as doing in the novel—solving everyone's problems!

'Oh, Gis, don't say so. Until you told me I had no idea what the name of the author was. I only know that they say this book, *Put money in thy purse*, is very clever and amusingly wicked. Are we in it? Oh, I see by your face that we are! Oh, dear! Whatever will Gerard say?'

Gis put an arm around her. 'Don't fret, Aunt Torry. You're not in it, but Uncle Gerard is, and the Schuylers generally, and so am I. But only in passing. It is clever, and yes, wicked. He must have grown up a lot to have written it. It's very powerful. Best to say nothing to Uncle Gerard about the possibility of Nicholas being involved until you have some proof. We may be wrong.'

'Oh, I'm so glad I met you, Gis. You're always so sensible. I'll do as you say. I suppose the truth about the identity of the author must come out sooner or later.'

'Exactly. It's going to be a runaway best-seller. The publishers have been pushing it; the word was out that it was dynamite before its official publication day. Arthur Merlin's name is made. He can probably name his own price for his next book.'

Torry gave a great sigh. 'Half of me wishes that Nicholas has written it because it would mean that he has achieved something. The other half of me is horrified by what his father is likely to say. And we still don't know where he is!'

'Keep mum for the moment, though. With any luck Uncle Gerard won't even read it.'

Luck was not with them. At that very moment Gerard was sitting in his study running rapidly through it and occasionally stopping to laugh heartily at the cuttingly satiric descriptions of his friends and enemies. His private secretary, James Hawksworth, had slipped *Put money in thy purse* into his briefcase, recommending it to him as he did so.

Waiting for an important telephone call to come through, Gerard had picked the book up, meaning to glance through it, but had found himself unable to put it down...

Until he came to the passage about him, the Schuylers and Padworth which Gis had read to Gerry!

Gerard let out the sort of roar which had his secretary scuttling in from the anteroom.

'What is it, m'lord?'

'Have you read this damned thing, Hawksworth?'

'No, m'lord. I understand it's dynamite.'

'Never mind about dynamite. It's libellous. We're both in it—and Padworth. He calls it Graveney. The scoundrel who wrote this is damned clever, but he deserves horse-whipping.'

'They say that it will make his fortune.'

'If someone doesn't shoot him first for his impudence. Get Stanton Harcourt for me on the telephone on Monday and we'll find out who the villain is.'

Torry joined him later to find him in a state halfway between anger and laughter. He thrust the book at her. 'You ought to read this, m'dear. We're all in it but you. It's scurrilous, but entertaining. I mean to find out who wrote it. Whoever it is knows Padworth and the political world intimately.'

Oh, dear! Gerard's blood was up. She wouldn't have needed Gis's advice to prevent her from telling Gerard of her suspicions about Nicholas.

'If you say so, dear,' she offered placatingly. 'After all, it's only a book.'

Gerard glowered at her for a moment. She smiled sweetly at him.

'Come and meet your guests, Gerard. I know that you had important business, but that must be over if you've had time to excite yourself over a silly novel.'

His face softened. 'Rightly rebuked, my dear. Hawksworth says that all the family have arrived.'

'All but Nicholas,' she could not help saying.

'Since he cut himself off from us of his own accord, he scarcely qualifies, does he?'

He saw his wife wince, and because after so many years he still loved her with the abiding passion he had felt for her as a young man, he said gently, 'You've heard nothing from him. I thought that he might have contacted you.'

'Nothing, but Gis told me not long ago that he's sure that he's well and happy.'

Gerard made a face. 'Do I wish him that? I'm not sure. For your sake, perhaps.'

'Not his?'

'Unless he's shown more character than he did before he disappeared—which I doubt.'

Nothing was to be gained, Torry thought, by pursuing the matter, and much might be lost, so she held her tongue while urging Gerard on to greet his family and friends gathered on Padworth's green and famous lawns.

* * *

'Bought the *Clarion* from you, John? You can't be serious. I didn't even know that you were retiring.'

Sir Charles was entertaining a few friends to dinner a fortnight after Nicholas had informed John that his bank had agreed to advance him the money to buy the *Clarion* on the strength of his aunt's legacy.

'Oh, it was a recent decision. I told young Allen of it in order to warn him that there would be a change of management and he made me an offer on the strength of a legacy and a bank loan. He paid the going price and I was happy to leave the paper in safe hands. He's a sound feller, straightforward and honest. He asked me to keep things quiet until his money came through.'

That's what Nicholas meant when he asked me to wait, thought Verena joyfully. He knew that he might buy the *Clarion*, which would make him a man of affairs, fit to marry me, and even Grandfather would find it difficult to refuse to allow me to marry him.

Piers saw the glow on her face and knew its cause. Jealous anger consumed him.

He frowned over his wine glass. 'A legacy, you say? How odd. I gained the distinct impression by his clothes and manner of living that he was a penniless nobody. Now he's suddenly found enough credit to buy the *Clarion*.'

'So did I.' Sir Charles frowned too. 'Think that he was penniless. You're sure it's all on the level, John? You have seen the colour of his money, I trust.'

'Quite sure. He went to London to arrange the loan a fortnight ago and the money came through yesterday morning. My solicitors are satisfied that everything is above board and we have arranged to visit their offices tomorrow to sign all the necessary documents. No, there's nothing dubious there, I'm happy to say.'

'Well, I hope that everything is fair and square,' grumbled Piers. 'Of course, it means the district's saddled with him.'

John Webster was suddenly angry. 'That is a most unkind thing to say. He's such a clever young fellow that he could well wish to make his way in London. West Bretton is lucky to have him and keep him.'

'Time will tell,' Piers muttered enigmatically into his wine glass. Privately he thought that he ought to set in motion his plan to discredit young Allen once and for all. With any luck Verena would be so disillusioned that she would turn to him for comfort, and enable him to live a quiet, carefree life again.

Chapter Ten

'Is it true, Nicholas, that you've bought the *Clarion*? Uncle John told Grandfather and Piers that you had last night. Oh, Piers was so cross. I can't think why he dislikes you so.'

'Sweet witch, he dislikes me because he thinks I took his girl away from him.'

Verena was indignant. 'I was never his girl!'

'I know that, and you know that, Piers doesn't. That's what conceit does to you. I was conceited once,' he finished mournfully.

'No, never. I don't believe that.'

'Well, I was. It's a failing in my family. We all think that we know what's best for us, and everyone else. Ah, here comes tea.'

They were having afternoon tea together in Bromley's. The waitress had smiled benevolently at them when she took their order. Everybody in West Bretton knew that nice Nick Allen and the Squire's daughter were sweet on one another and wished them well. Most of them were relieved that she was not going to marry Piers. Some of them were worried that the Squire might somehow be able to forbid the banns.

Neither Nicholas nor Verena had got as far as discussing marriage, although both of them had spent some time thinking about it. Mainly because they were both aware that the only way that they were going to be able to make love properly was when they were married.

In the meantime they burned.

'I'm sorry I wasn't able to tell you about buying the *Clarion* before, but it was important for me to see it through before anything was finally arranged. I didn't want to raise our hopes too much—and then have the whole thing fall through if I couldn't raise the money or John changed his mind.'

'What hopes?' asked Verena innocently—but her eyes were naughty.

'Don't pretend, sweet witch, that you don't know what hopes! I can propose to you now that I'm a respectable businessman, but I don't want to go down on my knees to you in such a public place as a teashop! The staff already have wedding bells in their eyes every time we come in!'

Verena was entranced. 'Where *do* you intend to propose, then?'

'Under the trees, down by the pool. Water's always romantic, don't you think? And then we reach the difficult part—when I have to ask Sir Charles for your hand.'

'No need,' returned Verena practically. 'I am of age, and I can make my own decisions and marry whomsoever I please.'

'True, but you must understand that it's important that I am seen to do the right thing. My station being so dubious and all that.'

'Your station doesn't matter to me,' replied Verena naughtily, 'so long as it's the station at which I want to get on the train.'

'I shall reward you for that piece of nonsense, whether

we are in public or not.' Nicholas picked up a piece of Devon scone lavishly adorned with Cornish cream and jam and held it out across the table for her to eat from his fingers. Which she duly did, licking them lovingly.

'Ooh, aren't they sweet,' whispered the waitress dreamily to the teashop's owner who had come in with a fresh batch of scones. Business was booming now that the summer had arrived.

'I wonder what the old Squire's thinking,' the owner whispered back.

'Don't matter,' retorted the waitress, practicality taking over from dreaming. 'She's her own mistress, ain't she?'

'Where d'you think they're going?' she asked the owner after Nicholas had paid the bill and he and Verena had wandered off down the main street, hand in hand. 'Somewhere nice, I bet.'

'None of your business,' snapped the teashop owner. 'Stop mooning and fetch table number three the extra hot water they asked for ten minutes ago!'

Nicholas was right when he had told her that he would propose to her in a romantic place. Down by the pool, among the scents and sweets of summer with the sun shining on the water, alone with his love, was the ideal place.

Gallantly he went down on one knee before her. On his way to his meeting with her in the teashop, he had decided that proposing to her was going to be the easy part. The difficult part was that he did not want to tell her yet that he was Arthur Merlin who had written the dragon books—and *Put money in thy purse*, and that this information must remain a secret. He wanted to take things slowly and not overwhelm her with too many new things at once.

He was a little worried that, when he finally told her, she would be unhappy that he had deceived her for so long. He hoped not, and that she would understand his reasons for remaining silent.

As for the other business about being a Schuyler, well...he was no longer a Schuyler, so that was that—'and there's an end on't' as a wise man had once said about something entirely different, but he liked the sound of it for he never intended to be a Schuyler again.

Verena's face, looking down on him, was so soft and loving, that he could hardly bring the words out. Afterwards he was to remember the glib young rake he had once been to whom words in such a situation had always come so easily. Now he could barely speak for the emotion which was choking him.

He took her hand—he always seemed to be doing that—but this time it was entirely appropriate.

'My heart's darling,' he murmured huskily, 'you know what I am about to say, and I will say it as simply as possible, for true love needs no fine words with which to adorn itself. Please say that you will marry me and I promise to try to make you happy, not only now in the first flush of our love when it will be easy, but in all the days which are to come—when sometimes it may be harder.'

He had used fine words to other women and they had meant nothing but that he wished to have an affair with them. Now, however, it was Verena, his true love, to whom he was speaking, and true love demanded that the loved object must be satisfied as well as one's self.

'Oh, Nicholas, you know that I will. Of course I will marry you.'

'To have and to hold until death do us part?'

'Particularly that. Without that it is not true love, but passing lust. I love you, Nicholas, with my mind as well as my heart. And I will try to make you happy, too.'

She had said aloud what was in his heart, too, and which

separated his feelings for her from all those he had experienced previously with the other women who had lightly passed through his life. No 'til death do us part' for them—or him.

'And now this,' he said, taking from his pocket a ring which he slipped on to her finger. It was a simple gold band, a half hoop of small diamonds—as delicate as she was. He had bought it with his own hard-earned money—it owed nothing to his Schuyler origins.

Verena held it out to admire it before putting out her hand to raise him up so that they stood facing one another, nothing between them, the two halves of the one who would soon come together, as he later said.

For the moment he said nothing, merely took her face in his two hands and kissed her on the lips so lovingly and gently that the tears stood in her eyes.

'We must be patient, my darling, and behave ourselves until we are married,' he whispered into her ear, his voice no more than a sigh, a light wind blowing.

Oh, how he would have laughed in the past at the mere idea of holding off until marriage—but the man who would have done that was long gone, and the new man respected his love and the conventions of their society which bade them to wait.

'I shall speak to your grandfather as soon as the legal business connected with the buying of the *Clarion* is safely over. What must be done must be done properly. I must be able assure him that I can support you in decent comfort. You don't mind waiting a little?' he asked her anxiously. 'But I don't wish to give him any excuse to show displeasure by not following the proper forms. We could marry without his consent, of course, but I would rather have it, for both our sakes.'

'Oh, I think that I can wait, so long as we can see as much of each other as possible until then.'

'But not quite all of each other yet, unfortunately,' returned Nicholas, his eyes naughty. 'Oh, my love, do you burn for me, as much as I burn for you?'

'Yes, of course. It's the oddest thing. When I am with you I feel that I am about to go up in flames any minute! You know so much, Nicholas, do you think that all lovers feel like this—and that they want so desperately to be part of the other?'

'Yes, my darling, but not all as strongly as we do.'

'And it's not only that,' she told him earnestly as they sat side by side on the grass, she admiring her ring, and he admiring her. 'I love being with you and talking to you as well—it's not just the desire to...' She trailed off, flushing rosily.

'I know—that's the wonderful thing about it. That we're friends as well as lovers. Not many are lucky enough to enjoy having both. I never valued the twin joys of being in love and being friends, because I never encountered them before. Now I have I know what I have been looking for all my life.'

Briefly and painfully he thought of his mother and father who, he now knew, had found the twin joys of mind and body united. For the first time regret at what he had left behind ran through him—as his cousin Gis had thought it might when he found himself.

Was he his own man, at last? Had loving Verena helped him to find that man? Thinking so, he took her tenderly in his arms.

'Let me reward you with a little gentle loving, my darling, for helping me to come to terms with life as well as love. It will be hard for us both not to go to the ultimate glorious end—but all the philosophers say that if we practise self-denial it will improve our characters wonderfully.'

Verena hid her face in his chest after saying, 'I sometimes wonder, my dearest heart, if any of the philosophers were ever in love to be able to proclaim that so easily. Or was it that they never practised what they preached!'

'Probably yes. The only one I ever met was a consummate rogue for all his great name as a philosopher and an aristocrat.'

He was thinking of Bertrand Russell who had once visited Padworth, and was as notorious for his unruly private life as he was famous for being a mathematician and a philosopher.

'I'm not surprised.'

'Well, let me surprise you a little before we part—but not too much, or we shall be in danger of forgetting ourselves.'

So he did—surprise her a little—and then he walked her to the gates of Marlowe Court. Before Verena left him she said, 'If you are not going to speak to Sir Charles yet, I shall take my ring off until you do. It would not be tactful or sensible to wear it. Either Chrissie or Piers is sure to try to make trouble for me if they see it.'

'Very wise,' he had said, kissing her again. 'Sleep well— if you can, my sweet witch.'

'And you,' her reply as she left him was saucy, and made him laugh.

In the night Nicholas remembered their idyll by Parson's Pool. Excitement had him waking several times, once because he thought that he had heard a noise outside. He went to the window but saw nothing, and Hercules, who slept in a kennel in the back garden, made no sound.

He lay awake for a little after that, but heard nothing

more, and fell asleep again, thinking that the noise must have been part of a forgotten dream.

After breakfast, he went out to Hercules' kennel—to discover it empty. This was not in itself disturbing, for he had been absent from it more than once, to return later in the day, looking almost sheepish.

He had not reappeared before Nicholas left for work, and when he returned in the evening, Hercules was still missing. For the first time he began to feel worried, and decided to look for him before he made his supper.

Could it have been Hercules that he had heard in the night?

He walked in the direction of Marlowe Court. Hercules always grew excited when he passed the gates to the Court, and it was quite possible that he had returned there to look for Jamie.

Which reminded him—Verena had rarely mentioned Jamie since she had been so worried about him after the specialist's visit. He had asked her once how he was, and been told that he was 'as well as could be expected' which was really no sort of an answer at all.

He walked up the drive to the Court, determined to ask Verena if Hercules had found his way back there. He thought not: she would surely have brought him home. He might even see Jamie again, if only by chance.

Verena ran into the entrance hall when told by the butler that he was enquiring for her. She took one look at him and asked, 'What's wrong, Nicholas?'

'It's Hercules. I'm sorry to say that he's been missing since the first thing this morning. I wondered if he had come back here to try to find Jamie. The butler thinks not.'

'No, we've seen nothing of him.'

Their voices attracted an audience. The drawing-room door opened and Chrissie stood there, eyes baleful.

'What's *he* doing here? You know that I don't like having him in the house because of his effect on Jamie.'

'Nicholas only came to ask after Hercules. He's missing.'

'Really?' Chrissie's perfectly plucked eyebrows made two twin arches. 'What a fuss about nothing! Couldn't he have gone to the stables to ask?'

Her spite was so manifest that both her hearers were nonplussed. They were saved by the kitchen door opening and Jamie bursting through it, Priddie in hot pursuit.

'It's the Dragon man! I thought that I heard his voice! Oh, sir, she won't let me see you, and you never finished your last story. And the butler says that Hercules is missing.'

Scarlet in the face, his mother hissed at him, 'You naughty boy! What are you doing here? You are supposed to be having supper in the kitchen with Priddie. And I am not *she*, you bad-mannered child, I am your mother.'

'Well, you don't behave like the mothers in the stories Priddie reads to me. Are you sure you are?'

Such an artless, but pointed, home truth from the little boy set the mouths of both Verena and Nicholas twitching. Chrissie looked as though she were about to burst. Priddie, casting her eyes to heaven, took Jamie's hand, and began to drag him out of the entrance hall.

This time it was Chrissie who was saved by a new arrival. The chief groom, Upton, came through the kitchen door. 'The butler said that you were enquiring after Hercules, Mr Allen. I've just this minute brought him in. He's in a basket in the kitchen. I found him down by the bottom meadow. He's been ill-treated and I think that one of his legs is broken. I thought that he was dead at first.'

Jamie gave a loud cry, wrenched his hand from Priddie's,

and ran to the kitchen door. 'Oh, poor Hercules! Do let me see him.'

Chrissie caught him by his jacket collar and hauled him back. 'No, indeed, you shan't. You've only just recovered from your latest attack, and I'm not having that bother all over again. Go to your room, and I'll send Priddie to you.

'Upton, I'll thank you to take Allen to the kitchen—it's his proper place, after all—and arrange for him to take his wretched animal home. It's no concern of ours. If you don't want to endanger your reputation further, Verena, you will come with me to the drawing-room and leave Allen to go his own way, which isn't yours.'

'Thank you, Chrissie,' said Verena, all prudence and good manners forgotten in the face of her stepmother's outrageous behaviour, 'for being so careful of my reputation when you are so careless of your own. I shall follow your example and do exactly as I please. Be sure to give my love to Piers when you go to his bedroom tonight.'

A ghastly silence followed. Chrissie, her face purple, and rendered mute for once, followed a sullen Jamie who had been hauled into the drawing-room by Priddie.

Nicholas said nothing, but thought a lot about this interesting revelation, and did as Chrissie had ordered him. He found Hercules in his old basket, being ministered to by Upton.

'He's in a bad way, Mr Allen. Best get him to the vet as soon as you can. He might be able to save him.'

'I'll come with you,' volunteered Verena. 'If you don't mind waiting whilst I fetch a cardigan.'

The vet, a friend of Nicholas's, obligingly left his dinner to examine Hercules. He agreed with Upton.

'Yes, I think that there may be hope here, but I'm afraid that he'll always be lame. Someone has given him a nasty blow on the head, as well. No fall did that. From what you tell me, he was probably left for dead. It's a dirty business, to be sure.'

'But why?' Verena burst out. 'Who would want to harm poor Hercules? What is the world coming to?'

Someone who might want to hurt me—or those at the Court—was all that Nicholas could think of by way of explanation. But he said nothing: he did not wish to distress Verena further.

They left Hercules in safe hands and Nicholas walked Verena back to the Court, both of them puzzling over Hercules' maltreatment. If Nicholas had not been such a popular a figure in West Bretton, Verena might have thought that it was aimed at him.

'What could be the point of hurting a little dog?' she asked before he kissed her goodbye at the main gates of Marlowe Court. He was only too unhappily aware that accompanying her to the house itself might be the cause of subjecting her to more of Chrissie's spite.

'I know, my darling, but try not to fret. It can only make you unhappy and won't help Hercules.'

'But who could possibly have done such a dreadful thing?' she asked him sorrowfully.

Nicholas could give her no satisfactory answer. Chrissie was the only person he could think of who might want to harm Hercules, but somehow he couldn't imagine her going so far as to attack the poor creature herself, and the idea of her hiring someone else to do so came, he thought, from the realms of fiction, not from real life.

He had long believed that one of the benefits of living in a small country town was the peace and quiet of the daily round, so different from the bustle of the city. This senseless attack on Hercules was thus a violation of all that he had come to value.

On the other hand, he had lived in West Bretton for three years and this was the first untoward incident which had occurred. He could only hope that it would be a solitary one.

Verena walked home sorrowfully to find that her two chief tormentors, Piers and Chrissie, had driven to a country hotel for dinner and that Sir Charles had decided on an early night. The kitchen supplied her with a scratch meal, and she was eating it in front of the big cast-iron kitchen range when the butler came in.

'Mrs Burton is on the telephone in the drawing-room asking for Mrs Marlowe. I told her that she was not in. She said that she'd like to speak to you instead. I asked her to hold on. I hope that I did the right thing; if not, I'll ask her to ring again.'

'Of course. She probably wants to arrange another meeting with my stepmother. I'll speak to her immediately.' Mrs Burton was the friend with whom Chrissie had spent her recent weekend.

She picked up the telephone, wondering what Mrs Burton wanted. 'Verena Marlowe speaking.'

'Oh, Verena, dear, so pleased to hear your voice again after all these years. I understand that Chrissie isn't in. I didn't even know that you were all back in the country, and I should so like to see her. We were at school together, you know. Please ask her to ring me urgently so that we may arrange a meeting as soon as possible.'

Verena stared at the phone which she was now holding away from her ear. She scarcely knew what to say.

'Verena! Are you there?'

'Yes, sorry. A fault on the line, I suppose,' she said desperately. 'Of course, I'll pass your message on.'

'Sweet of you. Bye bye. Give my love to young Jamie. I'm dying to see him! He must be quite a big boy by now.'

Verena put the receiver down slowly. According to Chrissie, she had already spent a weekend with her dear old friend—but she hadn't. Where had she been? And then Verena remembered. It was the weekend on which Piers had been away, too. Was that, in the light of their affair, merely a coincidence?

She couldn't ask her stepmother. Nor did she wish to speak to her and reveal that Mrs Burton had inadvertently given her away.

Instead she wrote a note which simply said, 'Mrs Burton rang and wished to arrange a meeting with you. I told her that you would ring back. Verena.' She pushed it under Chrissie's door for her to find when she came home.

In an office in Scotland Yard, Chief Detective Inspector Sutherland of the CID was talking on the phone to his counterpart in Exeter. Earlier in the day he had been sent for by the Commissioner, who had been subjected to pressure from all sides to send someone down to Devon to try to catch the gang who had been robbing country houses.

'First it was Lord Axminster who went to the Home Secretary and accused us of dragging our feet,' he had complained, 'and now we've had a message from Interpol telling us that they believe the robberies are not simply local, but are part of a highly organised cross-Channel conspiracy of thieves engaged in looting treasures from houses all over Europe.

'What's stolen over there is disposed of over here, and vice versa, so that it isn't easily recognised when it comes on the market. Most of it isn't stuff that's seen as remarkably rare, either, it's the sheer volume of what is being taken which is raising the money for them. Where they do lift something extremely valuable it's disposed of in secret to dishonest collectors and is never seen again.

'Interpol seems to think that one of the organisers lives in the West Country and knows exactly which houses to rob.

'To cap it all, I've had Special Branch on my back as well. They want to bring in some damned freelance who used to be with MI6 and is supposed to be a genius at sussing out things like this. He's retired, but will help if required. I've agreed that this damned business has been going on far too long, and I want you to send your best man and his sergeant to Exeter as soon as possible, to clear things up before this prancing amateur arrives.

'Fortunately, by a happy piece of luck, Exeter rang me this morning to tell me that they've had an anonymous letter putting the finger on some chappy who lives in West Bretton, which, in case you don't know, is a one-horse town in North Devon.

'The letter gives chapter and verse for believing that he's involved. Quite hard evidence, if the writer can be believed. Queer, that.'

'A falling out among thieves, perhaps?' Sutherland thought that it was time to put his oar in. 'Revenge for something or other achieved by shopping one's ex-mate?'

'Possibly, possibly. Who do you think of sending?'

'Cameron,' said Sutherland, who had a weakness for all his officers of Scottish origin.

'Well chosen. He's got that promising young sergeant, Finch, too. Brief them and send them down to save the day for our country cousins as soon as possible, if not sooner.'

'Aye, aye, sir.'

Now he was telling the man at the other end of the line that he was doing just that—but leaving out the bit about country cousins—and taking down a transcript of the letter.

'It's pretty detailed,' he told DI Jock Cameron and his attentive sergeant, before handing it to them. 'It says that there's a young man named Nicholas Allen who came to live in West Bretton three years ago, just before the robberies began. He has no obvious assets, took a job as a glorified office boy on the local paper, the *Clarion*. Not only does he possess an extremely expensive watch, but he has also suddenly found from nowhere enough money to buy the *Clarion* now that its owner wishes to retire. On top of that, he makes mysterious visits to London—one of them when the last big robbery took place.

'The suggestion is that he doesn't visit London at all—that it's just a blind for his activities with regard to the robberies. What's more to the point, the writer says that from time to time he keeps some of the valuable smaller stuff in a shed at the back of the labourer's cottage he lives in before it is moved on, and, quote, 'I have reason to believe that he has some stored there at present. Move quickly before it disappears.'

'It's signed, *A friend*.'

'Whose friend?' asked Cameron, grinning. 'Chummy's—or the law's? When do we leave?'

'Now. The officer in charge at Exeter police station has arranged for you to spend the night there. You can drive to West Bretton in the morning with their men, DI Ellis and Sergeant Yeo.'

Cameron's eyebrows rose. 'Four of us? Taking it a bit seriously, aren't we?'

'Upstairs wants this cleared up quickly before the Press gets hold of it. You know the headlines—''Scotland Yard slow off the mark again.'' What's more, this is a major operation involving Interpol which we're dealing with, and this is the first real piece of hard evidence we've had yet. Get cracking, lads.'

* * *

John Webster was tidying up his records in the office behind the shop. Nicholas was not taking over until the end of the month, giving him time to leave everything ship-shape. He heard the shop door open and walked to the counter to find two burly men there, strangers.

'Mr John Webster?'

'Yes. What can I do for you?'

'We think that you can help us with our enquiries,' said the larger of the pair, showing him a police badge. 'I'm DI Cameron and this is Sergeant Finch. I believe that you employ a young man by the name of Nicholas Allen?'

He looked around the shop and peered through the door into the office and the Press room. 'Is he here, sir?'

'Not at present. He's gone to North Bretton to interview a farmer there who's had a number of break-ins. Small beer, perhaps, unlike our recent spate of country-house robberies, but important to the farmer. Nick should be back any moment. Oh, and by the way, I don't employ him any more. I'm retiring, and he's the new owner.'

'So I understand, sir. Been here about three years, has he?'

'Slightly more.'

The Inspector made a note in his little book. 'Well, that confirms that,' he said cheerfully. 'You said that he had bought the paper from you. Any idea how he managed to raise the money?'

John said coolly, 'Why are you asking me all this? Why not ask him? He should be back any moment. You can wait for him in the office.'

'Oh, we shall be questioning Mr Allen later, you may be sure. In the meantime, it wouldn't hurt for you to answer a few simple questions, would it? Such as the one which I have just asked you... Oh, and can you tell us where he came from, or what he did before he arrived in West Bretton? That couldn't hurt him, surely?'

It was difficult for a man who believed in law and order to refuse to co-operate with the police.

'I understand that he was left a legacy by an aunt, and that he found the balance of the money by raising a bank loan on the strength of her small portfolio of stocks and shares. As for your other question…'

He paused because he had often wondered where Nicholas had come from, and who his family were—if he had a family, that was—and why he never spoke of them.

'I really know nothing of his life before he came to West Bretton, Inspector. From the occasional word he lets drop I assume that he is an Oxford graduate—but that is only an assumption.'

'He isn't a friend, then?' asked the sergeant suddenly. 'Just an employee?'

'Oh, I wouldn't say that. Yes, he is a friend. He's a likeable chap, very popular in the town.'

'But still a bit of a mystery man, you'd say.'

'Not at all.' John was nonplussed. 'Look, what is all this about?'

'Can't say—for the moment. Oh, what sort of motor does he run—anything fancy?'

'Not at all,' John repeated, beginning to look angry. 'He has a second-hand Morris. There's nothing fancy about him at all. He lives modestly in Jesse Pye's cottage—it used to be a farm labourer's—and is an extremely hard and intelligent worker. And that's all that I'm going to say.'

'Well, that's fortunate,' Cameron said with a smile. 'Because that's all I'm going to ask you. Have you any further questions, Sergeant?'

'Just one. Is he married?'

'No.'

'Engaged?'

'You said one.'

'It's an easy one, sir.'

'Oh, very well, no. But...' John stopped.

'He's walking out with someone, perhaps? If you don't tell us someone else will—and perhaps not as nicely.'

'Oh, have it your way. My niece, Sir Charles Marlowe's daughter, Verena, and he are great friends. And that *is* all. Wait in the back. I'll find chairs for you.'

The shop door opened, but not to admit Nicholas. It was DI Ellis, who had been questioning the bank manager, and had left his sergeant with him. He looked about to explode with excitement.

Cameron introduced him to John. 'DI Ellis—from Exeter. This is Mr Webster who used to own the *Clarion*.'

'Begging your pardon, sir, but could I have a word alone with Inspector Cameron and his sergeant?'

'Now, look,' exclaimed John, 'what exactly is going on?'

'All in due time,' replied Cameron shortly. 'In the meantime, some privacy, please.'

Privacy grudgingly granted, Cameron turned to his colleague.

'What is it, Fred? Found something, have you?'

'Indeed, I have. The bank manager was difficult at first—until I threatened him with a warrant. First he said that he never arranged a bank loan for Allen. It seems that the money Allen had paid for the *Clarion* arrived in the form of a bank draft and was for the full sum.'

'Oh, chummy, I think that we've just about nailed you down,' Cameron murmured softly, Ellis and Finch nodding agreement.

'You'll think so when you hear the next bit. Guess who the draft was from? Coutts, no less—to be paid into John Webster's account. The manager was so surprised that he rang Coutts to see if everything was fair and square. They said that it was—but refused to give any details other than that it came from an account they had held for—wait for it—three years. No mention of a bank loan.'

Cameron banged his hand on the table as though he was squashing a fly. 'Got you,' he said softly. 'It ties in with the letter, the time frame's right, and our man comes out of nowhere just when the robberies start. We shall need more than this, of course—but what a beginning.'

They heard the shop door open. Ellis looked at Cameron. 'Our man, d'you think?'

'Let's hope so. We'll go and see.'

Nicholas, who had been interviewing an angry man who had cursed the local police for their inefficiency and him for troubling him when he was trying to straighten up the mess which the thieves had left behind them, was a little surprised to find himself facing three large men in the small shop.

John, who had arrived on the scene too late to warn him that something odd was up, was prevented from approaching him by some adroit manouevring by Sergeant Finch.

'Mr Nicholas Allen, is it?'

'In person,' said Nicholas, his manner as friendly as always. 'What can I do for you?'

He was something of a surprise to the three police officers. They hadn't expected to meet a man built like a front-row rugby forward with a face to match. Cameron could understand why he was liked in the town. For all his size and strength there was something winning about him. Charm's an odd thing, Cameron had often discovered, and those who possessed it were not always the most handsomely obvious or the most worthy.

Nicholas Allen undoubtedly had it—which might explain

why, if he were a villain, he had, so far, been a successful one.

'You could help us with our enquiries, sir, if you don't mind answering a few simple questions,' and he waved his police badge at Nicholas, repeating his name and that of his colleagues.

'Oh, I always answer simple questions, Inspector,' Nicholas said with the smile which transformed his hard face. 'It's the difficult ones which are the problem!'

It would, he later thought ruefully, be fair to say that he had not the slightest idea of what was coming, for if he had he would certainly not have been quite so flippant. He assumed that the police were there to ask him about one of the stories on which he had recently been engaged.

That he could be the object of suspicion was the furthest thing from his mind. Even when Cameron demanded privacy again, he thought nothing of it.

'Now, how can I help you, Inspector? I confess that I'm a little baffled as to know why or how, but fire away!'

'So I will, sir. Nicholas Allen. Is that your name, sir?'

It was easy to answer that truthfully, for it had once been part of his name—and now was the whole.

'Indeed.'

The Inspector consulted his notebook. 'And you have lived here for three years, and have just bought the *Clarion*. outright, I understand, no loan involved? Is that true?'

To know that, they must have been investigating his account at the bank. For the life of him Nicholas couldn't think of any reason why they should.

'All quite true, Inspector. But why should you wish to know?'

'One moment, sir, and all will be made plain.' He changed tack. 'Where did you live, Mr Allen, before you came to West Bretton? What occupation did you follow?'

Nicholas's whole manner changed after a fashion which had the police officers staring at him. He had never looked more like his formidable father.

'What is this, Inspector? Why in the world should you wish to know of my past life?'

'You are not answering me, Mr Allen? Why?'

'My past is no concern of yours, Inspector. I can scarcely believe that idle curiosity brings you here to question my bank manager, and my friend and late employer about me. Suppose you tell me why you need to know—and then I might consider whether to answer you or not.'

He had not the slightest wish to tell the men before him of his true identity—even if it got them off his back. To do so would mean that the happy, anonymous life which he had built for himself in the West Country would lie in ruins once he was revealed to be a fabulously rich Schuyler.

And thinking of rich Schuylers, was it possible that his father had suddenly decided to trace him and had gone to the police for help and that was why they were here?

Surely not! He could imagine one police officer being sent to West Bretton to question him about his true identity, but not three. That suggested an investigation into a major crime. But what could it be?

He did not have to wonder long. DI Cameron was speaking.

'Mr Allen, I can say no more at the moment than that we believe that you can help us in our enquiries concerning the country-house robberies which have been taking place in South West England over the last three years. We have good reason to believe that you may be involved.'

'How can you believe anything so preposterous? John, tell them that they are barking up the wrong tree.'

'I'm sorry, Nick. They weren't frank with me, and I tried

to be as truthful as I could about you. I assured them that you were honest and hardworking—didn't I, Inspector?'

'You did, indeed, but that doesn't alter the fact that I need to question Mr Allen further. To save time later, it would be advisable for you to be as frank as Mr Webster has been, and tell me who exactly you are—other than someone who arrived in West Bretton virtually penniless three years ago,—and who suddenly found enough money to buy Mr Webster's paper outright.'

Nicholas folded his arms. 'I shall have to think about that a little before I answer.'

'You might like to reconsider your decision, Mr Allen. Not only is it not helpful, but it could do you harm.'

'So be it.'

'In that case, we shall have to ask you to accompany us first to your home, and then to the police station in West Bretton so that we may question you further.'

'Do I have to go with you? Am I under arrest? And why to my home? Suppose I say no?'

'Then I shall obtain a warrant for your immediate arrest on suspicion of being a prime mover in the robberies afore-mentioned. My advice, if you are claiming that you are innocent, is that you agree to accompany us.'

Nicholas said impatiently, 'This is ridiculous. I am not claiming to be innocent: I am innocent. But it seems that I have no alternative but to agree to do as you ask.'

'Very wise of you, Mr Allen. DI Ellis has his car outside. I believe that one way or another we may be able to clear up this matter satisfactorily very soon.'

'I do hope so, Inspector. I have work to do, a paper to get out tomorrow. I cannot imagine why you should wish to take me to Jesse Pye's cottage—it seems a long way round to the police station. Old Bull will have a fit when you take me in. He and I are great chums.'

'That's as may be, Mr Allen. Now, please come with us—and don't try to escape. Sergeant Finch is a judo black belt.'

'Then he may accept my congratulations,' snarled Nicholas, his temper finally fraying. 'And also be assured that I have not the slightest wish to escape—so he can keep his skills to himself.'

So chummy could lose his rag, could he? He'd been pretty cool so far. Perhaps it was the visit to his cottage which was troubling him.

In the back seat, carefully watched by Sergeant Finch as though he were a large tiger which might suddenly spring, Nicholas tried to work out why they were so insistent on visiting his cottage.

Finch's hand was on his arm as he was led to the doorway. 'Do I,' he asked politely, 'just invite you in—or do you invite yourselves?'

'Neither,' replied DI Cameron grimly, taking a piece of paper from his pocket. 'I have here a warrant which empowers me to search not only your cottage, but also all the outbuildings on your property.'

'Now you are joking, Inspector! Outbuildings, indeed. I've only one, that ramshackle old shed at the bottom of the garden which I never use. It leaks and it isn't even big enough to hold my Morris comfortably—if I had room for a drive to it. You needn't have gone to the trouble of obtaining a search warrant—I'd have given you permission to search everything without it.'

'Would you, Mr Allen?' Cameron was smooth. 'But seeing that I do have one, we'll never know whether you would have done, will we? We'll examine the shed first.' He walked to it, called back, 'I see that there's a lock on it.'

'There is?' Nicholas, still in Finch's iron grip, was

walked down the garden to the shed which he had not visited for weeks. 'I can't imagine where it came from. It's never needed a lock because there's nothing in it.'

'So you say. Fred, you smash the lock. Finch, keep an eye on Mr Allen. I'll stand by. We don't want chummy here saying that we planted anything on him, do we?'

He was so sneeringly confident that for the first time Nicholas realised that he might have good reason to be so. The sight of the battered lock on the shed door was enough on its own to worry him.

And then he thought of poor Hercules…

He didn't have time to think long. Under Ellis's professional ministrations the lock gave way, the door was flung open, and there, on the dirt floor, among the cobwebs, the grime and the late Jesse's rusty scythe and rake were three new-looking boxes…

'Well, well, well,' said Cameron softly. 'What have we here?'

Nicholas knew. He knew at last why Hercules had been attacked. He started to speak. Cameron silenced him. 'Best not to say anything yet.'

Ellis was wrenching one of the boxes open. He lifted out an object wrapped in paper. He tore the paper open to reveal a silver cup.

'By God,' he said softly. 'It's the Westermere Chalice! I never thought to see the real thing. I've a photograph of it in my car's boot. And there's more. It's part of the loot from Westermere Hall.'

Cameron turned to Nicholas. 'Nicholas Allen, I arrest you for being involved in the series of robberies in the South and West Country. I warn you that anything you say may be taken down and used in evidence against you. Cuff him, Sergeant, and we'll take him to the police station in West Bretton for questioning. Fred, I suggest that you stay here to search the cottage for further evidence. I'll send Finch for you with the car when we've got chummy here safely under lock and key.'

It was probably useless to protest, to say, 'I never saw this stuff before. I have reason to believe that it—and the lock—were put here on Wednesday night when my dog was attacked and left for dead.' But he said it all the same.

Cameron's look for him was a pitying one. 'Is that the best you can do? You've been caught bang to rights, laddie, and your best bet is to spill the beans and hope for a reduced sentence if you do, instead of keeping mum and pretending innocence.'

My best bet, Nicholas thought, is to keep mum, find out how strong the case against me is, for I'm sure by the way they've been going on that they know more than they say— and hope that there's a flaw in it big enough to drive a horse and cart through.

The only trouble is—how long can I go on being Nicholas Allen before I tell them who I really am, where the money to buy John's paper came from, and that it wasn't from the proceeds of stolen goods?

And what will my sweet witch say when she discovers that I can't meet her tonight because I'm in the nick!

Chapter Eleven

'Arrested! Nicholas has been arrested. Whatever for?'

Piers, who had just brought the news to Marlowe Court, smiled smugly at Verena who, shortly after lunch, had visited Nicholas's cottage in the hope that he might have returned home early. Outside it she found a large man opening the gate before getting into a car which had been parked in the narrow road.

She was about to open the gate herself when the man said, 'Visiting Mr Allen, are you?'

'Yes,' she had replied, her hand still on the gate.

'He isn't in at the moment, I'm afraid. You would be?'

The question had come out innocently enough. It was only later, much later, that Verena realised why it had been asked. Nevertheless his manner grated on her so that her reply was untypically haughty.

'I'm Miss Marlowe from Marlowe Court. Sir Charles's granddaughter. Why do you ask?'

Ellis, who thought that he might learn more from her if she wasn't aware that he was a police officer, said cheerfully, 'No reason, idle curiosity. Great friend of his, are you?'

Verena's stare grew haughtier. She answered a question

with a question, 'Have you missed him, too? Could I take a message? He's sometimes held up by reason of his work. I shall probably see him later this evening when he arrives home.'

Resisting the desire to say, 'Oh, no you won't,' Ellis shook his head. This pretty miss and young Allen were almost certainly sweethearts, with a relationship stronger than old man Webster had suggested.

'No need,' he said, adding equivocally, 'I can speak to him later myself.'

Remembering this, Verena realised that the large man had been a police officer—which made sense of his last statement and his earlier questions.

Sensing her distress, Piers's unkind smile grew. 'Apparently the police thinks that he's the man behind the country-house robberies and have taken him into custody.'

'What! They must be mad to believe that of him.'

Sir Charles said heavily, 'The police rarely act without sufficient reason, Verena. They must believe that they have strong evidence against him.'

Tears threatening to fall, Verena said, as bravely as she could, 'But to arrest Nicholas, of all people. He's not that sort of man, you know he isn't.'

Piers laughed scornfully. 'Oh, come on, Vee. What do you know of him? Or any of us, for that matter? Nothing, really. He arrives out of nowhere, is content to be cousin John's dogsbody, and then, out of the blue, finds enough money to buy his business. It's a wonder no one suspected him before!'

Chrissie, who had arrived earlier in this conversation, proceeded to back Piers vigorously.

'I can only say, my dear Verena, that the news doesn't surprise me. I always thought that there was something suspicious about him.'

'No, you didn't,' Verena exclaimed. 'You said that he was a perfectly divine man when you first met him, you know you did.'

'Well, that was before I got to know him better. He has deceit written all over him.' She turned a scornful shoulder on Verena. 'Really, my dear, you're such a child. Anyone could deceive *you*!'

Verena lost her temper again. It was becoming a bad habit of hers where Chrissie was concerned. The words flew from her.

'Really, Chrissie, really? Anyone, but not everyone, I do assure you. For example, I know that you deceived both Grandfather and me over where you went the other weekend. You said that you were visiting the Burtons—but unfortunately Mrs Burton told me when she rang the other night that she didn't know that you were back in England! So you should know all about deceit and deceivers, shouldn't you?'

Chrissie flushed an unbecoming purple; a bad habit of hers when cornered by her stepdaughter.

'How dare you misinterpret what Joan Burton said to you! Ring her for yourself and discover that she never said anything of the sort!'

So Chrissie had doubtless suborned her old friend! Ringing her would be useless. But Verena knew what she had heard.

Sir Charles, his old face sad, said mournfully, 'Really, Miss Verena Marlowe, I do not know what has come over you these days to cause you to make such an accusation against your poor dead father's wife. I must ask you not to come down to dinner tonight whilst I consider what, concerning yourself, my best course of action ought to be.'

'*I* know what has come over her,' exclaimed Chrissie

vengefully. 'That man has. Is he your lover, Verena? I suppose that he must be to influence you so strongly.'

Verena knew that nothing which she could say would help her, would merely sound like the bleating of the lamb about to be slaughtered. Sir Charles's anguish at her behaviour was written on his face, as was Piers's mocking glee.

'I won't dignify that with an answer,' she said steadily. 'I can only hope that "truth will arise although all the world will hide it from men's eyes".'

'Oh, we all know that you read books,' mocked Chrissie. 'A pity you ever stopped. It's a much less damaging occupation than the one you've recently been following.'

She appealed to Sir Charles. 'Now you know why I don't like her having much to do with James. Such a bad example for the poor child.'

There was no answer Verena could usefully make to that, either. She sighed, and said to her grandfather, 'I will obey you, sir, and go to my room. My very presence here is a cause of trouble. But I cannot take back what I said earlier, for that would mean admitting an untruth. I have been trying to decide whether it might not be for the best for me to leave Marlowe Court and make my living in London. Recent events have proved that I ought to do so. I shall make arrangements to leave as soon as Nicholas is cleared.'

'You'll be here a long time, then,' remarked Chrissie sourly.

'Now, my dear,' rebuked Sir Charles. 'I know that what has passed must have distressed you, but "least said, soonest mended" is a fine old adage to follow. Your stepdaughter has made what, under the circumstances, is a wise decision, although it grieves me to say so. Young James must be brought up well away from the bickering and strife which has been prevalent lately. Let that be enough.'

Chrissie's smile was poisonously triumphant. 'Oh, how right you are, sir. And forgiveness is a fine thing, too.' She threw a cloying glance in Verena's direction. 'I forgive you, my dear, and hope that you will behave more wisely in the future.'

Verena didn't want Chrissie's forgiveness, but she bowed her head before she left the room and wondered whether the police would allow her to visit Nicholas so that she might find out from him what was happening.

Of course, she believed him to be innocent, but what Sir Charles had said, of the police acting only when they had good cause, had frightened her a little. And so had Piers with his talk of them knowing nothing about Nicholas before he had arrived in West Bretton.

And if the police would not allow her to see Nicholas, she would visit Uncle John and try to find out whether he had anything hopeful to tell her.

Nicholas had been taken straight to a cell in the police station by a sorrowful Sergeant Bull, who had always liked him. He sat there trying to work out a plan of campaign whereby he could prove his innocence without giving his true identity away. It was going to be difficult.

The easy thing would be to tell them who he was, call in the might and power of the Schuyler influence and the battery of high-powered lawyers whom his father employed and who would doubtless see him free in no time.

But that would be to admit defeat. It would simply prove that as soon as the going was hard he would cave in, and allow himself to be saved by the very family from which he had driven away three years ago, vowing to make his own way in the future.

So far he had succeeded even better than he might have hoped, and he was not going to allow this setback to defeat him. He thought that he might be able to establish his innocence without much trouble. His first interrogation proved otherwise.

Cameron and Finch interviewed him in a tiny airless room whose walls were chipped white-glazed lavatory bricks and whose table and chairs were made of shabby, badly painted Victorian pine.

Cameron was characteristically brisk. 'Now, Mr Allen, you can save us a great deal of trouble by admitting what we all know to be true: that you are a member of the country-house gang—most likely an important member, if not the leader. The loot hidden away at your cottage proves your guilt. Circumstantial evidence such as that added to the question of your unexplained wealth and your mysterious past can only add to the case against you.'

Unmoved, Nicholas said, as simply as he could, 'Since I am innocent of the charge on which you have arrested me, I cannot confess to anything.'

Finch attempted to be persuasive. 'If you are innocent, Mr Allen, I can see no reason why you should not tell us of your past before you came to Devon.'

'No. It has no relevance to this business. What does have relevance is that on the night when the loot must have been placed in my shed, my dog, Hercules, surprised the conspirators who placed it there, was silenced and left for dead. I have evidence of that.'

'These conspirators, Mr Allen?' It was Cameron speaking now, all aggression. 'Who are they? Why should you have enemies who wish to see you convicted of a crime you have not committed? Can't you make up a better story than that to convince us of your innocence? No, no, what we do have here, I believe, is a classic case of thieves falling out. Why should you continue to protect those who informed on you, probably to protect themselves? Come clean—and take your revenge.'

'Informed on me? How?' As Nicholas might have expected, he received no answer to this question.

'Tell us who you are, where you came from, and where you got a large sum of money from to buy the *Clarion*, and I might tell you that. Oh, and the expensive watch which you are wearing? May I see it?'

'My watch? Why?'

'Please?' Cameron put out a large hand.

Nicholas unwillingly unfastened his watch and handed it over. He had smoothed off the names on the inscription on the back, and was pleased that he had done so. He cursed his untoward sentimentality in keeping it at all.

Cameron examined it closely. 'A Patek Philippe, eh? What house did you steal this from…Mr Office Boy?'

'No house. It's mine. My father gave it to me.'

'Oh, pull the other one. Your father, the millionaire, I suppose! This is getting tiresome. Finch, ask him about his supposed journeys to London.'

'My supposed journeys to London.' Nicholas stared at his interrogators incredulously. 'There's nothing supposed about them.'

'No? The last one coincided with the raid on Westermere Hall—as I suppose you know.' This was Finch, leaning forward terrier-like. 'Motive, opportunity, possession of the loot, refusal to speak of your past—criminal, is it? What more do we need to convict you? Save yourself a long sentence by confessing is my best advice.'

Nicholas began to laugh. To his hearers' surprise there was nothing hysterical in it. It was solid laughter, rumbling from a large chest. Nicholas did not remember that he had seen his father do exactly this in order to wrongfoot an adversary when engaged in hard bargaining.

'You are repeating yourselves, gentlemen. If it were not that I am involved I would find this amusing, Sergeant Finch. As it is—it's still amusing.'

'Share the joke with us, Allen,' Cameron snarled at him.

Nicholas registered that the 'Mister' had disappeared. He leaned forward to outstare the sergeant, whom he thought was the brighter of the two. 'The thought of what fools the pack of you will look when I prove my innocence. As I assure you I can.'

Finch flushed. His acid reply was never made. There was a rap on the door and Ellis put his head round it.

'I need to speak to you both urgently,' he said. 'Sergeant Bull will guard the prisoner for us.'

'Very well. Come on, Finch—you can carry on later.'

Bull sat down opposite to Nicholas with a twinkle in his eye. 'Not going to overwhelm me and try to escape, are you, lad?'

'Not likely.'

'Set of fools,' offered Bull comfortably. 'All your pals in West Bretton know that they're wasting their time with you.'

Nicholas smiled. 'It's nice to know that I still have friends.' He meant every word he said.

'Now, now, Nick, you don't live with a chap for three years in a town this size and not know his quality, do you?'

'Have you any idea what this latest development is about?'

'None, but it's excited DI Ellis. What can you have been doing, Nick? Getting ready to rob Buckingham Palace?'

'Something like that.' He lay back in his chair. 'Do you think that you could find us all a cup of tea when Laurel and Hardy come back?'

'Surely, lad. And a fag. No, I forgot, you don't smoke.'

'At times like this I feel like one, but best not. My father would never forgive me.' Because he was relaxed, despite his predicament, Nicholas's usual reserve about his past had disappeared.

Bull laughed. 'So you do have a dad! They're making a big thing of your refusal to tell them about your past. Why don't you do what they want, and then we can all go home.'

Nicholas was pleasantly short. 'Not yet. Not unless I have to.'

'Knowing you, it can't be shameful.'

'No, indeed. Quite the contrary. Now we'd better look solemn. They're coming back.'

Nicholas thought that he knew what Ellis might have found in the cottage and what he had to tell Cameron.

Alone with his fellow officers Ellis began his story. He had a large portfolio of papers in his hand.

'I've found some odd things about chummy which might throw a different light on him.'

'Oh, and what are they?' Cameron asked eagerly.

'You'd never guess. It appears that Nicholas Allen does have another name. Two to be exact.'

'So chummy *is* a villain!'

'Not exactly. Not in the way you're thinking. He keeps his private and financial papers in apple-pie order, by the way—just like his cottage. From them I've discovered that he writes and illustrates kids' books about dragons under the name of Merlin. My little lad loves them. No one in West Bretton knows that he's an author.

'I had a word with Bull about them without telling him why. He's full of excuses for Nick Allen, says he's a sterling figure, works hard for John Webster and all that. Nothing about him being a writer. There's more.' He broke off, grinning.

Cameron grew impatient. 'Look, Fred, I know that you think that you ought to be on the Halls. Just tell us, no fancy trimmings. I've had enough of that from him'—and he jerked a thumb in the direction of the room in which Nicholas and Bull were waiting.

'He's also written another book, not a kid's story, under the name of Arthur Merlin—and that's the real find. It's the latest best-seller, *Put money in thy purse.*'

Cameron said slowly, 'Tell me that again, Fred. You're saying that young Allen in there has written this notorious novel about the top nobs in society and the government that's going to make the writer a fortune, they say—if he's not horse-whipped to death before he earns it.'

'You've got it, Jock. There's still more. He was in London on the day Westermere Hall was turned over. There's a letter from his publisher to prove it. So that cock won't fight.'

'Forget that. Would what he has earned from the books be enough to enable him to buy the *Clarion*?'

'Not on its own. But add it to a supposed legacy and it might. Depends on the size of the legacy.'

'Damn. There goes part of our proof. Unless we can get a warrant to make Coutts disclose the details of the bank account from which the legacy came. But look at it this way, there's still his refusal to tell us of his past, and the stuff being found at his cottage, to explain. Plus the fact that the robberies began almost immediately after he arrived here. None of this points to him being innocent.'

Ellis shook his head. 'It doesn't point to him being guilty either. Even the stuff in the shed is only circumstantial. Is he still claiming he's innocent?'

'Loud and clear. But he's got a lot of questions to answer.'

'Look, Jock, I know that you believe that you've found our man, but don't you think that a little caution might be in order?'

'I might if it weren't that most of what we've found tallies with the anonymous letter. We've got chummy behind bars where he can't get away, and where we can question him. And there's another thing to consider. Interpol thinks that the men—or man—behind this know their onions. They know where to go and what to take. In other words, men of education. Our man is educated all right. Webster thought he'd been to Oxford, and I agree with him. He's a clever devil, whatever else. Look at his books. We're going to hang on to him—see if he'll crack.'

'Fat chance,' muttered Finch.

'Eh, what's that, Sergeant? Speak up, lad, if you want me to hear you.'

Finch risked giving his opinion. 'He's a tough, sir, whatever else. He'll not crack. Educated toughs are the worst of all.'

'Time will tell. Look, I've got an idea…'

Cameron's idea was lost for a moment. The telephone rang. 'Answer that, Finch. It's probably for us.'

It was. Finch held the telephone's handpiece out to Cameron. 'It's Scotland Yard. For you, sir.'

Ellis and Finch, watching and listening to Cameron's side of the call which consisted mainly of 'Yes, sir,' 'No, sir', and 'Of course, sir,', were joined by Sergeant Yeo, who had been making enquiries around the town about Nicholas Allen and his activities. As he was later to report, he had met little co-operation, and much hostility.

Cameron finally hung up the handpiece with an enraged bang. 'Seems,' he said disgustedly 'that Special Branch has insisted that they're sending along their big-pot roving freelance who'll no doubt tell us all how to do our job! He's already on his way. We've to find lodgings for him. I'll get Bull on to that later.

'What I'd really like to do is clear this up before he gets

here. You have a go at him this time, Fred. Change of scene won't hurt.'

'OK by me. Who's the big pot, though?'

'Name's Schuyler. Ralph Schuyler.'

'Oh, oh, a very big pot indeed. War hero and one-time member of MI6—or so rumour says—and related to *that* family. This must be an important case. I'll start on Allen immediately. Come on, Yeo.'

But he had no more luck with Nicholas than Cameron had. Bull brought them all, including Nicholas, tea and scones—buttered, no jam—when Cameron and Finch joined in the fun later.

'Anyone would think that I was about to start another Great War by the amount of top brass needed to question me,' Nicholas drawled as he drank tea strong enough for a teaspoon to stand up in and ate his buttered scones with relish.

'You do know that I've had nothing to eat since breakfast and it's now mid-afternoon? I would have thought that it was torture by starvation you were using to try to make me talk if Bull here hadn't included me in the tea party.'

'See that the prisoner has something more substantial to eat, Sergeant Bull, when this session is over,' commanded Cameron nastily. 'Can't have him complaining to his MP about police brutality, can we? Let me recapitulate, Allen, this is the impasse we've reached. You assert that there's nothing sinister about the fact that you refuse to tell us of your past life, and can offer no explanation to account for the loot in your shed.'

'Well, I have explained where the money came from to buy John's business, and you know that my visits to London weren't mysterious—unless visiting one's publisher is to be considered vaguely criminal. As for the stuff in the shed—that was put there to implicate me, the attack on my dog occurring after they woke him up.'

Cameron sneered at him. 'Oh, yes, that business about a deep conspiracy to involve innocent Mr Nicholas Allen in the country-house robberies. That won't wash other than in films and thrillers by Sapper and Sidney Horler. Who would want to do such a thing to you?'

Nicholas spread his hands. 'Now that I can't tell you. Perhaps it was simply a diversionary tactic to draw attention away from the real criminal.'

'Who would have to know you well enough to write us a letter giving chapter and verse about you and your goings-on. So he's reasonably local.'

'True. But he didn't know me well enough to know that I was Arthur Merlin, did he? Or that I raised the money legitimately.'

Cameron gave up. The day had been a long one and this fellow Schuyler would be arriving before it was over, and would doubtless want to tackle chummy before he settled down for the night.

'See that Bull feeds the prisoner,' he ordered Finch, and to Nicholas, 'We've not finished with you yet. A night in the slammer might cool you down a little and convince you to tell us the truth.'

Nicholas was taken back to his cell, to wait for Sergeant Bull and his delayed lunch. He thought wistfully of Verena and of his lost appointment with her. He wondered whether she had heard the news of his arrest, and what she thought about it. He hoped that she would believe in his innocence.

Verena had decided that she must try to see Nicholas later that afternoon. She was rather hazy about whether prisoners were allowed visitors. Nevertheless she fetched her handbag, cardigan and straw hat before setting off for West Bretton.

She met Piers in the Entrance Hall. He was carrying a small suitcase and a lightweight summer coat.

'Where are you off to?' she asked abruptly, a little surprised. Nothing had been said about his going away.

Piers was all friendly charm. 'Oh. To town for a few days. Take in a few shows, look up a few old friends. Be back after about a week. Need a break from rural bliss, you know. And where are you off to? To West Bretton, I suppose, to visit your favourite criminal. May I offer you a lift?'

He said this very airily. He had decided earlier that it might not be a bad thing to leave the scene of the crime, as it were, until Nick Allen had been taken to Exeter Gaol. So far everything had gone swimmingly, and with luck, even if they eventually let young Allen go, it might be some time before they did.

In the meantime there would be no more robberies—to add fuel to the police's belief that they had caught the criminal organising them.

'Thank you, Piers. Yes, I am going to see Nicholas, if they will let me. I know that everyone at Marlowe Court believes that he is guilty, but I still can't believe it.'

'Oh, love does odd things to a person's common sense. I'm sure that Sir Charles is right. The police usually know what they are doing. Hop in, old thing. Don't want to miss the train.'

Nicholas and Sergeant Bull were playing cribbage in his cell when Verena arrived. Mrs Bull had provided him with an excellent lunch. A Cornish pasty, new potatoes, fresh garden peas and a thick gravy. Strawberries from the Sergeant's garden made a splendid ending for the meal.

The duty constable, another old friend of Nicholas's, took them both the news that Miss Marlowe from Marlowe Court had arrived at the police station and was asking to speak to Mr Allen. He refused to call Nicholas the prisoner.

'She's here,' exclaimed Nicholas, forgetting his winning hand. 'What an absolute brick she is! Do let her speak to me, Sergeant.'

'I'm not rightly sure that I ought to. Constable, the visiting officers have all gone to Bromley's across the road for egg on toast or whatever they're serving today. Go and find out whether she may.'

Cameron and his cohorts arrived a few minutes later, full of Bromley's good food—and resentment against the unkind stares of the locals, and their even more unkind remarks about the police's ill-treatment of Nick Allen. 'What do they furriners know about us, anyway?' being the usual loud comment designed to be overheard and to put them in their place.

'Who is she, anyway?' Cameron asked Bull.

'Sir Charles Marlowe's daughter. He owns Marlowe Court, the big house down the road. He's been a magistrate for donkey's years. Friend of the Chief Constable—wouldn't do to offend him.'

'Oh, let her see him. So long as Finch is present.'

'She's not likely to be trying to help him escape,' offered Bull. 'Seeing who she is.'

'Ah, but he might say something incriminating whilst he's off his guard. Finch must be there.'

Finch led Verena into the interview room, and placed her chair on one side of the table and Nicholas's on the other.

'Sergeant Bull will fetch him,' he told her.

How would Nicholas look? Would he be wearing handcuffs? Were they treating him properly? Verena's notions of what went on in police stations were extremely hazy.

To her relief and joy Nicholas looked as he always did. Calm and in command of himself.

'Where's the screwdriver and the jemmy?' he asked her, winking naughtily at Sergeant Finch. 'The crook's girl friend always smuggles them in. Usually in her handbag. Yours doesn't look big enough.'

'Oh, Nicholas, don't joke. It's not funny. Everyone at the Court is being so unkind, but I'm sure that you're innocent. I can't believe that they've any real evidence against you.'

He leaned forward, and regardless of the watching Sergeant he kissed her lightly on the lips. 'Sweet witch, I joke because as a poet once said, "And if I laugh, 'tis that I may not weep." Regardless of that and in fairness to the police, they did find part of the proceeds of the robbery at Westermere Hall in my shed—which had suddenly sprouted a lock.'

'A lock on Jesse's shed? He never had a lock on it. No one ever locks things up in West Bretton. But how did the loot—and the lock—get there?'

'Remember the day when I discovered that Hercules had disappeared, and we found him half dead with his leg broken and his head injured, and we took him to the vet?'

'Of course, I do. How could I forget it?'

Nicholas half-turned towards Sergeant Finch. 'Are you listening carefully, Sergeant? I wouldn't like you to miss any of this. I believe, my darling, that Hercules woke up and started to bark at whoever was fixing the lock and putting the boxes in the shed, and that they disposed of him—but not quite efficiently enough. I thought I heard something in the night—but by the time I woke up properly and went to the window, I couldn't see anything. I've twice told the assembled coppers this—to no avail.'

'It would make sense, wouldn't it?' said Verena excitedly.

'So it would, but they're so sure that I'm the master criminal behind the robberies that they don't believe my explanation about Hercules' injuries.'

'Suppose I told them,' she offered eagerly. 'They'd have to believe me.'

'You already have told them, just now. Look at him, Sergeant Finch is all agog. Trouble is—' and he kissed her again, on the tip of her nose this time '—they will only believe that I have you in my wicked spell and that you will say anything to save my bacon. Now that they've chucked me in the slammer, you're a proper gangster's moll, my love—except that you haven't got a gat in your handbag.'

'What's a gat, Nicholas? And how can you be so cheerful?'

'A gat is Yankee slang for a gun, and I'm cheerful because I'm innocent. You know, I've just kissed you three times, and you haven't kissed me back once. Don't you think I deserve at least one little peck?'

Verena blushed. 'But he—that sergeant—is watching us. I don't like to.'

'It's his fault if he has to watch us making gentle love instead of plotting together to rob another country house. Come on, Vee, remember the motto of the Order of the Garter, to which your revered ancestor, Sir Beverley Marlowe, belonged. *"Honi soit qui mal y pense."* Evil be to him who evil thinks. Kiss me—and shame the watcher.'

So she did. Still blushing, she leaned forward and gave him a ladylike kiss on the cheek.

'Splendid. You must do it again sometime—a bit lower down, and more to the left! And how is the ineffable Piers taking my sad news?'

'Ineffably—as you might suppose. He's off to London tonight.'

'And Chrissie, the ultimate bottle blonde?'

Verena gasped. 'Is she? Is she really? I always thought that it was natural.'

'Alas, no. You are a trusting soul, my sweet—as Sergeant Finch would tell you—since he must know that you believe me innocent.'

'How do you know about Chrissie's hair?'

'Alas, a gentleman never tells. I knew an actress once— are you listening, Sergeant, my lost past is surfacing?—and she told me a great many similar secrets.'

'Aren't you worried that your lost past might worry *me*?'

'No, for you must be aware that I have lived the life of St Francis of Assisi since I came to West Bretton—apart from one fling with the late lamented Daisy Goring. The actress is as lost as my past. My present is all that matters— and you are the nicest thing in it.'

'Well, so long as the nicest thing isn't the actress—or Chrissie, who has been her usual charmingly spiteful self where you are concerned.'

'Ah, but I am not concerned. Seriously, Vee, do not worry too much on my behalf. All is not yet over. Try to convince Sir Charles and John that I am not the villain they might think me.'

'But who is, then? Who has done this to you?'

'For the life of me I can't think. Probably I'm just a usefully innocent sprat thrown by the sharks to keep the coppers away from them.'

'As simple as that,' she said despairingly, fetching out her handkerchief, 'and as a result you are in prison.'

Nicholas saw that the tears were about to fall: the tears which he had been holding at bay by his cheerful impudence ever since she had entered the interview room.

'You are not to cry. I forbid you to cry. Sergeant Finch forbids you to cry. His superiors will think that he has been ill-treating you—and that would never do. Even worse if they thought that I had been ill-treating you—they would simply add that to the list of charges against me.'

Verena's tears dried up. Against her will she began to laugh.

'You always do that to me, my dearest,' she said tenderly. 'Make me laugh.'

'Better than making you cry. I see that Sergeant Finch is growing restive. I fear that our time is up.'

The Sergeant rose and confirmed that it was.

'One kiss before we go.' Nicholas leaned across the table, took her face in his hands, and gently, oh, so gently, kissed her on the lips. He whispered lovingly, 'May we meet again soon in better circumstances, my love. No, don't cry, I absolutely forbid it,' for he had seen the tears threatening to fall again.

'I shan't,' Verena told him, but her mouth trembled precariously. 'I'll be brave, I promise you.'

'That's the stuff. *Nil carborundum*, my dearest dear, and if you don't know what that means I'll translate it for you the next time that we are alone. It's *au revoir*, remember, and not goodbye. Give my love to Hercules when you visit the vet.'

She watched the Sergeant lead him back to the cells, her heart going with him.

On the way out of the station she met Sergeant Bull, who took one look at her wan face and said, 'Don't worry, Miss Marlowe, I'll look after him as much as they'll let me. I'm sure that they're all barking up the wrong tree, and I'm afraid it may be some time before they bark up the right one. Let's hope that this chap that they're expecting tonight has more sense than this lot.'

He had meant to comfort her and he had. In the same way her presence had comforted Nicholas. Somewhere outside the police station, the real world went its way, and with luck, it might not be long before he rejoined it.

Chapter Twelve

Piers Marlowe had travelled in one direction, Ralph Schuyler in the other. He had caught an early afternoon train and arrived in West Bretton before anyone expected him.

He was not quite what Cameron and his cohorts had expected when he walked into the room where a blackboard had been set up, showing the dates of the robberies and the information which they had gathered about Nicholas.

Finch had insisted that they enter up the attack on Hercules even though Cameron had dismissed it as irrelevant to their enquiries.

'Why?' asked Cameron, exasperatedly.

'Well, sir, it's like this. I read a Sherlock Holmes story once—'

Cameron had interrupted him with a bellow. 'Why are you wasting my time with your literary preferences, Finch? We've a job to do here.'

'If you'll allow me to finish, sir. He was investigating a crime which took place in the night, and he said something like, ''I'll draw your attention to the curious incident of the dog in the night-time.'' The person he was speaking to said,

''The dog did nothing in the night-time,'' and Sherlock replied ''That was the curious incident''.'

'Meaning what, for God's sake, Finch? You'll try my patience once too often one of these days.'

'Meaning this, sir. In this case the curious incident was that the dog was undoubtedly injured, and was meant to be killed at around the same time that the stolen goods were hidden in the shed. If the goods were planted there, it would explain an otherwise unmotivated attack. We've had good evidence that Allen is a popular figure around here, and Sergeant Bull tells me that the locals were upset by the attack on the dog.'

'He has a point,' put in Ellis tactfully.

'*If* you accept that chummy is telling the truth. Oh, very well, Sergeant, chalk it up.'

Finch was doing as he was told when Ralph walked in. He was escorted by Sergeant Bull, who had been asked to stay on duty until after his arrival.

'Mr Ralph Schuyler to see you, Inspector.'

They stared at him. At his perfect tailoring, shoes by Lobb, hair cut by someone equally the master of his trade—and at his compact muscular body that Savile Row tailoring could not conceal, and the hard cold face above it.

The other thing which struck them was that he bore an odd likeness to the man they were investigating. He had the same thick glossy hair, strong chin and amber eyes.

Bull, who had been in the late war, recognised him immediately as an ex-soldier, as did Cameron, a little reluctantly. He had hoped to be suitably contemptuous of some untrained gentleman interfering in the activities of good hard-working professionals. It was plain that this man was no languid amateur.

'I would be grateful,' Ralph said, after introductions had been made, 'if, before I said anything, you would brief me on the state of play.' He gestured at the blackboard. 'I can see that you have all been working hard.'

Cameron led him through their operation ever since he had been given the anonymous letter, which he handed to Ralph for his inspection.

'Hardly a watertight case yet,' was his comment at the end. 'A number of promising pointers to Allen's guilt have been shot down. You say that he's undoubtedly this writer, Merlin, who's causing all the excitement at the moment?'

'No doubt at all. We found the contracts for the children's books and the novel when we searched his cottage. A meticulous man, young Allen. DI Ellis had no difficulty in sorting out his affairs when he examined his papers.'

'Hmm.' Ralph picked up the chalk and advanced on the blackboard. 'But you're all convinced that he is the man?'

Silence followed. 'Do I construe that as assent or dissent?' he drawled, after a fashion which reminded Finch, at least, of the man he had recently heard talking to his girl.

Probably just the way the nobs carry on, he reflected. Then, Hey, hang on a minute—that must mean that Allen *is* a nob!

'No matter,' Ralph continued. 'Let's make a list of reasons why he could be innocent.'

Cameron contributed nothing. Ellis and Finch offered the dog, and the destruction of the letter's suggestions that the trips to London and the money to buy John's business were proofs of guilt.

'On the other hand,' Cameron said, 'we must take on board the loot found in his shed, his refusal to speak of his past—and his expensive watch. Glorified office boys don't usually own Patek Philippe's.'

Bull said in his bluff fashion, 'Evidence of character, sir, from we who have known him since he settled here. He's a popular fellow, and no mistake. Hardworking and a good pal. Member of the cricket club, the Marlowe Arms darts team in winter—though he doesn't drink much—and helps with the British Legion. All good points in my book.'

Ralph looked at him. 'Ex-soldier, are you, Sergeant Bull?'

'Aye, sir. I was in the Guards. Demobbed Sergeant Bull, lucky to be alive—and you, sir?'

'Infantry like yourself. Would you rate him as a good chap to depend on in a tight corner?'

'That I would. I got to know them as were, as well as them as weren't, before I left the Army.'

Cameron said morosely, 'With due respect, sir, this isn't getting us very far.'

Ralph said, gently for him, 'Given we know nothing of his origins, and that he may—as you suspect—have a criminal record, the opinion of a man of Sergeant Bull's experience is worth hearing. Now, I should like to speak to the prisoner alone.'

'Alone, sir?'

'Yes. He knows you all by now. One thing about him that you are all agreed on is that he is clever. We can take it that he now knows you as well as you think that you know him. He won't know me—or what to expect from me—and so he won't have any defences erected against me before I even walk into the room to question him.'

'Makes sense,' agreed Ellis.

Finch decided to share his belief with a man whom he thought was more open-minded than Cameron. Cameron was a good copper with a good record, but if he had a fault it was that of making his mind up rather early and refusing to change it.

'One thing, sir, which has only recently struck me. I think that whatever he is now, he was once what we call, begging your pardon, sir, a nob. He's more like you than us—or the townsfolk—if you see what I mean. It's a way of speaking more than anything else.'

Silence fell.

'Interesting,' agreed Ralph. 'I'm looking forward to meeting him.'

'Insolent young bastard,' growled Cameron.

'Even more intriguing,' said Ralph. 'Set it up, Sergeant Bull. We've no time to waste.'

Nicholas was wondering how much longer he would have to wait before his supper arrived. His stomach, as well as his watch which Cameron had reluctantly handed back to him, told him that it was abominably late.

When the door opened it was Sergeant Bull. But no tea, alas, ready to lead him to the interview room again.

'I thought that they weren't trying to starve me into sub-mission, but it looks as though they are,' Nicholas an-nounced cheerfully. 'If it isn't tea or supper, what is it this time?'

Ralph had asked that the prisoner should not be given his name. 'The less he knows of me, the better, for the reasons I have given you. If he has been a nob, he might know who I am, and what I was. I don't want him alerted in any way. Just tell him he's going to be questioned again.'

'Big pot from London is going to tackle you next,' Bull told him. 'Seems a fair-minded chap.'

'Unlike Cameron, would you say?'

'Not for me to comment, Nick. Here you are.'

Nicholas sat down in the cheerless little room. 'This is getting boring,' he announced to the walls—and began re-hearsing, as Ralph had predicted, what he might say to 'the big pot from London'.

Matters weren't about to stay boring for very long. The door opened and his new inquisitor walked in.

It was his cousin Ralph.

Piers had reached London earlier than he had expected. He had rung up one of his latest flames before he had left Marlowe Court.

By seven o'clock he was in Gertie Wilde's flat. She greeted him with enthusiasm. After all, Piers Marlowe was rich, had an old name, and was great fun. For an actress who was at present resting in the theatre but was appearing regularly in British films he would be a catch.

Gertie had been involved in an unsavoury divorce, and since then her career had faltered. But she was still as lovely as ever, and good in bed, too. It was the best thing she did.

Her maid let Piers in. 'Madame's not ready yet. She asks you to wait in the drawing-room.'

Piers was restless. His plans seemed to be going well—so far. On the other hand, once he had reached his flat he'd had a telephone call from Switzerland which was rather worrying. It warned him that some depressing news had come through which might suggest that Interpol was on to them. And it wasn't the arrest of Allen to which he had been referring.

He roamed round the room which was full of trophies, knicknacks and photographs in ornate frames. He picked them up, looked at them distractedly and put them down.

There was a largish photograph at the back of a whole group of them on the grand piano. Its frame was even more gaudily elaborate than usual. He leaned over to see why it was so blessed—to stare at it disbelievingly.

Smiling at him was a younger version of Nicholas Allen! It was a head-and-shoulders studio portrait and was signed with a flourish in one corner—All my love, Nicholas.

Precisely at that moment Gertie entered the room, to find Piers approaching her, the photograph in his hand.

'Tell me, Gertie, who the devil's this?'

His whole manner was so unlike that of the man she knew that Gertie was suddenly afraid of him.

'Why?' she stammered. 'Why do you ask?'

'Answer me,' he gritted through clenched teeth. 'Who is he?'

'Nothing to do with me now. An old flame from years ago. I should have thrown it away.'

'For God's sake, Gertie. Answer me! Who is he?'

'It's Nicholas Schuyler. Nicholas Allen Schuyler to be exact. I told you, he's long gone.' Only jealousy, she thought could explain Piers's flaming anger.

Piers felt as though the whole world had fallen in on him. 'One of *the* Schuylers, is he?'

'Are there any others?'

'That's enough, Gertie. Have you seen him lately?'

'No one's seen him lately. He disappeared from society three years ago.'

Three years ago Nicholas Allen Schuyler had driven into West Bretton. Of all the people in the world, he had chosen to frame a member of one of England's most powerful families!

And no wonder his face had seemed vaguely familiar. His photograph and his wild doings—on and off the Brooklands race track—had been regularly featured in the London dailies.

Sooner or later Allen would acknowledge who he was in order to save his skin, and the search for the sender of the letter would begin—and his recent informant was sure that they were all on the edge of being discovered even without that.

Piers flung the photograph down so hard that the glass shattered.

'Sorry, Gertie. Got to go.'

'What? Now? You've only just got here!'

'Damnation, Gertie, do you never listen to a word I say? I'm going. Now.'

He was out of the door as he spoke. He had left all his personal belongings—many of them incriminating—at West Bretton, and he had to return there to recover them before leaving England for good. Fortunately all his earnings from the robberies were safe in a Swiss bank.

All the way back to West Bretton he damned Nicholas Schuyler for taking Verena from him and depriving him of oany chance of giving up the dangerous game which he had been playing.

A spectator would have found it difficult to decide which of the two men in the interview room was the more surprised since each of them displayed an admirable poker face to the other.

Ralph was the first to speak. 'Well, well, if it isn't my nephew, Claus. And in the chokey, too, the last place I would have thought to find you.'

'So, you are the big pot from London, Uncle Ralph—or should it be Cousin? I never quite know which. And do call me Nicholas, if you please. Claus is long gone. Does that last quip mean that you have been looking for me?'

'No, indeed. I'm simply in the middle of doing my duty for King and Country. Although your cousin Gis did tell me when we were last together at Padworth that he had a notion that I might be meeting you soon. He thought that the circumstances would be odd—but not, I think, so odd as a prison cell.'

'Oh, so he's still at his tricks, is he? Doesn't he find it

troublesome to be so infallible? He's been rivalling the Pope lately.'

This irreverent comment set Ralph smiling. 'You always had a wicked tongue, Nicholas, and now I know that you have a wicked pen, too. I wonder what your esteemed father would say if he knew that you were the author of *Put money in thy purse*?'

'A lot—and none of it complimentary. I think he'd prefer the dragon books, don't you? No satiric nonsense there. Sergeant Bull told me that you—or rather the big pot from London—were to be my latest inquisitor—so, inquisit away, big pot. Don't let my being your relative stop you. After all, I am a renegade—the Schuyler who got away. I wonder how much my esteemed parent spent trying to trace me. Or did he simply decide to let me stew in my own juice?

'And do sit down so that I can, Ralph. I'm weak at the moment from lack of food.'

Ralph sat down opposite to him. 'I've talked to the police officers on the case, and I have heard from them about your denial of complicity in the country-house robberies. Now you tell me your story.'

'OK. I think that we can skip the past that I refuse to reveal to them—you know that already. Here goes.'

With admiral lucidity and precision Nicholas went over everything which had happened to him since he had bought the *Clarion* from John Webster and had found that Hercules was missing.

He also gave Ralph the details of his trips to London, 'on the latest of which I accidentally met Cousin Gis. He told me that I was happy—which I already knew. He didn't warn me that I would shortly be banged up in the nick. His crystal ball must have been on the blink that afternoon.'

Ralph made notes in a small book, occasionally stopping Nicholas in order to ask him to repeat something.

When Nicholas had finished he made no reference to what he had heard, but said instead, 'You didn't tell them your real name—or anything of your past. Why not? Any question of your not having enough money to buy the *Clarion* would have flown out of the window immediately. They would have treated you much more carefully, too. Schuyler is a name of power.'

'Oh, dear, Uncle Ralph, I thought that you were cleverer than that. Why do you think I changed it? I wanted to be myself—not someone who always had a brand on them marked ''handle carefully''. I know that I am innocent, and that on the evidence they have the authorities would find it difficult to put me in court, let alone convict me, and I preferred to hope and work for salvation as Nick Allen, not as a Godalmighty Anglo-American wunderkind.'

Ralph nodded. 'Yes, I understand that. My surname hasn't always been an asset for me.'

He changed the subject again. 'They tell me, or Finch tells me, that you have a girl friend locally and that she has visited you.'

He looked at his notebook although he knew quite well what he was going to say next. 'Miss Verena Marlowe. Her grandfather is a JP and a great friend of the Chief Constable and the Lord Lieutenant of the county. You didn't think to ask him for help?'

'He doesn't approve of her having much to do with anyone as lowly as Nicholas Allen.'

'Nicholas Schuyler would be different. Your silence as to your origins is commendable as a point of principle, but in practical terms it hasn't been exactly helpful. Tell me, Claus…I mean Nicholas, have you lately been in the habit of making visits to Switzerland?'

Nicholas stared at him. 'Is that a serious question?'

'Eminently so. Answer it, if you would.'

'Look, Ralph, I've been living almost entirely on my pay from John Webster, on my income from the dragon books and I have occasionally drawn a small, a very small amount of money from a non-Schuyler legacy which I have deliberately not used very much because I preferred to live on what I could earn myself. Bearing that in mind, it didn't leave anything over to pay for trips to Switzerland.

'Furthermore, John Webster and the entire town of West Bretton will tell you that I've never been away from it for more than three days at a time. I admit that I've had a large advance for the novel but that, together with money from the legacy, is what I used to buy the *Clarion*. Does that answer your question?'

'Oh, yes. Leaving aside that we are related and that I know you well, I am satisfied of your innocence from what you—and the detectives outside—have told me. Putting everything together, there is no case whatsoever for holding you any longer, or even for considering that you should have an eye kept on you. I believe that the loot was either planted on you to be left there until it was collected—or better still, that you were set up as a suspect so that the police would waste their time chasing you.'

Nicholas said coolly, 'If so, they succeeded admirably on the last count. What interests me is how did they know that the loot was in my shed?'

'Because of an anonymous letter, and—do admit it—the details in it matched your apparently dubious background. The dates fitted, the stolen goods were in your shed, you wear an expensive watch; although apparently poverty-stricken, you can easily find the money to buy a business, and you also make mysterious trips to London. All but the goods in the shed have now been accounted for.

'There is, however, besides what I have already suggested, a plausible explanation for them which puts you in the clear. The key to that is, as Sergeant Finch says, the curious case of the dog in the night-time which must have been attacked when the loot was brought here.

'Besides that, I know some things about the thieves which neither the officers of the Met, nor the locals, know which makes your guilt extremely unlikely. All of this means that I shall tell them that you are in the clear, and that this decision has nothing to do with our being uncle and nephew, although DI Cameron will doubtless make disbelieving noises when I tell him this. Strictly speaking, I should have taken myself off the case when I entered this room and recognised you.

'But, and it's a big but, I believe that you, all unknowingly, hold the key to the mystery of who wrote the letter, and who better than I to help you to find it? I'm going to ask you to be patient and to stay apparently a prisoner overnight. I don't want the writer of the note to know that his plot has failed.'

Nicholas sighed. 'You're asking a lot of me, dear uncle—a night in the nick on a hard bed. I suppose so, if you say so.'

'Oh, I think that we might secretly arrange something better for you than that. You may not know that the townsfolk here think highly of you. Hardworking, honest, good at your job, cheerful and in love with the Squire's daughter. They didn't believe for one moment that you were a thief. You've become a model for the industrious apprentice—which would surprise your father more than a little.'

Nicholas laughed. 'After which flattery, put on with a trowel, I will, of course, consent to remain a suspicious character until the morning.'

Ralph rose. 'I'll go now, not only to recommend that

you no longer be considered a suspect, but also that to-morrow we have a session with you where we try to dis-cover why you were framed, as the Yankees say, and who could have done it, because he must be heavily involved with the country-house gang. I hope you understand that I shall have to give your identity away to the police because I must declare my relationship with you.'

Nicholas said sorrowfully, 'I do understand, but I can't say that I'm happy about it. If you had been anyone else…' He left the sentence unfinished.

'Exactly. I shall, of course, ask them to keep your real name a secret. There is one more thing that I must say to you. When all this becomes public, as it will once the case is solved, then your identity might be revealed anyway.

'You're a journalist, so I'm sure that you're realistic enough to know that what I'm saying is the truth. Which brings me to my next point, and that is your father and mother. Your mother is still very upset and hurt by your disappearance—and so, I believe, although he says little, is your father.

'When you first left Padworth, most of the family thought that it would not be long before you surfaced again, asking for help—although Gis and I never did. You proved them wrong, and what you have done at West Bretton, as well as your success as a writer, also proves that you could make a career for yourself without family influence to help you. In some ways you are the most remarkable Schuyler of all.'

Nicholas said shortly, 'What are you really trying to tell me, Ralph?'

'That you should make your peace with your father and mother. Oh, he doesn't like your novel, but he admits that a clever man wrote it. As for your mother, she has grieved for you ever since you left. She often says to me and Gis,

"If only I could know that he is safe and well." Think about it, Nicholas. You could make that concession because you've nothing left to prove.'

The habit of the last three years was strong in him. 'Yes, I will think about it, but I'm making no promises.'

Ralph's nod was cool. 'There's also another thing which you ought to consider, and that is whether you are playing quite fair by Miss Marlowe in not telling her, not only who you really are, but also that you are Arthur Merlin. I must say, by the by, how much I admire your choice of a name there. A neat conceit.'

'You're not going to talk me round, Ralph, by throwing compliments at me—I value them about as much as I did the criticisms which I lived with for twenty-six years. I'll repeat my earlier answer. I'll think about it. One thing, you may tell the police who and what I am, but no one else. If anyone is to do that, it must be me. It's my secret and you are not my keeper.'

Ralph had to be content with that. He acknowledged to himself that young Claus had grown into a formidable man who was more like his father than he might care to acknowledge.

He left him to tell Cameron and the others of his relationship with Nicholas and his belief that he was innocent.

'A Schuyler! You're sure of that?'

'I've known him since he was born.'

'In that case you shouldn't have interviewed him, you know that…sir.' Cameron's voice was reproving.

'Yes, I do know that—on the other hand, I have other knowledge which I used when I questioned him. Interpol has a different informant, who revealed a great deal about the operation and how it was run which ran counter to the notion that young Allen was masterminding it. He said that he didn't know who the criminal overlord was, but that he was a society gent who lived in London as well as in the West Country. Now all the evidence shows that Nicholas Allen does not live between London and West Bretton or visit Switzerland.'

Cameron said, 'Interpol's informant might be no more accurate than ours.'

'Ah, but he also told us of other things which I am not at liberty to divulge to you but which are known to be accurate. Very little about yours was—as your blackboard shows.'

'Your nephew might be a minor figure in the conspiracy, though.'

'Not on what is known of him. For one thing, he wouldn't have had the time—look at what he's been doing for the past three years and try to fit being even a minor member of the gang into that.'

Grudgingly Cameron conceded that the big pot was right.

'And you will also agree that we free Allen, but ask him to remain an apparent prisoner tonight in order to deceive whoever planted the loot and sent the incriminating letter. We can all meet tomorrow morning to see if we can work out who did send it—and why. We've had a long day and could do with a pint at the local and then bed. We shall be all the brighter for it in the morning—besides, we might hear some useful gossip in the local.'

Everyone but Cameron brightened up remarkably on hearing this. Bull said that he would join them there later when he had arranged for Nicholas to use the spare bedroom in the police house near the station.

Finch said after Ralph had left the room, 'I always thought that Allen was a nob.'

'But a Schuyler,' marvelled Ellis, 'and Lord Longthorne is his father!'

Cameron was not to be won over, 'Aye, and a bloody

cunning devil he is for all that he's a friend of royalty and a multi-millionaire.'

'Cunning made him a multi-millionaire,' asserted Finch, 'and this chap's cunning, too.'

'Which chap?' offered Ellis. 'Mr Ralph, or Mr Nicholas?'

'Both,' grunted Cameron. 'As artful as a wagon load of monkeys—and about as pretty. Come on, let's have a pint, some crisps and a fag. We've earned them.'

Chapter Thirteen

Earlier Verena had arrived back from her meeting with Nicholas to find Chrissie, Priddie and Jamie having a violent argument in the drawing room. At least Chrissie and Jamie were.

'I won't, I won't,' Jamie was yelling. 'I won't go with Priddie to the seaside unless Vee can come with me.'

'Well, she can't,' Chrissie said shortly. 'You know perfectly well that you're to have as little as possible to do with Vee because she encourages you to behave badly which brings on your attacks.'

'No, she doesn't. I've had more attacks than ever since I haven't been allowed to be with her. I think I'm starting one now. So there!'

'Oh, Jamie, you naughty boy, do as your mother tells you,' bleated Priddie.

They were so busy shouting at one another that none of them noticed that not only had Verena arrived, but that Sir Charles stood in the anteroom's open door, having been attracted by the noise. Normally he would have considered eavesdropping to be very much not the done thing, but some sixth sense kept him silent and observing.

He was on the point of reproaching himself and leaving,

when Chrissie saw Verena, and said acidly, 'Oh, you're back from your visit to the criminal classes, are you? You must enjoy wallowing in the mud and no mistake!'

Jamie shouted, 'You're not to talk like that to Vee. She's kind to me and you never are. You don't like her because the Dragon man does—and besides, she's prettier than you are.'

Chrissie's anger at this was so fierce that she gave the little boy an open-handed slap so severe that it brought him to his knees. Once there he began to pant violently in a vain attempt to breathe, his face slowly turning blue.

Verena ran forward to help him, but Chrissie pushed her out of the way, shouting at James, 'Stop that immediately. I know that you're only trying it on.'

'No!' exclaimed Verena. 'He's not. Can't you see that he's unable to breathe?'

'Oh, you always encourage him in his insolence. He's only doing it to gain attention. If you stand back and take no notice, he'll recover soon enough.'

'Oh, no, he won't,' said Sir Charles advancing into the room. 'The boy's in agony. Help him, Verena.' His old face was fierce as he looked at his daughter-in-law. 'This was your doing, Christina, and no-one else's. Don't stand there wringing your hands. Miss Pridham, telephone for the doctor immediately.'

Verena laid Jamie gently on his back and began to stroke his wrists, speaking to him in a soothing voice. 'Don't try to breathe, Jamie, just pretend you are in bed and nothing's the matter. You've had a bad dream, but it's over.'

Gradually, under her ministrations, his colour returned and his breathing became normal. Sir Charles lost his agonised expression. It was the first occasion on which he had seen his grandson suffer such a severe attack.

Chrissie, however, was not prepared to let the matter rest.

'There, I told you so. There was nothing wrong with him. We've sent for the doctor for nothing. He will be pleased to be dragged out on a Saturday. I blame you, Verena, and your association with that man...'

She got no further. Sir Charles said, 'Be quiet, Christina. Whatever else he may have done, young Allen has not caused this. And you should thank Verena for helping James, not abuse her. Verena, my dear, when Miss Pridham returns I should like to speak to you alone in my study. Christina, I think that it would be better if you retired and left Miss Pridham to look after James until the doctor arrives.'

Chrissie opened her mouth to defend herself, but Sir Charles waved her away. 'Exactly,' as she was later to complain to Piers, 'as though I were a common criminal.'

Sir Charles had not long to wait for Verena who entered the study not knowing whether she was to be praised for what she had done for Jamie—or blamed for visiting Nicholas.

'Granddaughter,' said Sir Charles heavily, 'I believe that I may have done you a wrong. I have listened to your stepmother's complaints about your behaviour and have never questioned them. I may also have done young Allen a wrong, though I am not so sure of that. What I am sure of is that I must somehow protect my grandson. I understand from what Christina said that you have just visited young Allen while he was in custody. Is that true?'

'Yes, Grandfather,' Verena replied bravely, not sure what was coming next.

'How was he? Did he offer any explanation for his arrest? I believe that the evidence against him appears to be pretty conclusive.'

'He said that he is innocent, and I believe him. We both

think that Hercules was injured because he interrupted the thieves who were putting the stolen goods in his shed.'

Sir Charles thought for a minute. 'Do you genuinely believe him to be innocent, my dear? Answer me truthfully, not allowing your feelings for him to influence your reply.'

'Yes, Grandfather. I believe that he is.'

'I believe that you have good instincts, which unfortunately is not true of your stepmother. I had no notion…' He stopped without clarifying what he meant—but Verena knew without being told that he was referring to the brutal blow which she had given Jamie.

'I am a magistrate. A personal friend of both the Lord Lieutenant and the Chief Constable of the county. I believe it is my duty to go to the police station and discover how matters lie with young Allen. John Webster also believes him to be innocent. I shall visit the police station the first thing in the morning.'

'Oh, thank you, Grandfather!' Verena exclaimed and, regardless of Marlowe family protocol which demanded that one should never show emotion, she threw her arms around him and kissed him on the cheek.

'I can't have him freed, you know, just on my say so,' said Sir Charles, grasping Verena's hand and holding it in his for a moment. 'You do understand that?'

'Yes, yes, of course! The wonderful thing is not only that you are prepared to help Nicholas but that you believe me. Father would have been so happy. He asked me to look after Jamie.' She did not say why, because she thought that Sir Charles was beginning to understand why.

A good breakfast inside him, thanks to Mrs Bull, Nicholas accompanied the Sergeant to the station. Cameron and his cohorts were already there, soon to be joined by

Ralph, immaculate as always, his sardonic face giving little away.

Another blackboard had been brought in from the village school, and Ralph began to write a series of questions on it, questions which had to be answered, he said, before the investigation could continue.

'I have asked that Mr Allen be present this morning because I believe that he may be of help to us in answering them,' he told his audience. 'They mainly centre, for obvious reasons, on the attempt to implicate him. Whoever wrote the letter knew a great deal about him and, we must assume, either saw him merely as a handy person to involve and so send the police up a wrong track, or as someone against whom he bore a grudge and was therefore seeking a nasty revenge on him.

'In either case, the man must be local—known to Mr Allen and also to you, Sergeant Bull, and some of the townsfolk.'

'If the letter was motivated by spite,' put in Nicholas slowly, 'then it's also possible that I might have upset someone by doing my job as a journalist.'

The discussion went on for some time as all avenues of possibility relating to the first point were explored. Just as it reached the end, the duty constable came in and said that Sir Charles Marlowe had arrived and wished to speak to the officers in charge of the investigation. He had rung the Chief Constable in his capacity as a JP and he had given him permission to do so.

Ralph said cheerfully, 'Send him in at once. One more contributor who knows all the local villains could be of great help.'

Sir Charles stared at the assembled company and at the sight of Nicholas sitting free among them.

'Do I take it,' he said, 'that Mr Allen is no longer a suspect?'

Ralph, once Sir Charles had been introduced to all present, assured him that he was not. 'Our investigation has cleared him completely. At the moment he is helping us with it—but not in the usual understanding of the term!'

All the police officers present laughed heartily. Sir Charles said, 'Then my task is completed. I came here to see if I could be of assistance to him.' He made as if to leave.

Ralph said quickly, 'Please do not leave us, Sir Charles. I believe that if you would consent to join our discussions you could be of assistance to us all, not merely to Mr Allen.'

He looked across at Nicholas and smiled ruefully. 'I think that I ought first to inform you that the young man you know as Mr Nicholas Allen bore quite a different name before he arrived in West Bretton. He happens to be my nephew, Nicholas Allen Schuyler, the youngest son of Lord Longthorne.

'Preferring to make his own way in the world, rather than to rely on his famous family to do it for him, he chooses to use only his first two names. He asks that you respect that decision and continue to think of him as Nicholas Allen. Although he is wealthy in his own right, he prefers not to use that wealth, but to live on his wages at the *Clarion* and from his earnings as the writer, Mr Arthur Merlin.'

Couldn't have put it better myself, thought Nicholas, watching Sir Charles's face change when he heard the news. I'd bet a golden guinea that Sir Charles has never heard of Arthur Merlin!

'Indeed, indeed.' One could almost hear the wheels turning in Sir Charles's head, thought Ralph and Nicholas simultaneously and cynically. The marriage of Miss Verena Marlowe to Mr Nicholas Schuyler was quite a different thing from that of Miss Verena Marlowe to unknown Mr Nicholas Allen.

Nicholas said quietly to Sir Charles, 'I would prefer it, sir, if you would allow me to tell Miss Marlowe who I am myself.'

'Indeed, indeed, most proper,' said the old man, beaming at him.

Cameron sighed and looked at the ceiling as Sir Charles sat down. One more local idiot to bear with. The friend of the Chief Constable and the Lord Lieutenant was hardly likely to be of the slightest use to man or beast.

He was soon to be proved wrong again—a habit which he was acquiring in this investigation.

'Have you any enemies that you know of, Nick?' asked Ralph. 'I know I've asked this question before, but bear with me if I ask it again.'

'Well, I do know that not everyone loves me,' said Nicholas slowly. 'I would be an odd sort of journalist if everyone did! But I know of none who might want to do this to me.'

He looked across at Sir Charles. 'Your cousin, Piers Marlowe, is annoyed that your granddaughter Verena and I have an understanding—I must be frank and tell you that she has agreed to marry me—but we decided to wait until I could come to you with hard evidence that I could support her. I understand that Piers has proposed to her and that she has refused him.'

Cameron said, 'To shop you for the country-house robberies would be a bit extreme as revenge for that, surely.'

'Exactly,' said Nicholas.

Sir Charles, who half an hour so ago would have been horrified to learn that Verena had accepted Nicholas, was now delighted. What a splendid match! The Schuylers might be Anglo-American *nouveau riche*, but Lord Longthorne was highly thought of everywhere—and this was his son.

After that, discussion was fierce—but went nowhere. Ralph, who always played his cards close to his chest, on the principle that it wasn't always an advantage for everyone to know everything—a habit he had acquired when working for MI6—threw a new card on the table. At least it was new for everyone but Cameron.

'One thing I learned from my unknown informant which I have so far not revealed was that the organiser of the robberies in England makes frequent—sometimes lengthy—visits to Switzerland in connection with the European end, and has a secret bank account in Zurich. Does that help us in any way?'

Silence followed. Cameron muttered, 'That certainly lets Mr Allen off the hook.'

'Exactly. Yes, Sir Charles, what is it? You wish to say something.'

Sir Charles said, 'I have to tell you that my cousin Piers Marlowe has frequently blackguarded Mr...Schuyler, but more to the point, he often visits Switzerland. He has a flat in Zurich—something which has always puzzled me as I know that he was left very little money and has no regular occupation. After the War he joined a broker's house, but soon left—he said that it tied him down. Despite that, he never seems to be short of money.'

He looked around the table, his face ghastly. 'I hope that I am not wronging him, but if Mr Schuyler has an enemy it is my relative. He would know of Jesse Pye's shed—and also which houses to rob since he has been a regular visitor to all of them—and Marlowe Court has been spared. I fear that I see why, now.'

Cameron said grimly, 'He would certainly bear investigation. Is he at Marlowe Court at the moment, Sir Charles?'

'No, he left for London yesterday. He was not sure when he would return, but he left most of his personal belongings behind, so I assume that he will be coming back before long.'

'And his London address is?' asked Cameron, fetching out his little notebook and beginning to take it down at Sir Charles's dictation.

Ralph looked around the table. 'We are agreed that this could be a most fruitful line of enquiry. Much of the evidence would appear to support the supposition that Mr Piers Marlowe might be our man. Cameron, I suggest that you get in touch with Scotland Yard immediately and ask them to send men round to his flat as soon as possible.

'Any more suggestions? No, if not, since it's almost lunchtime we'll adjourn until two o'clock. By then we ought to have some news from London. Since, through no fault of our own, we wasted time investigating Mr Schuyler, I don't wish to compound it by pursuing another false trail.'

Sir Charles said hesitantly to Nicholas, 'If Mr Ralph Schuyler will allow, I would like you to return with me to the Court for a meal. It is the least I can offer you since I find that I have been wronging you since I heard of your arrest.

'I know that Verena will be delighted to learn that you are freed from all suspicion. I cannot, of course, inform her that Piers is now under suspicion until we have further, more concrete, evidence. I have been over-hasty once in judging my man, I do not want to be so again—but I am fearful.'

Nicholas thanked him. 'But with your permission I wish to speak to my uncle for a moment before we leave.'

Permission granted, he caught Ralph in the act of leaving with the others.

'Ralph, I've changed my mind. I would like you to ring my father and mother and tell them that I am well and living in West Bretton. Give them my address and nothing more. It's up to them then what they do.'

Ralph clapped him on the shoulder. 'Good man. You've done the right thing, I'm sure you'll not regret it.'

'I wish I was as sure of that as you are.'

Gis had said he would want to rejoin the family and he had been right. Whether it was seeing Ralph again and not feeling in any way inferior to him despite his unfortunate situation, Nicholas didn't know, nor did he care. Life's wheel had turned full circle and he was ready to go home again.

He was whistling joyfully as he walked to Sir Charles and the waiting car.

Verena had spent part of the night by Jamie's bed and had been relieved by Priddie after midnight.

'You must get some sleep, dear,' Priddie had said kindly, as though she were a child again.

She was down late to breakfast to find Chrissie yawning and moaning about Jamie's latest attack: the doctor had diagnosed it as a severe one, so she could no longer claim that he was putting it on, and the knowledge annoyed her.

In the middle of her complainings there was a noise in the entrance hall and Piers's voice could be heard.

Chrissie jumped to her feet. 'No, it can't be Piers. He only left for London yesterday, saying he wouldn't be home until next weekend—whatever can be the matter to bring him back so soon?'

She ran into the hall to find out, Verena following her

more slowly. She had not the slightest interest in Piers's goings-on, but this one was so odd she was intrigued.

Piers, looking haggard, but dressed with his usual care, was busy explaining something to Chrissie about having to return to pick up some stuff he had inadvertently left behind.

'And please don't detain me. I've left my car outside and I want to be off again as soon as possible.'

With that he dashed upstairs. Chrissie, staring after his disappearing figure, said, 'There's something wrong, I'm sure. He's so unlike himself. And where's his man?'

'No business of ours.' Verena was brisk. 'I'm off to see how Jamie is. Care to come with me?'

'What? Oh, no. I wonder what Piers is up to. I know he's up to something.'

Piers as a subject for conversation was decidedly not to Verena's taste. She shrugged her shoulders and set off to see her stepbrother, whose mother showed no interest whatsoever in his condition.

Chrissie dithered at the bottom of the stairs for some minutes before making up her mind. She set off up them, reached Piers's room and, without knocking on the door, walked in.

He had all his clothes, books, papers, and personal trinkets on the bed, and was packing a pair of large cases as though the devil were after him.

'What are you doing?' she demanded shrilly. 'You're leaving, aren't you? For good. Have you forgotten that you said that if you ever did you'd take me with you?'

'Oh, come on, Chrissie,' snorted Piers, folding shirts and stuffing them higgledy-piggledy into a case. 'You know perfectly well that you can't come with me. I'm damned sure I'm not dragging that invalid child of yours around Europe.'

'Oh, no, Piers, you don't get away as easily as that. I've no intention of taking Jamie with us. I'm sick of him—he's nothing but a millstone around my neck, and I'm sick of that stiff-necked old man and his purer-than-pure grand-daughter. I shall be happy to leave them all behind. If you don't take me with you, I shall tell the police what I know—and then where will you be?'

Piers stood stockstill. 'And what the devil do you mean by that?'

'You know perfectly well what I mean. I don't trust you a yard so I've been listening on the extension to the tele-phone, watching where you go and what you do. You're up to your neck in the country-house robberies. You sent that letter about Nick Allen, and you're the one who put the stolen goods in his shed, you and that man of yours. I watched you. So, take me with you, or you're done for.'

'I'll be on the run,' he said desperately. 'You can't want that.'

'I'll tell you what I want—a life in the sun, far from this dreary hole, on the money you've got squirrelled away in Switzerland. Come on, Piers. We're good in bed together and I'm cleverer than you, aren't I? So I can help you. I mean what I say about the police.'

'Very well, then. Pack your bags and meet me in the stables where I've left the car.'

'And you won't trick me? Promise.'

'What—and have you run to the police? No fear.'

'Good. I shan't be a jiffy. No need to take too much. We can buy what we want abroad. And if the police don't twig what you've been up to, we can come back again. With any luck Jamie will snuff it and you can be Sir Piers and I can be Lady Marlowe.'

It would be more like taking Lady Macbeth with him than Lady Marlowe, but he had no alternative—and she *was* good in bed—so together they packed the car, climbed into it and left Marlowe Court for good or ill.

Nicholas had never thought that he would drive to Marlowe Court in its owner's Rolls Royce. Immediately before they turned in at the gates a car passed them, travelling at such speed that their chauffeur only narrowly avoided colliding with it.

Sir Charles exclaimed, 'Good heavens! I could have sworn that it was Piers who was driving that car. But it's not his, and he's in London. I must be seeing things.'

Nicholas had thought that the woman passenger resembled Chrissie, but decided that he, too, must be mistaken. In any case, his mind was on meeting Verena and what she would say to him when she saw that he was free and that he was with Sir Charles. They had only just entered the house when the drawing-room door opened and Verena rushed into the hall on hearing their voices.

She took one look at them, and to Nicholas's joy she ran towards him, flung her arms around his neck, and kissed him, almost weeping with excitement and relief.

'Oh, Grandfather,' she said, eyes brimming, 'thank you for bringing him back to me.'

'No thanks to me,' said Sir Charles gruffly, touched, despite himself, by their openly expressed affection for one another. 'He had already been freed by the time that I arrived, and cleared of all complicity in the robberies. I have brought him home to take lunch with us.'

Verena stood back, her eyes shining. 'I always knew that you were innocent, Nicholas. I never doubted that they would have to let you go in the end.'

'Well, you knew more than I did then,' Nicholas grinned back at her. 'There were times yesterday when I was sure that I faced a long stretch on Dartmoor!'

'Lunch will have to be put back to one forty-five,' said Sir Charles, looking at his watch. 'I'm sure that you young things would like to be alone a little before it.'

This generous offer surprised Verena, but not Nicholas, who knew that his revealed identity as a Schuyler was responsible for it.

She was about to leave the room with him when she remembered that she ought to tell Sir Charles of Piers's sudden return.

'Oh, Grandfather,' she said. 'It's the oddest thing! Piers arrived back this morning quite unexpectedly, just after you left for West Bretton. So he'll be present at lunch, too.'

To say she was surprised by the reaction of her hearers to this news would be an understatement.

'Piers! Here?' exclaimed Sir Charles. He rang the bell for the butler. 'I shall send for him at once. He has a great deal of explaining to do. Be a good fellow, Nicholas, and ring the police station to inform them that he has returned to Marlowe Court.'

The butler's reply to the request that Mr Piers Marlowe be sent for and asked to attend Sir Charles in his study immediately was as follows. 'I have to inform you, sir, that Mr Piers's stay here has been an extremely short one. He has already left again.'

He paused for dramatic effect, and added, 'Mrs Hugh Marlowe left with him. They both of them took a great deal of luggage with them, and seemed to be in a hurry.' After another significant pause he added an important rider.

'Mrs Marlowe did not take Master James with her. He is unaware that his mother has left without him.'

Nicholas, who had Ralph on the other end of the phone, immediately passed these interesting titbits on to him.

'Right,' said Ralph, 'find out the colour and the make of his car, and if possible, its registration number. I'll try to have him traced and stopped before he gets too far away. Has he been gone long?'

Sir Charles exclaimed, 'So, I wasn't mistaken. It *was* Piers driving the car which nearly hit us at the gates. He can't have got very far yet. He'll probably take the London road.'

Nicholas passed this message on, too. The butler, always on the ball where Marlowe matters were concerned, immediately gave him the details about the car which Ralph had asked for. None of the staff liked or trusted Piers, or would be surprised to learn of his dishonesty.

Verena exclaimed, 'What's happening? Why do the police want to speak to Piers?' and then, 'Oh, was it *Piers* who put the stolen goods in your shed, Nicholas?'

'I fear so, my dear.' Sir Charles was magisterial. 'Worse than that he may have been the organiser of the recent country-house robberies. There's nothing more that we can do now—except eat our lunch in peace and wait for further news.'

Verena put a hand on Nicholas's arm. 'What a wicked thing to do to you. How could he?'

'Never mind,' he said gently. 'It's all over now; the police are after him. I don't think he'll get very far. And your grandfather is right, we must watch and wait.'

'And,' he said, after Sir Charles had gone, his smile a mixture of love and naughtiness, 'now, my sweet witch, that we can be alone together, we must celebrate my release. Before I do so I have something important to tell you, which I ought to have told you before. Could we go outside, d'you think? I've been indoors quite long enough during the last twenty-four hours.'

They found a stone bench in a quiet corner of the terrace which overlooked Parson's Pool and the distant hills beyond it.

'What is it, Nicholas, which is so important that you must tell me at once? Don't you think I have had enough excitement recently to last me for the next six months?'

'Yes, indeed. I don't know whether you will think my news exciting. It's this,' and he told her without preamble, and with no explanation, that his real name was Nicholas Allen Schuyler and that his father was the famous Lord Longthorne, maker and breaker of governments.

To his astonishment Verena immediately began to laugh. 'So that's why Grandfather was being so friendly to you, and suggested that we would like to be alone. Poor Nicholas Allen wouldn't do for Miss Verena Marlowe at all, but I suppose that rich Nicholas Schuyler will.'

'Something like that. But I'm not rich, Verena, nor have I lived for the last three years as though I were, nor do I intend to be so in the future. I know that I have a large share of the Schuyler fortune in Coutts Bank, but I haven't touched it since I became Nicholas Allen because I didn't earn it.'

He laughed a little ruefully. 'You are an amazing girl, you know, to take this in your stride.'

'Well, after Piers has proved to be an international criminal, your really being a Schuyler seems quite tame. It makes you more respectable, not less, you know.'

'Yes, I do know.' Nicholas grimaced. 'That's why I ran away and changed my name. Being a Schuyler and rich tied me down. It meant that a lot of avenues in life were closed to me, and they were the avenues I wanted to walk down.

'Like being a painter. I wasn't allowed to go to art school and until I reached West Bretton three years ago I had given up painting and drawing through sheer disappointment that my ambitions in that quarter had been thwarted. It was only when I began to write the dragon books that I started to draw again. That's another thing I should have told you. My pen name is Merlin, Arthur Merlin.'

'Better and better,' said Verena softly. She leaned forward to kiss him. 'Poor Jamie will be delighted to learn that you really are the Dragon man, and will immediately demand that you write another book.'

Nicholas kissed her back. And if Verena's kiss had been innocent, his was not. The sight of her was rousing him so much precisely because he had feared that she might be lost to him for ever.

Now that that danger was past he wanted to celebrate his freedom. He put his arms around her and began to caress her, gently at first, and then more strongly.

Verena was in heaven. The hands which stroked her neck and her breasts—Nicholas's hands—the mouth which kissed hers—Nicholas's mouth—were together causing her to feel the strongest pleasure which she had ever experienced.

When she gave a little moan, and began to kiss him back as enthusiastically as he was kissing her, and also added her caresses to his by stroking his neck and running her hands through his thick black hair, she excited Nicholas so much that he drew away from her.

'No more,' he said, panting, for his desire to make real love to her was a sweet agony which demanded to be satisfied. 'We are public here. We might be called to lunch at any moment, and I wouldn't want us to be found in what the *News of the World* describes as an intimate and compromising position.'

Her expression was as naughty as his when she teased him with her answer. 'Only if you promise me that we can be in an intimate and compromising position as soon as possible after we are married.'

'Oh, it will be quite in order then—demanded, in fact.

Its absence would be a cause for nullity and social disgrace. That's what having a marriage licence does for you—licence being the proper word!'

Verena smoothed down her dress. 'Because you are a Schuyler, do we have to be married at St Margaret's, Westminster, and live in a huge house with lots of servants?'

'Certainly not. We shall buy something better than Jesse Pye's cottage, but nothing grand, I assure you. A nice little house is all I want; I ran away from a large and splendid one to make sure I found it. There won't be any room for lots of servants.'

'That's a relief,' said Verena frankly. 'Did you really run away?'

'I have to confess that I did. I left all my many relatives behind, as well as my fortune. By an odd coincidence the man leading the investigation into the robberies is my uncle, Ralph Schuyler. He's monstrously clever, but not as clever as my cousin Gis Havilland. Now, he really is a sort of junior Einstein. Their cleverness used to overwhelm me, but not any more. Not now I've found you and my destiny.'

'You seem very clever to me,' said Verena frankly and truthfully. 'I've heard of your cousin, of course. He's quite famous. But what did your mother and father think when you ran away?'

Nicholas was suddenly ashamed. 'I don't know. You see, until Ralph arrived at the police station yesterday, no one had the slightest notion of where I was or what I was doing.'

'Oh, your poor mother!'

'Yes, I know. It wasn't until I fell in love with you that I began to question what I had done. I met Gis by accident in London, and he told me that I would. As usual, he was right—a nasty habit of his! This morning I asked Ralph to ring them up and to tell them where I live—and that I am well and happy. After that, it's up to them. They may not want me any more.'

He looked into her eyes. 'Oh, Verena, I had to get away. I was so unhappy and ill-behaved that I was heading for a nasty end. I was the dog with a bad name and I damned nearly got hanged. When I stopped calling myself Schuyler it was as though a magician had waved a wand and I became someone else. Without turning into unknown Nicholas Allen I could never have created Arthur Merlin.

'Would you mind very much if I stayed Nicholas Allen? I don't want the other man back. You wouldn't like him.'

'Oh, I don't believe that, but if it would make you happy, then I don't mind being Mrs Allen. It will be a great deal easier to be Mrs Allen than Mrs Schuyler when I go shopping, and no mistake. No one will ever be able to spell Schuyler correctly!'

'Good girl,' he said, kissing her chastely on the cheek, instead of the lips so to dampen down not only his rampant carnal desires but Verena's as well. She was looking at him as though she would like to eat him.

'I think I can hear the bell. It must be time for lunch—which is just as well, since I can't trust myself to behave properly much longer. After it I shall ask Sir Charles for your hand so that we may be alone together as much as we like, and no one will care what we are doing. It's one of the pleasures of being formally engaged.'

They went indoors hand in hand to be affectionately greeted by Sir Charles. His granddaughter was settled for life which was one worry over and done with.

His three other worries, which concerned Chrissie, Piers, and what to do about poor abandoned Jamie, had still to be resolved.

* * *

Piers drove as though the devil himself were after them. He had decided to make for Southampton and cross to France. He wanted to be away and out of England before the police caught up with him. Every car which followed closely behind him was a source of worry because he feared that it might be one of theirs.

Chrissie's unwanted presence was like having a bad boil on the back of his neck which he couldn't pretend didn't exist. She prattled and chattered about their future life together until he could have strangled her. Her main effect on him was to make him drive even faster to get the journey over.

Thirty miles from West Bretton a car began to follow them, hooting insistently, and demanding to be allowed to pass them on the narrow road which Piers was hogging by driving in the middle.

His paranoiac fear of detection translated the hooting into a request to stop. The hooting persisted until they came to a byway which motorists usually avoided since it was very narrow and ran through lonely country. Piers decided that it would be safer to leave the main road and take this circuitous route to Southampton which the police might not know of.

To his relief the hooting car did not follow them. 'You see, it was as I said,' Chrissie offered in an 'I told you so voice'—she had been complaining about his wild driving for the past twenty miles. 'It wasn't the police. I'm sure they haven't had time to catch us up.'

'Oh, do shut up, you silly bitch! Whatever did I do to deserve you?' grunted Piers, and drove even faster. The byway ran through high hedges which concealed fields on one side and woodland and scrub on the other. Its road surface was poor, and Piers's frantic passage along it caused the car to jolt violently, throwing up clouds of white dust. Chrissie immediately began to complain that they should have stayed on the main road.

Her moans only served to cause Piers to go even faster. The wicked flee when no man pursueth, and Piers's guilty conscience had him fearing that a police car was hiding behind every corner.

His patience finally snapped when Chrissie shouted, 'Oh, do slow down, I'm sure we shall have an accident!'

In turning to curse her for this further slur on his competence as a driver, Piers failed to see that the road, hitherto a straight one, now followed an ancient field line and took a sharp bend to the right. In consequence his car travelled straight on at high speed through a break in the hedge, ploughed through some low scrub and finally plunged into a shallow lake which the hedgerow had hidden from their view.

The car turned over as it entered the water, trapping them both inside. The impact mercifully knocked Chrissie unconscious, but Piers was not so lucky. Upside down, he tried desperately to free himself, but the car sank deeper and deeper into the water, and all his efforts remained fruitless.

It was to be a year before some surveyors, measuring the land for sale, and inspecting it as they went along, discovered that in the lake's shallow waters a car and its two passengers had been waiting to be resurrected—but not brought to life again.

All that the police knew was that they had lost Piers's trail. It was to be some time before information filtered through that neither he nor Chrissie had been seen since they had left Marlowe Court. So far as the authorities were concerned the pair of them had brought off a grand disappearing act, and left the police in particular, as Ralph said ruefully, 'with egg on our faces.'

* * *

As usual, once the annual grand Schuyler reunion was over, Nicholas's father and mother left Padworth for their Park Lane home in London.

They were sitting down to a leisurely afternoon tea after a hectic week of business and socialising when Gerard's secretary put his head round the door.

'Mr Ralph Schuyler is on the telephone in your study, m'lord, asking to speak to you. Most urgently, he said.'

'Oh, if Ralph thinks something is urgent then I must be on my way at once,' said Gerard, putting down his teacup, and walking briskly from the room.

He returned a few minutes later, the oddest expression on his face.

'What is it, Gerard?' asked Torry, laying aside the copy of *Punch* which she had been idly skipping through. 'What did Ralph want? Was it official business?'

Gerard shook his head wryly. 'You wouldn't guess, my dear, not in a thousand years, so I shan't tease you by asking you to try. Bluntly, he has found Nicholas.'

'What! I didn't know that he was looking for him.'

'He wasn't. He came upon him purely by accident. How, he says, is too long a story for the phone. Nicholas is apparently living in some obscure town in North Devon called West Bretton. He has been resident there for three years— since shortly after he left Padworth, in fact. He is well, happy, and, in his terms, successful. At his request, Ralph gave me his address, but no other details of his life. Ralph thinks that he wishes to be reconciled. He says that he's greatly changed.'

Torry leapt to her feet. 'Oh, Gerard, this is wonderful news. I have worried about him ever since he disappeared. You have no urgent business at the moment—why should we not go and visit him at once, if not sooner? Oh, please say that we may.'

A sudden thought struck her amidships. 'Oh, dear, Gerard. Before you consent I ought to tell you what Gis discovered about Nicholas and what he has been doing.'

She looked so doleful that Gerard put a consoling arm about her. 'What is troubling you, my love? Of course, if you wish it I shall take you to West Bretton, to Jesse Pye's cottage which is now Claus's home—although Ralph did say that he wishes to be known only as Nicholas.'

Torry said, a trifle feverishly, 'It's this. Gis read that new book, *Put money in thy purse*, and said immediately that Nicholas must have written it. There were things in it that only he could have known. And I knew that he must have written it for the same author was responsible for the children's dragon books; the stories in them are identical with the ones which I used to hear Nicholas telling the Schuyler children. So Nicholas must be Arthur Merlin. He always wanted to write and draw. How wrong we were to discourage him.'

Gerard said slowly, 'So you think that he wrote that book which pilloried me—and the family.'

Torry waited for his outburst of anger; instead, as she afterwards conceded, in true Gerard fashion, he did the unexpected.

He began to roar—with laughter, not with rage.

'So he's the villain who pinned me down on the page as neatly and accurately as an entomologist pins a butterfly to a specimen board. And his analysis of political life and chicanery proves that he must have been listening carefully and shrewdly to the life which went on around him at Padworth and in London. He'd have made a splendid politician, no doubt of it.'

'But he didn't want to be a politician. You will take me to West Bretton, won't you, Gerard?'

'We shall set off in the Rolls as soon as our cases are

packed, stay overnight in Salisbury, and arrive at West
Bretton by late morning, or early afternoon. I shall tell
Timson to pack my horse-whip.'

'Oh, Gerard, you won't!'

'Teasing, my dear, only teasing. If you are right, I can't
wait to see what the young villain has made of himself.
Ralph sounded proud of him.'

'Will my mother ever come back, sir?'

Verena had taken Jamie to Nicholas's cottage on the
morning after his release and Piers and Chrissie's flight.
She was carrying a child's cricket bat, a single stump, and
a tennis ball. The atmosphere at Marlowe Court was doom-
laden. Sir Charles had spent the morning on the telephone
with various authorities trying to assist them in their search
for Piers. Ralph had visited him before he left for London
in order to say goodbye to Nicholas and to thank Sir
Charles for his help.

Sir Charles had told Jamie that his mother had gone on
a visit—but he had already heard the servants' gossip, not
only about her flight, but about her previous 'goings-on'
with Piers.

For some reason Jamie thought it inadvisable to ask his
sister what 'goings-on' were. He decided that he would ask
the Dragon man instead when Verena told him that
Nicholas was back at Jesse Pye's cottage so Jamie would
be able to visit him again.

They found Nicholas in his garden, watering some let-
tuces which had grown limp whilst he had, as he slangily
informed Jamie, 'been banged up in the chokey'.

He offered them lunch, but they had already eaten, so he
cut himself several doorsteps of new bread, buttered it lavishly, and ate it with huge chunks of Cheddar cheese.

Pound cake from the bakery in West Bretton, shared with Jamie, followed that.

'Sure you won't have any?' Nicholas waved the cake knife invitingly at Verena. She saw his face drop when she confirmed her refusal, watched it brighten up again when she changed her mind. After that he brewed strong tea which they drank while Jamie leafed through the big dragon book which he had admired on his first visit.

'I shall put on weight if I visit you too often,' Verena offered as she wolfed the cake down. Love, she had discovered, was improving her appetite, not destroying it.

'Eat on, my darling, I don't like skinny women,' returned Nicholas, cutting himself another slice of cake. 'I like a nice handful rather than the collection of skin and bones which is so fashionable today.'

'No chance of the latter,' and Verena looked ruefully down at her neatly rounded figure.

'Oh, plenty of exercise will soon run off any fat.' Nicholas was having a tough time of it since, with Jamie present, he was unable to satisfy what he was later to tell Verena were his base carnal instincts. 'As soon as I have finished lunch we shall have a game of cricket on what is laughingly known as Jesse Pye's lawn.'

This was a rough patch of green sward to the side of the cottage, and to which the three of them repaired to play single-wicket cricket, where Jamie, to his great delight, scored more runs than the Dragon man and his sister put together.

Before that, once he was alone with him, he had asked Nicholas his question about his mother to which Nicholas had replied evasively, 'Oh, I suppose so, don't you?'

'Well, I don't want her back. I heard the housekeeper say to the butler that she wasn't surprised they had run off together what with all the goings-on between my mother and Uncle Piers. What did she mean by goings-on?'

Nicholas was mercifully saved from answering this by Verena returning from doing Nicholas's washing up.

'Something grown-ups do which is no business of little boys.'

'Like going to work, or playing golf?'

It was now Nicholas's turn to rescue them both from Jamie's remorseless logic by saying loudly, 'Cricket, everybody.' He picked up the stump, the bat and the ball and led the way through the side gate on to Jesse's lawn.

They were so engrossed in their game that they did not hear the Rolls Royce arrive and stop in front of the cottage...

Gerard's chauffeur drove him and Torry to West Bretton, stopping only for them to eat a light luncheon at a country hotel which had been recommended to Gerard—who, like his son, loved food—for its cooking.

On arriving in the little town, they had asked their way to Jesse Pye's cottage, which they found was up a narrow, but reasonably surfaced, road.

'Only cottage down it,' they were told. 'Drive on past Marlowe Court and you can't miss it. Mr Allen lives there now. He's the new owner of the *Clarion*.'

This titbit intrigued Gerard, since he had noticed the *Clarion*'s shop window and facia board when they had driven past it.

Both of them were surprised by its humble nature when they reached the cottage. The word cottage in their experience covered everything from a largish house to a veritable shack. This cottage was obviously a one-room up, one-room down building, with a lean-to kitchen at the side, and almost certainly an earth closet at the back, out of sight.

The front garden had a few flowers growing in it. At the back was a flourishing kitchen garden.

'Nicholas lives *here*,' said Torry faintly.

'So Ralph said—and look—' Gerard pointed through the side-window of the Rolls '—"Jesse Pye's cottage" is written on a board let into the gate.'

The chauffeur opened the door for Gerard to get out. He immediately heard the sound of cheerful voices coming from the field next to the cottage. They were those of a man, a boy and a young woman.

'Wait a moment, my dear,' he said to Torry. 'Let me investigate. I don't think that we have come to the wrong place, but we might have done.'

He walked into the cottage's front garden to discover another, makeshift, gate leading to the field from which the voices were coming. He pushed it open quietly, so that the owners of the voices remained oblivious of his curious presence—and Gerard saw, for the first time in three years, his youngest son.

Nicholas, a tennis ball in his hand, was facing a little boy who stood before a single stump flourishing a small cricket bat. In front of him, and slightly to Gerard's right, was a young woman wearing a pretty blue-and-white striped summer dress. She had her back to him.

His son bowled a gentle ball, underarm, at the small boy who gave it a merry whack. The ball soared in Gerard's direction. He caught it, and as Nicholas turned to follow its flight, he threw it back to him, saying as he did so, 'Caught Gerard, bowled Nicholas—but I believe that I've caught Nicholas, too.'

All three now turned to look at Gerard. The boy, his bat held in front of him, ran to him, saying, 'You caught me, sir, and it's your turn to bat now. I say, sir, why do you look exactly like the Dragon man?'

Nicholas, a hand on Jamie's head, said to him affection-ately, 'He doesn't look like me—I look like him. He's my father, Jamie.'

'Your father? I didn't know that you had a father.'

Gerard, taking the bat from Jamie, said gravely, 'Oh, we all have fathers, Jamie. Even old men like myself once had a father.'

He waved the bat at his son before taking up his position before the single stump. 'Explanations later. We must finish the game first.'

Nicholas began to laugh. 'Like Drake playing bowls be-fore fighting the Armada, eh? Nevertheless, I think intro-ductions to the players are in order first.'

He turned to the pretty girl—who, like Jamie, was struck by the resemblance between the two men—saying, 'My dear, this is my father, Lord Longthorne. Father, this is my fiancée, Miss Verena Marlowe of Marlowe Court, and this young man is Jamie Marlowe, her half-brother.'

Gerard gravely acknowledged them in proper form. He saw at once that Miss Marlowe's beauty was for the con-noisseur, being that of bone and character, not the super-ficial kind created by powder and paint, and the trick of youth which would disappear with age. He conceded that his son had chosen well.

She also showed her character by not being excited or distressed by his sudden arrival and unorthodox behav-iour—even though Jamie appeared to think it quite normal for a beautifully dressed man in city clothes to appear from nowhere in order to take part in his game of cricket.

Nicholas looked hard at his father before adding, 'And I am Nicholas Allen.'

'I know,' said Gerard. 'Also, I am told, known on oc-casion as Arthur Merlin. Time to bowl.'

Not quite, though, for Torry, tired of waiting for Gerard

to return to the car, had followed him to Jesse Pye's lawn, and was walking through the gate to it.

'Have you come to play cricket, too?' Jamie enquired of her eagerly.

Torry who, as Gerard's wife, was used to finding herself in odd situations, replied gravely, 'No, I've come to watch my big boy play,' and she turned her smile, still dazzling in her old age, on her son.

Impulsively, his face working, Nicholas, dropping the ball he held, advanced on his mother, who was holding out her arms to him, and saying, 'At last!' He threw his own arms around her and hugged her to him.

Torry's tears flowed freely—all those which she had suppressed for three long years. Nicholas, who until he met her again, had had no idea how much he had missed her gentle but deep affection—so like Verena's, he later came to realise—was equally moved.

When they eventually stood apart, she said wonderingly, 'How big you are! You surely can't have grown!'

'You've forgotten how much bigger I was than my brothers and cousins,' he told her, 'and before I forget my manners, let me introduce you to my fiancée, Miss Verena Marlowe, and her little brother, Jamie.'

Jamie, hopping from foot to foot, said impatiently, 'When are we going to start playing cricket again, Dragon man? I want you to bowl at the man who looks like you so that I can catch him out.'

Verena, who was as moved as Nicholas by this unexpected arrival of his lost father and mother, said reprovingly, 'Come now, Jamie, you mustn't talk like that to Mr Allen's parents. You must be patient.'

'Little boys are never patient, my dear,' said Torry, kissing Jamie on the cheek. 'And big boys rarely are. I think I can see a big boy who is impatient, too.' For Gerard was standing before the single stump, child's bat in his large hands, watching his changed son's loving greeting of his mother.

Ralph had said on the phone, 'He's become formidable in his self-assurance.' He had not added, 'He's just like you must have been at that age,' but he had thought it.

Gerard could see what Ralph had seen—the determination behind the charm, the sign of a man who was supremely sure of himself.

He called to Nicholas. 'Come on, are you going to disappoint the little fellow?'

'Certainly not.' Nicholas turned to his mother. 'You may be umpire here—as you are at Padworth.'

He walked to his sweater, which had been placed on the ground as a marker, and bowled a gentle ball at his father, who responded by lofting it towards Jamie who stood, his cupped hands outstretched, ready to catch anything which came his way.

He duly did so. Gerard shook his head in mock disgust. 'I must be out of practice to fall for a dolly drop like that.'

Nicholas, retrieving the ball which Jamie had thrown to him, said, 'I didn't know that you could play cricket, Father. I thought that baseball was your game.'

'Ah, there's a lot that you don't know about me, matched only, I suppose, by what I don't know about you.'

With which cryptic comment he handed the bat back to Jamie, and they played for a little while longer until Verena said, 'I think, Nicholas, that we ought to offer your mother and father a cup of tea. They must have had a long journey from London.'

'And the chauffeur,' agreed Nicholas. 'Is Chester still with you, sir?'

'Indeed,' said Gerard. He held out his arm to his wife, and they all, except Jamie, walked to the cottage. Jamie was sent to fetch Chester to join the tea party—something which Chester had never done before.

Both Gerard and Torry were surprised by the simplicity of Nicholas's cottage, and, despite his evident lack of servants, by its cleanliness and order. Everything was spick and span, quite unlike his rooms at Oxford which had been notable for their disarray.

It was he who prepared afternoon tea for them all, leaving Verena and Jamie to get to know his parents better. He could hear them laughing and talking. Jamie had taken a liking to the father of the Dragon man who looked so much like him.

Tea over—Chester drinking it, at his insistence, away from the main party on a joint stool by the hearth—it was agreed by both women that he should drive Torry, Verena and Jamie to Marlowe Court to be introduced to Sir Charles, leaving Nicholas to make his peace with his father.

To their mutual surprise, once they were alone, they were struck dumb, not through embarrassment, but because each of them found the other to be so different from either their memory or expectation of the other.

Gerard found that Nicholas had grown strong and self-reliant, and because of this Nicholas did not find his father as intimidating as he had done in the past. For the first time they met as equals—and were aware that they did.

Gerard broke the silence first. He said, 'Ralph told me that you were greatly changed, but otherwise told me nothing of your life. Gis believes you to be the Merlin who wrote the children's dragon books and that sensational novel—and has so persuaded your mother. The little boy called you the Dragon man, so I suppose that Gis, as usual, is right.'

Nicholas laughed, 'As usual! I suppose that I had better

bring you up to date with the career of Nicholas Allen—but before I do, I must tell you that I do not intend to change my name back to Schuyler. I hope that doesn't hurt you. I have to emphasise that I would never have used my real name to save myself when I was falsely accused, and only Ralph's arrival on the scene revealed to the police that I was that strange and powerful bird, a member of the Schuyler family.'

Gerard shook his head. 'On the contrary, you may do as you wish. If calling yourself Nicholas Allen has wrought such a profound change in you then I am happy to leave matters as they are. After all, our name, I have recently discovered, is not really Schuyler. The Captain adopted it to make himself appear more respectable.'

Relief poured through Nicholas. 'That being so, I am happy to continue with my tale.'

As both Torry and Verena had hoped, they sat down companionably for the first time in years, and Gerard was more than satisfied by what he heard from his once-errant son.

'And so you intend to continue living in West Bretton. But I would hope that you would not bring that pretty young woman to Jesse Pye's cottage to live. She deserves better than this.'

'Indeed, no. We are agreed on a modest villa on the outskirts of the town. I shall continue to run the paper and to carry on with my writing. I shall keep in touch with you all now that my self-imposed exile has been breached.'

When, after further conversation, they heard Chester return with the Rolls to drive them to the Court and they rose to go, Gerard offered Nicholas his hand.

'Let us forget the past,' he said, 'and greet a happier future. The way you have chosen is not the one I would have planned for you, but it seems to have tamed what Gis once called ''your wayward heart''. I believe that it is way-ward no longer. Let us shake hands on it.'

So they did, and all the constraints between them dis-appeared, never to return.

Verena and Nicholas sat in the gathering dusk on the terrace at the back of Marlowe Court. They had left the busy drawing-room—unnoticed, they wrongly thought—and were sitting decorously side by side and holding hands.

'I'm so happy that you made your peace with your father, Nicholas,' Verena said. 'You did make your peace, didn't you?'

'Yes, and it was easier than I thought that it might be. I feared that he might be in a frightful bate over the novel, but it turned out that he admired it! He thought it very clever and told me that I was quite the young Disraeli, and if I carried on in his footsteps I might also end up as Prime Minister after beginning by writing a political *roman à clef*!'

He laughed wryly, and Verena asked him, 'And do you, Nicholas? Wish to be Prime Minister?'

'Not at all. And so I told him. My idea of fulfilment is quite different. I'm happy here with you at West Bretton.'

'But will you always be? From what I know of your family, it is exceedingly ambitious.'

'But I'm not. At least, not in their way. I think that I'm like my mother. I've discovered that I want to make the lives of those around me happy. Does that sound conceited and pious?' he asked her anxiously.

'Not at all. It's why you looked after Jamie and why you wrote the dragon books.'

She paused and said, surprising him a little, 'There is ambition in *Put money in thy purse*, though.'

'Clever girl! But that's not surprising since you're my

sweet witch, and witches are notoriously clever. I want to write at least one more like it, but ultimately I hope to write a kinder book—about life in West Bretton, and the countryside. After that, who knows?'

Verena's eyes shone. 'Oh, how splendid'

'And now, my sweet witch, let us talk of more important things. How about a stroll to that somewhat larger bench down in the rose garden where we are out of sight and sound of the house?'

'Oh, whatever for?' Her voice was innocent but her eyes were not.

He caught her roughly to him. 'You know exactly why, my dearest girl. We are to be married—and soon—so we are permitted to misbehave ourselves. I promise you that we shan't go all the way, but we will take a few steps in the right—or do I mean wrong?—direction.'

'Then the rose garden it shall be! We've been good for far too long, and I really feel like misbehaving myself with you tonight.'

They walked down the steps—and did.

Misbehave themselves—a little.

Until at last, with great difficulty, they tore themselves apart.

Nicholas said hoarsely, 'The sooner we marry, the better. You do want it to be soon?'

'As soon as you like. I would want to be married in the church here—but will it hold all your family?'

'Oh, I want a quiet wedding and I'm sure you do, with just Mother and Father, Sir Charles, John Webster and Jamie will do. Later, in the autumn, after the honeymoon, I shall take you to the November the fifth celebrations at Padworth and introduce you to the clan.

'Ralph has assured me that he and the police will not

reveal my true name to the Press. I shall remain Mr
Nicholas Allen if it is necessary to refer to me at all.'

'I think that you will find that there are many in West
Bretton who will want to be present at the church,' Verena
told him.

And so they did. Coming out after a simple ceremony
they found that Sergeant Bull had assembled all the West
Bretton cricket team, bats held high, to make an archway
for them to walk through!

'And I'm not even a regular member of the side,'
Nicholas marvelled to the good Sergeant at the reception.

'Ah, but you're always ready to help out, Nick—and not
just on the cricket field, either.'

'That's the nicest compliment I've ever been paid,'
Nicholas told Verena later that evening when they arrived
at the hotel in Newquay where they were to spend their
honeymoon.

She smiled demurely at him, and leaning forward whispered in his ear, 'Do you think I might be able to come up
with a better one later tonight?'

'Oh, I hope so, I do hope so,' Nicholas returned, his eyes
eager. 'I shall try my best to make it possible.'

And so he did: to such good effect that Verena, lying in
his arms, royally satisfied by his lovemaking, all her dreams
at last having come true, gasped out, 'Oh, Nicholas, I'm
glad we waited. Oh, I do love you so, I can't believe I
should have enjoyed myself half so much with anyone else.
I'm so glad I never married Roger Gough, or Piers, or any
of the men in India… You are my *preux chevalier* and no
mistake.'

'And I'm glad I waited for you. When I think of the
women I might have married… Come here, my darling, and
let us celebrate our nuptials again as the parson called our

wedding this morning. I like that word nuptials, don't you? It sounds so important.'

'You must put it in a book,' whispered Verena drowsily, 'and then we must write our own and hope that it has a happy ending.'

'Oh, and what book is that, my sweet witch?'

'The book of life, of course.'

'Then let us begin to write it straight away, remembering that well begun is half done, and that the night is not yet over.'

They turned into one another's arms again and started out on their long and happy journey together.

Epilogue

The stars had turned and wheeled, the earth had travelled on and a year had gone by. The grand Schuyler reunion at Padworth had come round again. It was four years since Nicholas had driven away to find a new life and a new love, and now he was back again, his own man at last, with the one woman beside him.

The clan were seated on the lawn having afternoon tea. Nicholas was talking to Gis, who had his youngest son on his knee. Verena, who was expecting her first baby in the autumn, was engaged in a long conversation with Gis's wife Thea, whom she had discovered when they had first met in November to be a sister soul.

Opposite to them, Ralph and his wife Claire and their young children were relaxing in the shade of the giant cedars for which Padworth was famous. Various other grown-up Schuylers and Havillands were scattered about the grounds.

Jamie, who in the continued absence of his mother had been made a ward of court with Nicholas and Verena, at Sir Charles's insistence, as his guardians, was playing rounders with assorted children of the clan. His asthma was no longer so troublesome and he was growing tall and strong. A year ago the noisy Schuyler small fry would have frightened him, but now he held his own with them.

A month before the gathering, the Press had highlighted the discovery of the car in which Piers and Chrissie had met their deaths. The mystery of their disappearance was a mystery no longer.

'They went into the lake only thirty miles from West Bretton,' Ralph was saying to Nicholas and Gis, 'and there we were, wasting our time, examining sightings of them from all round the world. If our Swiss friends had only told us that the money undoubtedly standing in Piers Marlowe's name in a bank in Zurich had never been touched, we might have guessed that something untoward had happened to them.'

'I must remember that,' drawled Gis, bouncing his baby boy on his knee. 'Are you listening, Junior? If your papa ever embarks on a life of crime, he must fly immediately to Zurich to bank the dibs!'

Nicholas said, 'One good thing is that Verena and I will be able to adopt Jamie now we know that his mother will never come back to claim him. The poor little lad still has nightmares in which she arrives on our doorstep and takes him away. Sir Charles told Verena and me not to go to the funeral given the circumstances of their death and Verena's condition.'

He looked around the grounds, trying to remember how he had felt four years ago—and failing. His happy life with Verena, soon to be crowned by the birth of his first child, would have seemed then like an impossible dream. He could not have foreseen that he would return, not as a prodigal, but as a fulfilled and happy man, secure in his success as a writer and a newspaper owner.

His coming child kicked against the hand he had gently

placed on what Verena had unromantically named her bump. She smiled contentedly back at him.

'Happy?' he asked her, to be answered with,

'Of course, are you?'

'More than I expected,' he said. 'More than I deserve.'

'Never that,' she told him, stroking the hand which stroked her. 'And I like your family. I recognised Gis immediately from what you had told me about him. He is even cleverer than I thought. What you didn't tell me is how kind he is. He doesn't *look* a bit like you, but you're very alike in character.'

'We are?' Nicholas stared at her.

'Oh, yes. Didn't you know? I've been talking to Thea and she agrees with me. You're like Ralph, too. She calls you the terrible triplets. You all make the same awful jokes.'

Nicholas thought about what she had said. He had never told anyone of the flash of horror he had felt on the occasion when he had touched Piers.

For a moment he had shared Gis's strange intuition—and he knew why Gis disliked it. On the other hand he had also experienced more than once a strange intuitive joy when he had been with Verena—and he could not regret that. He wondered briefly whether Ralph possessed the same odd talents. Perhaps that was what had made him such a successful member of MI6—a deep knowledge of his fellow men.

What did surprise him was to learn that he was not the white blackbird of the Schuylers which he had always supposed himself to be. He was a true member of the family, even if his ambitions were not so lofty as theirs. In every way that mattered he had come home.

He lay back in his chair. Nicholas Allen he had named himself, Nicholas Allen he intended to be, but at heart he would always be Nicholas Schuyler. He dropped his hand to take Verena's in his. She squeezed it gently.

Like him she was enjoying the bright day and the company. She had been a little frightened at the prospect of meeting Nicholas's formidably clever family, but she was finding them both kind and considerate—even his redoubtable father. And life with Nicholas was never dull, even if they did live in what Chrissie had once contemptuously christened 'that backwater, West Bretton'.

She fell into the easy contented sleep of the heavily pregnant, but happy, woman.

Gerard and Torry, coming out of the great house, looked out across the lawn at them, contented family men all. At Gis and Ralph, each with a child on his knee, and at Nicholas, soon to be a father for the first time.

Gerard said, 'Reformed rakes are said to make the best family men and, looking at that little collection, I am inclined to believe that the saying may be true.'

Torry took his hand and kissed him on the cheek. 'You should know, my dear! You should know!'

* * * * *

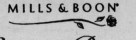

MILLS & BOON

Historical Romance™

Coming next month

A BARGAIN WITH FATE
by Ann Elizabeth Cree

A Regency delight from a new author!

Michael, Lord Stamford needed a pretend fiancée to keep
his family at bay. Rosalyn had to accept Michael's
proposal if she was to regain her brother's estate.

DRAGON'S COURT
by Joanna Makepeace

Intrigue at Henry (the Welsh dragon) VII's court

Anne Jarvis has watched her father pay fines to the king,
and she wanted a husband who would give her a peaceful
life—Dickon Allard wasn't that man!

On sale from 6th November 1998

*Available at most branches of WH Smith, Tesco, Asda,
Martins, Borders and all good paperback bookshops*

FIND THE FRUIT!

How would you like to win a year's supply of Mills & Boon® Books—FREE! Well, if you know your fruit, then you're already one step ahead when it comes to completing this competition, because all the answers are fruit! Simply decipher the code to find the names of ten fruit, complete the coupon overleaf and send it to us by 30th April 1999. The first five correct entries will each win a year's subscription to the Mills & Boon series of their choice. What could be easier?

A	B	C	D	E	F	G	H	I
15					20			

J	K	L	M	N	O	P	Q	R
	25						5	

S	T	U	V	W	X	Y	Z
			10				

4	19	15	17	22

15	10	3	17	15	18	3

2	19	17	8	15	6	23	2	19

4	19	15	6

4	26	9	1

7	8	6	15	11	16	19	6	6	13

3	6	15	2	21	19

15	4	4	26	19

1	15	2	21	3

16	15	2	15	2	15

C8J

Please turn over for details of how to enter →

HOW TO ENTER

There are ten coded words listed overleaf, which when decoded each spell the name of a fruit. There is also a grid which contains each letter of the alphabet and a number has been provided under some of the letters. All you have to do, is complete the grid, by working out which number corresponds with each letter of the alphabet. When you have done this, you will be able to decipher the coded words to discover the names of the ten fruit! As you decipher each code, write the name of the fruit in the space provided, then fill in the coupon below, pop this page into an envelope and post it today. Don't forget you could win a year's supply of Mills & Boon® Books—you don't even need to pay for a stamp!

Mills & Boon Find the Fruit Competition
FREEPOST CN81, Croydon, Surrey, CR9 3WZ
EIRE readers: (please affix stamp) PO Box 4546, Dublin 24.

Please tick the series you would like to receive if you are one of the lucky winners

Presents™ ❑ Enchanted™ ❑ Medical Romance™ ❑
Historical Romance™ ❑ Temptation® ❑

Are you a Reader Service™ subscriber?   Yes ❑   No ❑

Ms/Mrs/Miss/Mr ....Initials ....
                                         (BLOCK CAPITALS PLEASE)

Surname...

Address ....

....

....Postcode..........................

(I am over 18 years of age)   C8J